Table of Contents

Prologue: Class Up

I was standing in the main hall of the huge church that lorded over the town square in Melromarc. The enormous dragon hourglass stood in the center of the hall, a commanding presence.

"Every time I come here I end up feeling the same way. That thing looks more ominous than holy."

"I feel the same way, Mr. Naofumi."

"The red sand is so preeeeety!"

My name is Naofumi Iwatani.

Back in the real world, I was an average *otaku* college student in Japan.

I actually ended up here sort of by accident. I was killing time in the local library when I found an old book called *The Records of the Four Holy Weapons*. I started flipping through it only to black out and wake up again in the very world the book had been describing. I'd been summoned to serve as the Shield Hero.

Apparently the whole world was living under the threat of something called the waves of destruction.

Pretty soon I found out exactly what that meant. There were temporary waves that came at specified times. When the wave came, massive hoards of monsters appeared and attacked any person that happened to be living nearby.

People from this new world had summoned me from my own world to help them fight against the waves.

When I'd first arrived I was very enthusiastic—what could have been more exciting than adventuring in a whole new world? But then I met that *woman* . . . . Even now, most of the populace distrusts and hates me. It was all because of this woman, who was now officially known as Bitch. She had framed me for rape, lied about me, and dragged my reputation through the mud.

It was all a lie, but I was chased out of the kingdom and sent out into the world by myself. My ruined reputation basically ensured that I would never find another adventurer to travel with me.

Well, that's what I'd thought at the time. Apparently I'd been mistaken.

In the end, and I'll explain it all later, I ended up falling behind the other three heroes that had been summoned. They effectively got a head start on leveling up.

So not only was I unable to secure any help—I was also forced to fight in the battles of the waves.

I did what I could to level up, and I managed to stay alive for a while.

Eventually, I was able to take down some enemies that

the other heroes had failed to defeat, but just when I thought things were looking up for me, I was framed for an even more serious crime.

The country that had summoned me was called Melromarc. It was a human-supremacist country and ruled by a queen.

Apparently the royal family was matrilineal, and the throne was passed down through the women in the family.

The princess next in line for the throne was named Melty—and they framed me for her kidnapping.

Melty was Bitch's younger sister. She was . . . feisty, to say the least.

Her mother trusted Melty much more than she trusted Bitch, and so she appointed Melty first in line to inherit the throne.

I soon realized that there was only one way to clear myself of the charges that had been brought against me—I had to find out where the queen was and go visit her myself.

Ultimately, I was able to meet the queen and clear my name.

Once everything was out in the open, it was clear that the real perpetrator behind all the misery that had been heaped upon me was the national church in Melromarc—the Church of the Three Heroes.

The gist of their dogma was that there were four weapons

that represented their respective heroes. Of the four weapons, three were worthy of worship, while the other was worthy of derision.

You've probably already guessed, but the hero worth the derision was the Shield Hero—me.

So the reason for my persecution had its roots in the national religion, and whether or not I had raped anyone was not really the issue.

The reason for all of this lay with the neighboring country, the country where demi-humans ruled. Melromarc had been locked in war with them for generations.

Demi-humans were basically just like humans, except that they all had certain characteristics in common with animals. So while they looked and behaved like humans, they sometimes had animal ears or tails.

At first, I wasn't really sure what all that was supposed to do with me, but apparently the demi-humans had taken to worshiping the hero.

So in the end, the citizens of Melromarc, as well as its king, had taken up arms against me because of religious dogma.

Even now I get pissed off just thinking about it.

Moving on—there was a single person that stood behind the whole conspiracy to ruin my life. It was the high priest of the Church of the Three Heroes. Eventually we came face-to-face and fought. I won, and that basically wrapped up the story of my persecution.

But in the middle of our battle, I had to summon a cursed shield to defeat the high priest. The shield was called the Shield of Wrath, and I used its strongest skill, blood sacrifice.

It was a complicated skill that damaged me as much as him. I was able to defeat him in the end, but I had to pay the price—the skill sapped my stats and left me incapacitated and cursed.

I was, however, able to prove my innocence. I finally found myself on equal footing with the other heroes. And the queen had decided to make the official religion of Melromarc the Church of the *Four* Heroes.

"It really seems like you only use your talents to make Mr. Iwatani suffer."

"Yeah, it really does."

The queen of Melromarc had declared that the king who had been standing in for her would be officially renamed Trash. She was in the middle of torturing him—by incasing his body in ice.

To punish him for his actions as king while she had been away on diplomatic missions, to punish him for persecuting me, she'd changed his name and taken away his royal position.

"ARRRRGGHHHHHH!"

I looked at Trash—he was encased in ice up to his neck.

He wore a look of agony, but he wasn't broadcasting it to the queen who punished him. He was staring at me.

I wished I could have taken real joy from seeing his pained expression . . . but I couldn't.

There was something sad about it, but I had to keep watching.

He'd been sneaky, conniving. He'd done all he could to help the church accuse me of kidnapping princess Melty, and now he was receiving his due punishment from the real ruler of the country.

But Trash hadn't been involved with actions the church had taken on its own.

A part of me thought we should just exile him and send him out into the world empty-handed. But if we weren't careful who knew what something like that could lead to? Furthermore, their first daughter, Bitch, had been punished as well. She'd been stripped of her royal title, renamed Bitch, and would have to live the rest of her life as an adventurer with the pseudonym Whore.

Furthermore, in her mother's absence it seems Bitch had been living the high life off the Crown's coffers. She now bore the responsibility of paying back all the funds she'd used to finance her own extravagance.

On the surface the queen seemed to be an honest, decent human being.

Recognizing the true threat of the times, the existential crisis faced by the whole world, she'd abandoned the national zeitgeist of human supremacy and reached out to their national enemy, the Shield Hero, for assistance. It seemed like she genuinely wanted to bring me into the fold.

She hid her mouth behind a folding fan and appeared young, probably in her late 20s. She was very beautiful.

To think that she had already given birth to two daughters—it didn't really seem possible.

"ARRRRGH!"

Trash was still encased in ice, leaving only his neck and head free. He was staring at me hatefully.

It was a simple cause and effect. He was the one that summoned me here, and then he went out of this way to make my life a living hell. The punishment was fitting.

I turned to the queen and suggested she move on.

"I think that's probably enough for him. I'd rather you go ahead and let me participate in the class-up ceremony."

I've probably said enough to sum up the current state of affairs, and the beleaguered history of my persecution here. Now it was time to take a solid look at the problems I was still facing.

For whatever reason, this world I found myself in functioned much like a game. Everyone had levels, and they could level up by defeating monsters and accruing experience points.

When you leveled up, your abilities tended to grow more powerful as well.

When your abilities got stronger, your stats increased, which would enable you to battle stronger monsters that previously would have defeated you easily.

That was one of the more interesting aspects of the world: the harder you worked, the more powerful you became, and the power was immediately useful.

But of course there were problems with the system as well.

As the Shield Hero, I was equipped with the legendary shield from the moment I was summoned here. The shield's abilities severely limited the amount of damage I was capable of doing. In fact, even if I attacked an enemy with my bare fists and pummeled it all day long, I was unable to do any appreciable damage at all.

Not that it was all bad news. The shield came with an enormous defense rating and a number of very special skills.

All that was well and fine, but if I was unable to deal any damage on my own, I was effectively prevented from participating in battles by myself.

As if that weren't bad enough, the persecution and reputation I was suffering under made it impossible to find anyone that would consider traveling with me.

"Huff . . . I suppose you're right."

"Are you finally finished?"

Raphtalia whispered to herself, her exasperation evident.

Raphtalia was a girl that traveled with me. When I was unable to find anyone that would help me, I ended up buying her as a slave. It was the only way I could get an attacker on my team.

She was a demi-human, so she had as hard of a time living in Melromarc as I did.

She had the ears and tail of a *Tanuki*, and I think she was called a "raccoon-type" demi-human. When I'd bought her she had only been a little girl. But apparently demi-humans' physical bodies grow in response to their level, so she grew up very quickly as we battled our way through the countryside.

Now she looked to be around 18 and was a cute, attractive girl.

When the first of the waves of destruction arrived, she lost the village where she'd grown up—and both of her parents.

After traveling together for so long, I'd come to see myself as a sort of surrogate parent to her.

In a way, she felt like my child. She was an accomplice I could depend on.

"Still, I could watch Trash get tortured all day . . . ."

I flashed Trash a smile.

"Mr. Naofumi!"

THE RISING OF THE SHIELD HERO 5

"Grr . . . shield!"

"BE QUIET!"

The queen immediately put a stop to Trash's protests while Raphtalia put me on notice.

As if I didn't know. Raphtalia was always very serious.

Still, she kept a close watch on me. Whenever it looked like I was going to lose control, she stepped in and tried to put out the fire.

"Master! When is this gonna be over?!"

"Soon enough."

The girl who just whined at me was named Filo.

At the moment she looked like a little blonde girl. A prominent cowlick stood up from the crown of her head, and she had small angel-like wings protruding from her back.

She was one of my companions too.

She's . . . a little harder to explain than Raphtalia though.

"What's taking so long?"

I'd originally bought her egg from a lottery-like game with plans to keep her as a pet.

When the egg hatched, a filolial emerged. Filolial were large bird-like monsters that were often seen pulling carriages down the street.

However, if a filolial was raised by a hero, it would grow into something else altogether.

I guess that was what caused it. At some point, she gained

the ability to transform into this young angel-like human form.

Had she been a human, she would have looked like a young girl around 10 years old. Her real form, for whatever that's worth, was a large bird.

When in her bird form, she was actually something called the filolial queen.

She had a powerful attack and was a very important member of my team, but because she was originally a bird she had a tendency to be louder and more obnoxious than necessary.

We sometimes traveled around the country selling wares to raise funds. Whenever we camped in the fields, she was invariably the first one awake—and she'd wake me the second she woke up.

Furthermore, Filo ended up becoming best friends with the younger princess, Melty, when we traveled together.

Personality-wise, she was a very naïve little girl, with a tendency to make inappropriate outbursts at inconvenient times. Honestly, she'd be a lot cuter if she'd learn to keep her mouth shut.

"You're thinking something meeeean!"

"I guess that's true."

Raphtalia and Filo both could be very perceptive. Whenever it looked like I was turning rude thoughts over in my mind, one of them would immediately notice.

Anyway, those two are my closest friends here.

So the reason that we were in the church gathered around the dragon hourglass had to do with the leveling up system in this world.

The leveling system actually has a ceiling in place—not for heroes like myself, but for normal people in the world.

Raphtalia and Filo had both reached the leveling limit—which was level 40.

If anyone wanted to level past 40, they had to go through something called a class-up ceremony.

The ceremony itself utilized the dragon hourglass, which was controlled by the country.

The hourglass itself had other uses. For one thing, it was a countdown to the arrival of the next wave of destruction. But it also served a necessary role in the class-up ceremony.

We had already tried to go through the class-up ceremony once before, but Trash had stepped in and prohibited us from participating.

That was all well and fine for me, but he had created a situation where neither Raphtalia nor Filo was able to level any further.

When all the investigations and talks were over, I addressed this issue to the queen, and she summoned Trash to get the truth out of him.

But Trash was equivocal, giving excuse after excuse. It took encasing him in a block of ice to get him to speak the truth—but he eventually did.

I grinned as I watched him confess. I guess it makes me look bad to admit that though.

I didn't care. That man had made our lives a living hell for months. Couldn't I take some degree of pleasure in his downfall? Anyone that saw me smiling at his misery would think I was a bad person though.

"By the way, what happened to the sisters that lived here?"

The last few times I'd come to the church it was filled with nuns who treated me terribly. But now when I came to the church all the nuns were gone. They'd been replaced by soldiers.

"They accompanied the high priest to the battle field and have therefore all been arrested."

That seemed reasonable. As far as I was concerned, they deserved whatever they got.

"Okay, so what do we need to do to have the class-up ceremony?"

"First tell us who would like to participate in the ceremony."

A little while ago, when I thought we couldn't participate in the ceremony, I had no idea what to do.

I didn't see any other options, so I decided to go to Shieldfreeden, which was a country of demi-humans, to see if I could do it there.

But just as we tried to leave for Shieldfreeden, we got

mixed up in the whole princess-kidnapping affair. Did it mean that we'd be able to class-up here after all?

For now, I'd just do as the queen asked. She wanted to know who needed the ceremony, so I sent my gaze over to Raphtalia and Filo.

"Me!! I want to go first!"

Filo threw her hand into the air, desperate to go first.

I looked over to Raphtalia, who nodded in agreement.

"Alright, let's have Filo go first."

"Yayyy!"

Filo stepped forward with confidence.

"Now then, stand in a relaxed way, touch the dragon hourglass, and focus your mind."

"Like this?"

Filo turned back into her monster form and slowly reached out to touch the glass.

When her feathers brushed the glass, the red sand inside swelled and rippled in waves before beginning to glow mysteriously.

"Very well. We shall now begin the class-up ceremony."

The queen snapped her fingers and soldiers appeared and surrounded the dragon hourglass. There was a large and complicated pattern cut into the floor, a series of grooves that crisscrossed the area. The soldiers knelt and poured a liquid into the grooves.

"What's that? Do you guys hear that?"

"Keep focusing."

"Okaaaay!"

Filo slowly closed her eyes and raised both of her wings.

The hourglass was filling with a faint light, and the light was echoed back by the magical pattern on the floor.

Filo stood in the center, and the light grew stronger until she was completely enveloped in it.

"Now then, chose your desired future."

"Hey! I can see something!"

Filo's eyes were closed.

Just then, a small, somewhat warped image of Filo appeared before me, a flashing icon of sorts, and branches extending from the icon like . . . . To borrow language from games, it looked like a sort of growth tree.

"And this is the monster that you will choose? Mr. Iwatani, please decide."

Like I've just described, Filo is actually a monster. Monsters that you use in your team can be controlled with a monster control seal, which allows the owner to control the monster by hurting them if they disobey or ignore orders. It basically gave me the right to control her life and death.

It seemed that her owner, myself in this case, had the right to decide whether she participated in the class-up ceremony too.

"Guess I can control that too."

A filolial growth chart appeared before my eyes, splitting off into many directions, each indicative of new possibilities.

And yet, I . . . .

"Filo, this is something you should decide on your own. It's not my choice."

I rejected the choice, and a new option appeared, asking if I would like the monster to choose on her own. I chose yes.

"Oooh! I can see so many things! Which one should I choose . . . ?"

Filo closed her eyes and an expression of joyful anticipation spread over her face as she considered the possibilities.

I could have chosen for her, but Filo should have some say over how she spends the rest of her life.

I decided to tell Raphtalia the same thing.

"Raphtalia. I already went over this with Filo, but after the waves are finished and I return to my own world, you need to live on your own. So you need to decide your path for yourself. Okay?"

"I would have been okay with any future you'd chosen for me."

"You have to choose."

" . . . Very well."

She nodded, looking somehow disappointed.

But it would be worse if I chose and later had to regret my decision.

I trusted her—that was enough reason to let her decide on her own.

So what would Filo pick?

I looked over to see that the feather standing up from her head was now glowing.

"Huh?"

The light grew stronger and seemed to vibrate before flashing brilliantly.

It was so bright that I was blinded for a moment. I blinked a few times to get my bearings, then looked again at Filo.

Her appearance hadn't changed very much. But the vertical feather on her head seemed somehow more splendid than before.

It looked like . . . a small crown.

"The class-up ceremony was a success."

"I see that."

I opened up Filo's status menu to take a look at what had changed. The star symbol that had been next to her level earlier was now gone, which probably meant that the level ceiling had been removed.

That must mean that she could now level far beyond the previous cap. I looked at her actual stats and discovered that most of them appeared to have doubled.

So that's how powerful the class-up ceremony really was.

"Heh . . . This is pretty impressive."

Filo's stats had always been better than average, and now she was substantially stronger than she had been.

I decided to compare her stats to my own to see how far ahead I was only to discover that her stats had surpassed mine!

Of course, I meant compared to my stats before the curse had lowered them.

The only stat of mine that was higher than hers was my defense rating!

"I couldn't pick . . . ."

Filo had turned back into her human form and came running over to me with tears in her eyes.

"What's wrong?"

"I wanted to learn how to spit poison, but then, before I could pick one of the paths I wanted, another option showed up and picked itself."

A while back we'd been fighting some monsters that were able to spit poison. Ever since then, Filo had sort of romanticized the notion.

She doesn't need to spit poison because she already has a poisonous tongue.

"Well it looks like that cowlick of yours is glowing now."

"Erm . . . ."

"Filo, don't lose hope. When you start to get stronger, you still might learn how to spit poison."

Raphtalia tried to cheer up Filo.

"Really?! Then I'm gonna try real hard!"

"Okay Raphtalia, you're next."

"Oh, alright."

Raphtalia reached out and touched the hourglass, just as Filo had.

And just like last time, the soldiers in the room all knelt and poured a viscous liquid into the grooves on the floor. Just then—just like last time—a flashing icon appeared in my field of vision.

Right—I selected to refuse the choice . . . .

But just then, Filo's cowlick split in two and one of the cowlicks came flying straight at me.

"Huh? What?! Filo!!"

"It's not me!"

What did she mean by that? Did she mean that the new cowlick was somehow moving and acting on its own?

Raphtalia was looking over at us, her eyes wide and surprised.

"Mr. Naofumi?!"

The floating cowlick caused a new potential line of growth to extend from Raphtalia's growth tree—one that hadn't been there before—and the new growth line selected itself.

"Ahh?!"

Raphtalia suddenly yelped.

The whole area was engulfed in flashing, blinding lights.

A column of smoke appeared. The whole thing seemed to be proceeding differently than Filo's class-up ceremony.

A moment later, the smoke dissipated, and Raphtalia appeared standing where it had been, coughing, but looking otherwise healthy.

"Are you okay!?"

"Y . . . yes. I'm alright, but . . . ."

What was happening?!

I was worried, but I opened the status screen to check on her. Just as with Filo, the star had vanished, and most of her stats had doubled.

"What happened?!"

"I don't really know. Some option automatically selected itself. It filled me with a horrible feeling of dread, but everything seems to be just fine."

"Well that's good . . . but what is going on? Why are your class-up directions being decided on automatically?"

"Who's behind it?"

"I don't know. But Filo's cowlick was originally given to us by Fitoria, right?"

"You're right. "

When we were in the middle of the whole princess Melty-kidnap debacle, we'd come across a legendary creature—the queen of the filolials herself.

Filo and the queen talked about a lot of things, and in the

end the queen gave Filo this cowlick, saying that it would help her in the days to come.

She also did something to my armor—saying it would help us. In return, she only commanded that I find a way to bring the heroes together.

If I wasn't able to get the heroes to cooperate, she warned that she'd have to see us killed.

"What does it mean?"

I looked over at the queen. Her eyes were shining.

"You don't say? I've wanted to meet with the filolial queen for ages."

"That's not what I'm asking!"

The queen seemed to know a lot about the heroes, but according to Melty, she'd also spent some time exploring legendary lands.

Maybe she had a personal interest in exploring ancient legends?

Her daughter, Melty, harbored a deep-seated interest in filolials. Like mother like daughter, I guess.

Regardless, it wasn't the time or the place to wax poetic on inherited traits.

"How are you two feeling?"

"I feel stronger than I used to."

"The feather from the filolial queen . . . I wonder what it all means?"

The queen sighed, looking disappointed.

"I know that certain special tools can be used during the class-up ceremony to achieve certain special effects. I don't know what this means, but I'd like to assume it's a good thing."

"Right . . . ."

"How much have their abilities improved?"

"From the look of it, most of their stats have doubled."

"DOUBLED?"

The queen was shocked. Was it safe to assume that the growth was more dramatic than usual?

The filolial queen's feather had somehow affected the ceremony. If it had raised their stats more than usual, I certainly didn't think that was anything to complain about.

"Typically the ceremony is considered a relative success if one of the items raises by 50 percent. Compared to the average outcome, this is very impressive."

As for our stats, there are all sorts of them: HP, MP, SP, attack power, defense, agility, strength, and so on.

I could keep going into more subtle stats, but there are at least this many main ones.

Well, Raphtalia and the others don't have SP. It might be a stat that only heroes share.

The "one item" that the queen mentioned referred to one of these stats. She meant that normally a stat, like attack power, would get a 50 percent boost.

"You don't say? Guess we got a good deal here."

But the two of them both seemed a little disturbed by what they'd been through. I guess I could sympathize with that easily enough.

Class-up . . . . As common a concept as it is in online games, the best thing about the system was that you had the agency to decide your growth path.

"Well . . . keep your chin up."

"I feel . . . I feel sad."

"I do too!"

"Shall we try to redo the ceremony?"

The queen suggested a redo. Was that even possible?

"Can you do that?"

"Normally it is only done for convicted criminals, but it is not impossible."

Apparently the ceremony could be reversed.

This whole time I'd been thinking of it as an analog to the job-change system you find in so many online games—which was typically a one-time thing that couldn't be reversed.

"With a 'level reset' we can return someone to a point at which they were unable to class-up. That will reset the changes, but they will also revert to level one."

"Level one? That doesn't sound good."

Considering the situation we were in, if either Raphtalia or Filo were to drop to level one, I wasn't sure we'd be able to carry on.

The next wave would be here soon, and I was sure we'd get involved in all sorts of petty conflicts before then.

Still, those sorts of punishments existed in games.

It seemed reasonable enough that they could exist in a world like this too.

The more I thought about it, the more it seemed wrong. How could you take all the work and effort someone invested in their leveling and just render it all moot in an instant?

"But what should we do?"

"I want to redo it!" Filo shouted. "I want to learn to spit poison!"

Her tongue was poisonous enough as is, but I'd leave that issue for another day.

"The feather on your head is what caused this, so I don't think that will work. The same thing would just happen again."

"Oh . . . ."

"Raphtalia? What do you think?"

"I didn't really have an idea of how I wanted to progress. I just wanted to be stronger, and I've become stronger—so I'm fine with this."

She was right. This co-opted class-up had resulted in much higher stat gains.

As a result, she was already much stronger than I was.

"Alright then . . . . Let's head back to the castle."

"Okay."

"But . . . Poooooooison . . . ."

"You're plenty poisonous."

"But . . . ."

And so our bizarre class-up ceremony came to an end.

We turned, leaving Trash collapsed before the hourglass, and made our way back to the castle.

Chapter One: The Heroes' Teammates

We took a carriage back to the castle, and when we arrived everyone was bustling to prepare the large hall for a feast.

"What's up with all this?"

"We are preparing a feast for Mr. Iwatani and the other heroes. In celebration of their swift and decisive victory."

"Hm . . . ."

I had been able to prove my innocence, and at least one major domestic dispute had been settled. I suppose that was worthy of celebration.

The hall was filled with long dining tables. Judging by the size and number, this feast was looking more expansive and impressive than the last feast—the one I'd fought Motoyasu at.

It had taken so long. I reflected on how long I'd been framed and persecuted. It felt like it had taken forever to prove my innocence.

I was ruminating on the past few months when the queen passed by. She was in deep conversation with a group of soldiers, nodding gravely.

"What's going on?"

"Oh . . . ."

I went over and asked her what was up. She cradled her head in her hands and whispered an explanation, clearly distraught.

Apparently during the preparations, Bitch had shown up in the kitchen. She'd wanted to be the one to bring me my meal at the feast.

She felt bad. She wanted to repent. She felt, apparently, that delivering my food would be a step on her path to reconciliation.

Then she forcibly took my meal from the kitchen and came marching out into the hall.

However, the queen had been prepared for any potential mishaps and had given orders ahead of time to deal with any issues Bitch might cause.

In the end, it was Bitch who ended up suffering.

Before Bitch could serve me my meal, she was required to sample it for poison.

"So what happened?"

"She was taken to a hospital."

Only a few hours had passed since she'd been read her punishment. How stupid was she to try something like that so soon?

My shield had given me resistance to poisons, so I'm sure I would have been fine. Still, recreationally imbibing poison wasn't one of my favorite pastimes.

Bitch didn't understand what "repent" even meant.

What was she thinking? Attempted assassination could get her the death penalty.

"How will she be punished?"

"I will see to it that she is. Bitch will only reap further hardships until she learns her place."

"How are you supposed to punish someone so unrepentant?"

"At least we stopped her before she got too far. Had she pulled off her plan, I would have lost your trust—and I've spent too long trying to earn it."

"Whatever. It was almost a sure thing that she'd try something. She never looked repentant anyway."

She wasn't very smart, but I suppose there was something I could admire in her stubborn persistence. What could get her so ruffled?

I could have gotten angry, but I decided to praise the queen for her foresight instead.

"Better keep a good eye out. If anything happens to me or my friends, that will be the end of our agreement."

The queen had stepped in to help me, so I'd decided to trust her for the time being.

I was really hoping that that trust would not turn out to be misplaced.

"I intend to keep you safe. You do not even know how

important you are to Melromarc and the world—but I intend to show you that as well."

The queen, as befitting one in her position, apparently had the foresight to order a 24-hour watch over Trash and Bitch.

"You've got a watch on Trash? Even as he sits encased in ice?"

"Naturally. Until the two of them settle down and cease their foolish plotting, I'll be receiving reports from my ears on the ground."

"Good."

The guests had begun to arrive. Once the hall was full, the queen began to make an announcement—full of royal bombast.

"I am Milleria Q. Melromarc. I would like to welcome you all to this feast, which is held in celebration, and to honor those of you who worked so tirelessly to end this painful chapter in our collective history. Please enjoy all that we have prepared for you."

The gathered crowd broke into uproarious applause. This feast was nothing like the last one.

"Wow . . . ."

Filo's eyes sparkled with unbridled anticipation as all the food was carried out from the kitchen and lined up down the center of the tables.

The room was divided into halves. One half was served

buffet style, while the other half was waited on as if it were a restaurant.

The most important guests were seated on the full-service side of the room. If they were still hungry by the end of the meal, they were free to move to the buffet side and continue eating.

Some servants appeared with shining plates of food for our table, and it all looked so good I couldn't stop smacking my lips.

I'd spent the last feast huddled in a corner, begrudgingly snacking on scraps. From where I sat now, that whole experience seemed like a joke.

"When we're done eating here, you can still go to the buffet and eat."

"REALLY?!"

"That's what they say. You can eat all you want. But you have to stay in human form, okay?"

"Okay!"

We finished our expensive and refined plates of food. Filo quickly cast her gaze at the buffet and, receiving permission, jumped up and skipped over to it.

Quantity over quality, I suppose. It was a very Filo way to see the world. Or should I say she cared about the quality in addition to the quantity. She was insatiable in every sense of the word.

She reminded me of a younger Raphtalia in a way.

I looked over at Raphtalia.

"What is it?"

Raphtalia caught me staring at her, and she flushed, embarrassed.

"You're still hungry too, aren't you? Go get some more if you want it."

"I can't eat that much anymore!"

"You better think more about your health. With all the daily fighting and hardship, you'd better get as much nutritious food as you can—when we have the opportunity."

Raphtalia sighed deeply. What did she want?

"Hey, Mr. Naofumi, what kind of girls do you like?"

"What?"

That came out of nowhere. But I didn't have any girls that I liked at the moment.

Actually, the whole topic just made me think of Bitch. I wish she'd stop bringing up topics like that.

"I mean . . . is there a girl waiting for you back in your own world?"

"What are you talking about? Of course not."

Did she think that was the reason I wanted to get back to my own world? What was she thinking?

The reason I wanted to get back to my world was simple enough: I hated this place.

They'd framed me for crimes, forced me to fight when I didn't want to, and the knights that were supposed to be on my side tried to set me on fire. Who would want to stay in a place like this?

Raphtalia sighed heavily, again.

"I don't know what you're getting at, but I'm going back home because I want to. That's all."

When all this was over, I'd go back home as soon as possible. Did she really need a reason?

Suddenly I remembered how'd I felt on the day after my arrival here. It had all seemed so great—I really did think I could have stayed forever.

The desire to stay had evaporated the moment Bitch had betrayed my trust.

I'd already known that, but working through those emotions again made me want to go home even more.

"Shield Hero!"

"Huh?"

I turned to see who'd called for me and saw the volunteer soldiers I'd worked with calling to me.

These were the guys that had come to me of their own accord before the last wave. They'd wanted to help me fight.

"It's so good to see you again, sir!"

"And you're all safe. That's good to know."

"Yes sir!"

One of them nodded, apparently very happy.

He even flushed bright red. This kid might have worshiped the Shield Hero as a member of the reformed Church of the Holy Four.

"Until we meet again."

"Yes sir!" they shouted in unison.

Just then, the other heroes filed into the hall.

Ren Amaki, the Sword Hero, came in first, followed by his retinue.

Ren was a teenager who always came off as cool and aloof. He was always dressed in blacks and dark colors.

He came off as the cool swordsman type. He was 16 years old, the youngest of the heroes.

He chatted with his team members for a little while before parting with them and sitting off on his own. I sensed some sort of distance growing between them.

The next to enter was the Bow Hero, Itsuki Kawasumi.

He seemed like he thought himself a real hero, traveling the world and righting wrongs. He was insufferable.

He called on the authority of the Bow Hero to cast himself as a friend of justice. He was so just—at least TWICE as just as everyone else.

He looked like he was younger than Ren, but he was

actually 17. He had naturally curly hair that flopped about agreeably. People would probably find him charming . . . I guess.

He looked to me like the type of guy that played piano, sensitive and suffering and all that.

But his sense of justice was so all-encompassing that he never listened to what anyone had to say. He seemed a lot nicer than he actually was, I guess.

I didn't have a very firm grasp on his character yet.

Motoyasu hadn't arrived yet. Maybe he had followed Bitch to the hospital to check in on her?

Regardless, he was the only one that hadn't yet shown up: Motoyasu Kitamura, the Spear Hero.

He traveled around with Bitch, and until I had completely proved my innocence, he treated me as if I were guilty beyond the shadow of a doubt.

Among the four heroes he was undoubtedly the most attractive. I didn't like him very much, but I'm obligated to admit that much.

He was a self-proclaimed feminist. He loved the ladies.

He never listened to what anyone had to say. Back when there was a bounty on my head, he completely ignored the dubiousness of the charge, decided I was guilty, and dedicated the majority of his energy to hunting me down.

They say he's loyal to his companions, which I suppose sounds quite lofty and nice. In truth, however, he was a fool to never doubt the suggestions delivered to him by his "friends."

It was his fault, in my estimation, that it had taken so long for the country to come to its senses and expunge the true evil from its lands.

Anyway, all three of the other heroes came from some alternative version of Japan—just like I had—and all three of them had experience playing a game that intimately resembled the world we had found ourselves transported to.

The book I'd been reading at the library, *The Records of the Four Holy Weapons*, had given terse descriptions of their character.

The Sword Hero was attractive and active, the Spear Hero was loyal, and the Bow Hero was a warrior for justice.

All that was well and fine for the sake of a story, but in reality the whole lot of them were pretty miserable to be around.

"Where's Motoyasu?"

The queen asked them as they filed in.

"He was very worried about your daughter's condition, so he went to the hospital to check on her. We've already sent for him."

"You don't say . . . ."

The queen waved a greeting to Ren and Itsuki.

Soon everyone had finished eating, and the hall was filled with dancing and song.

But the feast was . . . well it was certainly more festive than the last feast had been. I couldn't help but notice that it seemed to be attended by an entirely different set of people. There were less members of the nobility than I'd expected to attend, and a greater portion of the crowd seemed to be adventurers and soldiers.

It also looked like there were quite a few people from neighboring countries attending. I caught them trying to look at me from time to time.

The queen led Ren and Itsuki over to where I was sitting before she climbed the stairs to the stage.

"Huh? What's going on?"

"The queen wants us all together."

"I wonder why? Motoyasu hasn't even arrived yet."

"Apparently he's visiting the woman who tried to poison me."

"Poison?!"

"You know who I'm talking about, right?"

"Yeah. So it was true?"

"Maybe the queen made her drink poison?"

"No. I was with the queen at the time. She came in with a plate of food, and she was forced to take a bite of it. That's all."

"Really . . . ?"

We were still whispering back and forth when the queen turned dramatically and shouted.

"Now then, heroes! How did you enjoy the feast?"

"Wasn't bad."

"Very much. Quite a success."

"Now that my name's been cleared, it's a weight off my shoulders."

"How wonderful to hear."

Really though, it felt like all the hardship and absurdities I'd faced were finally being dealt with.

The queen stood there, nodding subtly to herself before she snapped her folding fan shut and began to address the room.

"In these regrettable times, members of our country have unfortunately done all they could to hinder the heroes' progress. I would like to do what I can to make reparations for this."

What did she mean by that?

"In the sea that borders our land lies a group of islands known as Cal Mira. They are in the midst of an impressive activation event. I would like to request our heroes participate in these activities."

What kind of island was she talking about? What did she mean by "activation?"

"Really?!"

Ren was so excited he jumped forward and nearly shouted.

"What's that?"

"Do you really mean there's a bonus field?!"

Now Itsuki was excited too. He stepped forward to stand in line with Ren.

"What are you talking about?"

I didn't know as much about this world as they did. Why wouldn't anyone tell me what was going on?!

"It seems that Mr. Iwatani is not aware of what I'm speaking of, so I will explain. 'Activation' refers to a phenomenon that visits these lands once every 10 years. While it is occurring, the normal bout of experience earned through battles is doubled."

I picked the important parts out of her speech. Here's the gist of it:

The Cal Mira islands were famous as a resort, but at the same time it tended to attract hoards of monsters in its more remote areas, where they would quickly acclimate to their new environment.

The islands were also famous because adventurers that wanted to level up would make for the islands in large numbers to fight these monsters. Every ten years, when the "activation" occurred, adventurers would descend on the land in even greater numbers.

In order to make up for the leveling experience I'd been denied by the actions of Trash and Bitch, the queen was offering us participation in the activation.

"Naturally, your boarding and transport costs have already been covered. I hope that you will all participate."

Had this been an online RPG, this would be equivalent to some kind of special event where players' experience gains were doubled.

So she was talking about double experience for simple enemies. It was the sort of thing any gamer would flip out for.

"Now then, before you heroes make your way to the islands, I was hoping you would participate in a friendly exchange of information. Please come with me."

"Information exchange?"

"Yes. In preparation for the increasingly difficult and dangerous waves, I believe the only way forward is to ensure more cooperation between the heroes."

"Is that really necessary?"

Ren spat the question as if he considered her suggestion absurd.

What was his problem? What did he think was unnecessary? Unlike the others, I didn't already know everything about this place. Didn't he know that by now?

"I believe so. I've heard that the heroes had difficulty coordinating their efforts during the last wave. I think it would be beneficial to discuss this."

" . . . ."

Ren was silent.

She was right though. When the last wave came, the other heroes hadn't even joined forces with the knights. So they were left all alone at the site of destruction.

Apparently if the heroes registered a group of reserve soldiers as part of their party's back-up battle formation, those soldiers would be automatically teleported to the site of the waves, whenever and wherever they occurred.

But none of the other heroes had taken advantage of the system.

So in the end, aside from the group of soldiers that had approached me, there were no other back-up troops around to help when the last wave had come.

"Aside from that concern, I wonder if it might not benefit you heroes to coordinate your efforts, combine your strengths and knowledge, and move forward together, as a unified body."

"You're right. If we want to survive the coming waves, we need to do as you've indicated."

Itsuki immediately agreed with the queen. But he was just saying what she wanted to hear.

If anyone were to protest at this point, they'd look like the bad guy.

Or, if anyone were to protest, they'd end up dying alone in battle.

I realized that I needed to agree as well.

Besides, Fitoria had told me that the heroes needed to cooperate if they wanted to stand a chance against the waves.

Before some of my recent experiences, I probably would have dismissed the possibility of cooperation outright.

They wouldn't have believed a word I'd said anyway.

But Ren and Itsuki had listened to what I'd said. They'd analyzed the church's story and found it suspicious.

If they'd done that for me, I could at least return the favor.

"Very well then. Let's set up a place to talk, here in the great hall. Heroes! Introduce yourselves and follow me."

We looked at one another.

"You heard her."

"We need to coordinate our efforts. What should we do first?"

"Why don't we introduce our teammates?"

"Good idea. Very well, I'll go first."

And Itsuki led us over to his other party members.

"These people have been traveling with me as party members."

Itsuki waved his hand at a group of people there, motioning so that Ren and I would understand.

"This is the first time we've officially met. Shield Hero,

and . . . yes, Sword Hero—though we've spoken before."

" . . . Yeah."

Itsuki's party members each stepped forward and introduced themselves.

It all felt natural and casual enough. In the middle of a feast there was no sense of tension or nervousness. The soldiers were ordering whatever they wanted from the waiters as if it were any other day

"I'm Naofumi Iwatani—the Shield Hero. Pleasure."

We introduced ourselves, and I made a mental note of each of Itsuki's friends.

So there were . . . five of them? One of them wore some flashy armor and kept his arms authoritatively crossed.

When he noticed my eyes moving in his direction, he quickly uncrossed his arms. It gave me the creeps.

"Ah, yes. Pleased to meet you. I am Master Itsuki's bodyguard, and I intend to fight for the good and safety of the world."

"Bodyguard?!" Ren and I shouted in unison.

That wasn't a word I was expecting to hear. Ren seemed to be just as surprised as I was.

What's wrong, Ren? You didn't know either? Ha! I had to keep myself from bursting out laughing.

Just who did Itsuki think he was? It took all my willpower to suppress a grin.

"Yes!" They all shouted together. "All five of us are Master Itsuki's bodyguards!"

"Excuse me! I'm terribly sorry it took so long to get this food to you!"

I turned to see a young girl carrying a tray piled high with various foods.

She better be careful. She looked like she was about to drop it.

"Ah . . . ."

Damn! I reached out and quickly snatched the tray to keep it from falling.

"I'm so sorry!"

This kid . . . she seemed kind of young.

She probably wasn't a day over 14. You could feel the immaturity.

She had a refined bearing though—and a pretty face. She must have come from a good family. She was pretty cute.

She probably had a weak resolve. Had Motoyasu been there, he'd have probably already been hitting on her.

She was a small girl. I guess she was part of Itsuki's party, but what did she do? Maybe she was a magic-user or something like that.

"You're so slow, Rishia! Go on, introduce yourself."

"Fu, Fueeeee! Okay!"

Then all spoke together again. "The SIX of us are Mr. Itsuki's bodyguards!"

Ren turned to me and whispered, "Didn't they just say there were five bodyguards?"

That's what I'd heard too, but there was no use in pointing fingers at this point.

"Don't say anything, just watch what they do."

The whole thing made me a little uncomfortable, honestly. But until their behavior became an issue, I would assume that Itsuki knew what he was doing.

"What do you think? Quite the dependable lot, these guys."

"Honestly I have plenty I'd like to say, but for now I'll just say that everything looks good."

I looked them over again, starting from the right, just to take stock. They all wore expressions of extreme self-confidence.

I'm sure they were all dependable enough, but I couldn't help but remember our battle with the high priest—during which they hadn't done anyone much good at all.

Itsuki was positively blushing with confidence, but I was still bothered by the guy in the flashy armor. There was something about the way he knit his eyebrows that didn't sit right with me.

He looked somehow condescending, but then I took stock of the whole party and realized they all had that look.

As for the Rishia girl—she was casting awkward glances

left and right, looking uncomfortable and unsure of herself.

"I hadn't really met any of them before, but you've got a weird group of people together here."

Ren chose his words with care. The group had given me the same impression.   "You think? They all seem normal to me."

What did he think was normal about them? Calling them "bodyguards" made the whole thing weird straight from the get-go.

I thought that Itsuki considered him some kind of world-weary general character, the sort that traveled the wicked world righting its wrongs. But here was his party referring to themselves as bodyguards.

I didn't know what to make of it—it was all too strange.

Itsuki went on to tell me each of their names, but I wasn't paying attention and immediately forgot them.

I was distracted by the guy in the flashy armor. He'd pointed his chin in my direction, and I couldn't shake the feeling that he was looking down on me.

It started to really get to me . . . . I decided to mention it.

"Itsuki."

"What is it?"

"Do something about this one. His face and his attitude are bothering me. He looks at me like he thinks I'm a criminal."

"I suspect that has more to do with your own attitude than his, Naofumi. Nothing about his behavior is bothering me."

"Mu!"

Itsuki . . . . That little word-dance was really obnoxious.

"Yeah, well. He makes a different face when you aren't looking."

"Shield Hero, you're probably just imagining it, don't you think?"

"We're talking about YOU! Stay out of it."

It sure looked like he hadn't spent much time teaching his "bodyguards" proper manners. It's probably Itsuki's fault. I imagined him talking bad about me for the last few months. His friends probably just picked up on the general mood.

Actually, they were from Melromarc to begin with, which meant that they were probably prejudiced against the Shield Hero from the very start.

"I've been curious about something."

Ren raised his hand.

"What?"

"You've been referring to Itsuki as 'master' but don't attach a title to either mine or Naofumi's names. Why is that?"

"Because the Sword and Shield Heroes have clearly not been performing as well as Master Itsuki has. That should explain the difference."

What did he just say?

I'm used to dealing with crazy people by this point, but that was just too much. What would make them think that? I looked around at the crowd, and each member of Itsuki's party, save one of them, seemed to be in agreement.

It was Rishia that seemed to not share in their opinion, the girl that Itsuki treated like a servant. I couldn't tell how she really felt, but she did seem stressed by the disagreement.

Ren sighed loudly.

"Just when I was wondering what you'd say . . . ."

I couldn't believe he had the gall to even mention our "activities!" And this from Itsuki, who snuck around and did his work in secret. How did he think the rest of the country saw him?

He might have liked the idea of fighting for justice in the shadows—but no one knew who he was, and no one talked about his "deeds."

"Activities? Is Itsuki, by far the most boring hero around, trying to act like he's done more than we have? You know, I haven't heard anything about what you've been up to. No one talks about it."

"Well, maybe that's because, unlike Ren and Motoyasu, I haven't been running around trying to get people to praise me. The best work goes unnoticed—that's just how it is."

Itsuki shot back, apparently surprised that he was being challenged.

What was that supposed to mean? No matter how you looked at it, it seemed like Itsuki was the one concerned with his reputation.

Did he just like to fancy himself an angel? Oh Itsuki, so brave! So noble! Saving the world and not even looking for credit!

"You fool . . . . Are you berating Master Itsuki?

"What are you going to do about it? I'm not nice enough to stand aside while someone insults me to my face."

Ren spat back, and I saw his hand move to the hilt of his sword.

"Fueeee!"

"Please stop that! Ren!"

Itsuki inserted himself between flashy armor and Ren.

"Itsuki, it looks like you still have some explaining to do."

" . . . ."

Ren spat angrily at Itsuki.

"Regardless, Ren and Naofumi are heroes just like I am, so please show them the respect they're due."

"Understood!"

Flashy armor shouted and bowed deeply to us. I wondered what he was really thinking.

"Alright, I'll introduce my people next."

Ren clipped and stalked off without another word.

A feeling of malcontent remained in the air, but Itsuki and I followed Ren across the room.

"Welcome! Welcome! It's good to meet you both, Shield Hero, Bow Hero."

"Oh, um . . . ."

Ren's party members were still eating, but when we approached they stopped and snapped at attention, treating us respectfully but looking nervous as they did.

After dealing with Itsuki's crew, I wasn't really sure what to make of it.

Anyway, there were four of them.

"I'm the Shield Hero, Naofumi Iwatani."

"I am the Bow Hero, Itsuki Kawasaki. I believe we've met a few times before."

I think I'd seen three of them before, on our first day after we were all summoned here. It looked like he'd acquired one more party member somewhere along the way.

"Pleased to meet you again, Shield Hero, Bow Hero."

"Sure."

The whole group was very polite and proper.

But I couldn't help remember the way they'd avoided me on the first day here, the way they'd all run to hide behind Ren.

I couldn't forget it.

I better stay on my toes—there's no telling what they really thought.

"I apologize for my previous actions."

"Huh?"

One of the men stepped forward, representing the group. He appeared to be a solider of some kind. He bowed to me.

"I'm sorry, under the previous king I, we . . . I didn't know what would have happened to me had I aligned myself with the Shield Hero."

The rest of them all followed suit, lowering their heads to me.

"I realize this is too little too late, but please accept our apology."

"Uh . . . okay."

They were all so . . . modest, I wasn't expecting that and was thrown of balance.

Based on the way I'd been treated for the last few months, I couldn't help but suspect ulterior motives.

"Mr. Ren, to what do we owe the pleasure?"

"They say they want us heroes to cooperate from now on, so we're going around introducing our parties."

"Is that so? Very well! However, I did want to confirm our plans for the coming days. What type of monsters should we focus our attention on?"

"What?"

Itsuki and I both exclaimed our suspicions at the same time.

"Apparently we are heading for the Cal Mira islands. We'll do our leveling there. See to it that you are all prepared."

Ren barked out the order as if it were the most obvious thing in the world—but that's not what had surprised us.

"Wait a second—what are you talking about? I want to hear from you all, not from Ren."

"Oh, well . . . um . . . We were thinking that we could split up and work on our leveling separately from Mr. Ren."

Well that should be simple enough, except that I had no idea what they meant.

I got the gist of it, but . . . what did it mean? Was it just another method?

It looked like Itsuki was just as confused by this all as I was, but he chose not to say anything about it because of the incident we'd just been through with his party members.

"What?"

"Um . . . ."

I guess if Ren was okay with it, there wasn't a problem?

"Do you typically operate separately from Ren?"

Itsuki's curiosity got the better of him. In response, the whole party nodded.

They went on to explain themselves.

Ren's plan was to introduce his party members to areas of the map where the monsters were in the ideal power range for effective leveling.

They were to battle monsters and raise their levels, collecting materials, ores, and tools along the way.

Sometimes they would come across monsters that were particularly strong, at which point they would team up with Ren to defeat them.

"Mr. Ren was also quite clear that we were to avoid taking any damage in our fights with monsters."

I had a fare amount of experience with online RPGs, so I'd seen this kind of thing before. Stronger players in charge of guilds or other organizations would often recruit weaker players like this and let them in on secret leveling spots and rare item drops.

That seemed to be what was going on here.

"You don't say? So that means that Ren is fighting on his own?"

Itsuki was glaring at Ren, his irritation evident. Ren didn't seem to notice.

Ren's party members were clearly interpreting his actions positively, but still—I could sense a lot of distance between them.

It was simple, I guessed. Ren didn't think it was cool to be tied to a party. He wanted to be on his own.

He might have a lot of experience with online games, but could he have always been a solo player?

It was a play style I'd seen before. People that liked to do what they could on their own—only teaming up with others to take on large-scale events or to battle powerful boss characters.

Or it could be that he was the type that was part of a very small guild and would only recruit people that already knew of it, watching over their growth and managing them as a new style of play. I could understand playing with the system on a game, but would he really do that here in a completely new world?

I'd seen this online before, I knew the type.

Well Itsuki was no different, traveling to appease his own sense of moral superiority. What a bunch of heroes these two were.

"It's Naofumi's turn."

"Sure."

I could only imagine how they'd react when I introduced Raphtalia and Filo.

I'd thought that Ren and Itsuki would understand, but after meeting their parties I wasn't so sure anymore.

"Alright, this way."

I led the two of them over to where Raphtalia was resting.

"Welcome back, Mr. Naofumi. What happened?"

"The queen wants the heroes to cooperate, so we're introducing our party members."

"I see, then allow me to introduce myself. My name is Raphtalia."

"My name is Ren Amaki. I am the Sword Hero."

"I'm Itsuki Kawasaki, the Bow Hero. I have a feeling we'll be seeing a lot more of each other. I look forward to it."

"If you don't hold us back, we might come to depend on you."

Raphtalia's mouth hung open in stupefied shock at Ren's comment.

The way he said it made his position clear: he obviously assumed that she would only hold him back.

"I don't think I've ever been a burden in a battle."

"Ren didn't mean to insult or disparage you. We've seen your true power in battle before."

Itsuki jumped in to cover for Ren. He was only making it more confusing.

"He's right. You're stronger than I'd thought."

"Very much so . . . though that reminds me. Where is the young girl with the small wings on her back? I think she was able to turn into a monster of some kind?"

"You mean Filo? She's probably over there."

Filo was . . . I think she was over at the buffet counter stuffing her face.

I picked her out of the crowd and called out to her.

"Filo!"

"Hm?"

Hearing me call, she finally abandoned her plate of food and came running over.

"What do you want, master?"

"Yeah well . . . I think you already know these two faces, but I've got to formally introduce you."

"Why?"

Filo looked troubled and took a step back.

"Are they like the spear guy?"

"No, no. Compared to him, these two are upstanding guys."

"Yes, I feel the same way."

"Oh? They kind of look like they'd get along."

We all seemed to be in agreement on that. No one was as crazy over women as he was.

"So go on and introduce yourself."

"Okay! Filo's name . . . MY name is Filo!"

She sounded so stupid . . . . Why slip into the third person to introduce yourself?

"My job's to pull master's carriage!"

She was very proud of herself for her work. What would a normal person think, hearing a small girl brag about dragging carriages down the street?

Both Ren and Itsuki winced awkwardly as they looked at me.

"My name is Itsuki Kawasaki. Pleased to meet you."

"I'm Ren Amaki. Try not to hold us back . . . though I can see you won't."

"Yeah! Nice to meet you! Bow! Sword!"

After giving their full names, only to be called by their respective weapons, Ren and Itsuki shot me the same awkward wince.

With the introductions finished, the three of us fell to silence.

They might have thought it strange that I treated Raphtalia and Filo as other humans, instead of just treating them like subordinates.

"Raphtalia, weren't you once a slave?"

"Yes."

Itsuki's mouth hung open. What was he implying?

"Is this a master-slave relationship? How do you think of Naofumi?"

"Now that you mention it, I suppose it was that sort of relationship. I never really think about it."

Hearing Raphtalia's response, Itsuki continued to look confused.

"Anyway, Mr. Naofumi has never given me any strange or uncomfortable orders. I know that he depends on me, and so I want to do what I can for him."

"Have you ever thought that you hate fighting? Or that you'd like to be free?"

"I haven't. If I were free, there's nowhere for me to go. My old village is gone. All I want is to keep fighting with Mr. Naofumi."

"Is that so?"

"Why do you only ask questions to get a complaint out of her?"

It's like they'd taken this introduction as an opportunity to root out my weak points.

"I guess you already had made up your mind about this before Motoyasu challenged Naofumi?"

"Yes, I had . . . . I'm sorry about that."

He seemed to mostly just let it all go, but something about Itsuki's face betrayed his true feelings. He looked over at me.

What did he want from me? Raphtalia had been a slave, but now she was a trusted friend.

Was I imagining it? No . . . I could trust what she said.

"Let's introduce our friends to each other and then go back to speak with the queen."

"Good idea. Raphtalia, go introduce yourself to Ren and Itsuki's teammates. We're going to have to cooperate from now on. I know that it will make you a little uncomfortable, but do your best to avoid a fight."

"Understood."

Chapter Two: Meeting of the Heroes

After Ren and Itsuki explained the situation to their parties, we went to visit with the queen.

When we met up with her, she led us all out of the hall and into another room. We went down a hall and then climbed a spiral staircase.

Finally we reached the room, which must have been at the top of a tower, judging by the number of stairs we'd climbed.

It was a simple room, furnished with a large, round table in the center.

It reminded me of *the* round table. There were chairs already set around it for us, and we all took our seats.

"Soon, Mr. Kitamura, the Spear Hero, will join us. Please wait just a moment for his arrival."

Ren and Itsuki, apparently troubled by all the free time, stared off into the distance—they must have been looking at their gaming menus.

It was a good idea, I opened my own status tree.

I'd sort of neglected it recently, having been too busy. This was a good opportunity to get back up to speed.

Five minutes or so went by.

A disgruntled looking Motoyasu stumbled into the room

and made no effort to hide the hatred in his gaze when he glared at us.

"Mr. Kitamura, I trust you've gone to see my daughter? This is her punishment for attempting to poison Mr. Iwatani."

"That's right, you'd mentioned that."

Ren's cool gaze fell on Motoyasu and the queen.

"Fearing that Mr. Motoyasu might be angry with the circumstances, I ordered a subordinate of mine to extract a confession directly from my daughter, Bitch."

Bitch was currently under the slave-sealing spell and was only able to speak the truth.

She was especially unable to lie to either the queen or Motoyasu.

He'd probably gone to see her in the hospital, and heard her confession for himself. Did he believe it? Apparently not.

"Bitch isn't in the wrong! This is all Naofumi's fault!"

"I believe my daughter has confessed. And I believe you have been included in the slave-sealing ceremony as a master, so she certainly is unable to lie to you. Were you able to understand the gist of her story?"

" . . . ."

"Regardless, please understand that this is no longer the time to get into petty arguments over my daughter. If you value her life, you will help us protect this world. Its safety is also her own."

Motoyasu's irritation was evident, but he swallowed his protest and took a seat at the table. It was time to get down to business.

With us all seated around the table, the room had taken on a real Arthurian atmosphere.

With both Motoyasu and myself seated there, which of us played the part of the betraying knight?

"Now then, let us begin to share information between the four holy heroes. I, Queen Milleria Q. Melromarc, will moderate the discussion. Let us begin."

"Sure."

"Gladly."

"So we should share information . . . ."

"What is there to talk about?"

The queen was supposed to moderate the conversation, but Motoyasu's displeasure was clear, and he spat his question with obnoxious spite.

He could have learned to keep his emotions to himself a little more. It was clear that he was upset, but HIS woman was the one at fault here.

"I will be moderating this discussion, so I might as well begin it. I'd like to start by telling you about the opinions of our neighboring nations, as well as our own country's subjects."

So the queen had something she wanted to say right from the get-go.

"I will be frank. I have received communications from other diplomats expressing concern regarding the heroes' ability to survive the coming waves—all the heroes aside from Mr. Iwatani, that is."

"WHAT?!"

The other three heroes shouted in disbelief.

"What is that supposed to mean?!"

Itsuki was the one who shouted the question, but Motoyasu and Ren nodded along.

"It almost sounds like you're implying that Iwatani is the strongest one here!"

"Then let me ask you something. Who among you landed the most effective attacks against the high priest of the Church of the Three Heroes? I've actually heard that the rest of you were effectively defeated before Mr. Iwatani was able to defeat the high priest himself."

"Um . . . ."

I liked the way this conversation was going.

The other guys had all played games similar to this world back in their own worlds, so they seemed to assume that they knew what they needed to do to power up—and yet, they honestly didn't seem to really be all that strong.

At the very beginning of all this, I had definitely been way behind the rest of them. But these days it seemed like I had made up for that initial difference.

Motoyasu had a pretty hard time defending himself from Filo, and that had been before she'd even leveled up.

I didn't know what their actual levels were, but from what I had heard, they'd all participated in quite a few battles around the world. I'd lost all that time when I'd traveled around selling items, and so I hadn't been able to class-up as soon as the others. Yet they had still lost to me in a battle. What did it mean?

And they were heroes too, so at the very least they should have been more powerful than your average, everyday citizen.

Trash had also given them all a substantial amount of money to start their travels, so they shouldn't have had any trouble in the money department either.

"The citizens of the world wish for the heroes to cooperate. I trust you understand what I am getting at."

"Very well."

The three wore expressions of deep disappointment, but they seemed to grasp the point of the meeting.

"Naofumi, why don't we hear from you first?"

"Why do I need to go first? The queen started this by addressing you."

"Well to be honest, I find your strength odd, considering the level that you and your teammates currently are. You're too strong. That ridiculous shield of yours also seems strangely overpowered."

"Yeah, I want to address that too. The Raphtalia girl, not

to mention that monster Filo, are both much stronger than I would have expected. It's not natural."

"Yeah. Little Raphtalia-chan and Filo can really hold their own."

These creeps. We were supposed to be sharing information, but instead they were using this as an opportunity to get me to do all the talking. They had some mixed up priorities.

I guess that meant with all they supposedly knew about the world, they weren't expecting to run into the curse series, or for Raphtalia and Filo to be as powerful as they were.

Then again, I couldn't just tell them whatever they wanted to hear.

"And what are you three planning on giving me in exchange for this information?"

"What?"

"Is that such a crazy question? Think back to the beginning of all this. You all sat me down and told me that the shield class was underpowered and weak. You cut me off and left me to my own devices. You didn't tell me anything. Now you want to know the secret of my power, but how am I supposed to know that you'll share what you know once you get what you want out of me?"

If I had information that they wanted, that put me at an advantage for any negotiations that were about to start. I didn't want to give that up.

If they wanted information out of me, they'd have to go first—they had to tell me everything that they knew.

"It's not like we purposefully kept secrets . . . ."

"Look at your help screen."

"I suppose we could have been a little more forthcoming with our knowledge, but . . . ."

The three of them all responded pathetically.

"However you spin it, none of you helped me. You might say 'look at the help screen' and try to act all cool. But would the help screen tell me the most efficient areas of the map for leveling?"

I had to really read their reactions if I wanted to get any information out of them at all.

Had I forgotten how to get information out of someone?

Sure, we were all trying to manipulate each other. If you wanted success in negotiations, you had to find some way to control the flow of the conversation.

I'd managed to create an atmosphere where they realized they would have to indulge me in information if they wanted to get anything out of me.

If I made one final push, maybe I could secure an advantage.

"Just like the rest of you, I have some secrets of my own. I think it's finally time we all had a real heart-to-heart."

"Ha!"

Ren snorted, obviously annoyed.

"And you know what else? You three need to realize that you've already lost against the waves once. If you mess up like that again, you're going to die."

"What are you talking about? That was a special event battle—you have to lose that one."

"What?"

"Yeah, if the heroes lose that battle, they just get carried to the hospital and they wake up there. You don't die. The story is set up that way."

"Yeah, it's as good as proven. Just look at what happened once we lost to the high priest—we woke up in the hospital."

What the hell were they saying? Were they out of their minds?

"What are you three saying? Occasionally I have trouble understanding what Mr. Iwatani is saying, but this is something new altogether!"

The queen exclaimed. She seemed very troubled. I felt the same way.

It's like the three of them had just claimed immortality in front of us. They thought that they would never die, no matter what they did.

"Well, just so you know . . . I actually defeated that high priest after you lost to him, so . . . ."

The three of them all shouted in unison again.

"There's no way a shielder could win that fight. It's because of that weird shield you have."

Damn, they were getting annoying.

If they lost, they'd just wake up in the hospital? Was that how their game worked? Did they honestly think this was just a game, and that these were only events to advance the plot?

Even though they lost I remembered how they'd condescended to me and my shield. It made me furious just thinking about it.

It . . . It was . . . .

"Anyway, that stuff doesn't matter. Let's move on."

Doesn't matter? These idiots were still treating everything like a game!

This was absurd—absolutely crazy! Their misunderstanding of the situation needed to be addressed immediately.

"You idiots. You know this isn't a game, right?! If you die here, it's all over!"

"Right, but we are protected."

"Yeah."

"Exactly."

There was just no reaching these people.

This conversation was making me very uncomfortable. Even with all the problems I'd run into since arriving in this world, this conversation might have been more dangerous than any of them. I tried to tell them all, but they just wouldn't listen. So what else could I do? I had to just go along for the ride.

I had to be strong enough to survive after they'd all died. With the way they were talking, that day might not be far off.

But wait . . . no. Fitoria had said that the waves would get more severe if the heroes died.

"So that's how you think the world works and you guys still tried to kill me? What would have happened if you'd succeeded?"

"What do you mean? You just would have died."

Itsuki said it like it was nothing.

So they didn't feel any hesitation at the thought of murder? As long as they got 'the bad guy' everything was just fine?

"I thought it was a little weird. I figured we wouldn't be able to kill you."

"I just figured you'd end up back in your own world. Crazy."

"Motoyasu—I should send YOU back to your own world!"

Why did he even think that would happen? What an idiot!

"Anyway, enough with thinking of everything like a game. Enough is enough! It's a miracle that you three are still alive at all!"

The three of them let my words blow by without comment. They didn't even respond. They wouldn't understand until the truth waltzed over and slapped them in the face—but by then it would be too late.

I sighed. "Anyway. You all better start talking. Tell me everything you know, right from the beginning. If you don't, then I don't have anything to tell you either."

"Well there's no avoiding it then, is there? It's a pain, but if you insist . . . ."

"Yes, and the heroes must also stop interfering with one another's successes."

"Whatever. Nothing will change in the end. Nothing at all."

They better start talking, and fast. I needed to know what I needed to do to get stronger.

They'd wrested control of the conversation through sheer idiocy, but it was time for me to take the controls back.

"And Itsuki," I started. "Certainly a hero that fights for justice would never take the side of liar to appease his sense of balance . . . would he?"

"Lies? I do not lie!"

"I wonder. What's less cool than lying, eh Ren?"

"Who knows?"

"And women don't like liars at all, do they Motoyasu?"

"No, they don't."

Was that enough? I hoped I'd sealed off the possibility of their continued lies before the conversation started moving again.

I imagined that Ren was very concerned with looking as cool as possible.

Motoyasu wanted the ladies to like him.

Itsuki was all about justice. Sure, he could define that however was convenient at the time—that's why I made sure he associated it with lying at the table. With that in his head, he'd find it hard to lie straight out.

With all the pieces in place, the three of them were more likely to tell the truth.

"Alright, Itsuki, you go first. Tell me everything right from the beginning."

"Why are you in charge?"

Itsuki knit his eyebrows together in annoyance but turned to the rest of the table and started talking.

"The heroes' weapons are unlocked by the materials that are absorbed into them. This also expands the skill tree that is available. The system is very similar to the game I used to play, *Dimension Wave*, but there are differences here and there."

"Huh? It's not the exact same?"

"No—but it's very similar. There are a lot of weapons here that I've never seen."

That would mean that he didn't know all there was to know about the different weapons in this world.

That made sense. If he had known all about the different weapons and their skills, then he should have known about the slave and monster shields as well.

"The biggest difference is probably that, in this world, when you change to a new weapon, the other weapons you have used remain available to you."

Ren and Motoyasu nodded along. So this place wasn't exactly like the games they were used to? That was kind of worrisome.

"I'll go next."

Ren raised his hand and started to speak.

"I'll take over where Itsuki left off. When a weapon is unlocked, certain equip bonuses become available to you."

I knew that I could trust that information, because I already knew it to be true.

"Still, the equip bonus system is a little different than what I'm used to from *Brave Star Online*."

"How so?"

"In my game, you normally learned skills by earning skill points through skills you already knew."

That made sense to me too. In games that I had played in the past there were skill points available to the player, and they could assign them however they wanted to customize their character.

I felt like . . . like if I could just unlock the skill tree of this one shield, then all the skills would suddenly be available.

Anyway, what really surprised me was that, despite all

these differences, the three of them still seemed confident that they were in the same game as the one they were familiar with from their own worlds.

"You're right. It was just like that."

"Yeah."

"But I think that only the heroes are able to unlock the entire skill tree."

I was starting to understand. Normal adventurers could only unlock certain portions of the skill tree, depending on the conditions that open up to them in their growth. Only the heroes, because of their legendary weapons, could unlock everything.

"My turn. If you hold a weapon type that you specialize in, you can copy them. I think they have a 'weapon copy system.'"

"What?"

What was that? I'd never heard of anything like that!

"Yeah, that's a lot different from the game I was used to, but I was able to get a really strong weapon for free, so it ended up being a big help."

"Well, we are heroes, after all. We do have some advantages."

"I'm sure everyone already knows this, but the weapon shop in the capital of Zeltbul, the mercenary country, has the best equipment."

The other two went along nodding with what Motoyasu said.

"What's that now?!"

I was so upset I practically screamed.

Weapon copying?

I'd never seen anything like that in the help menu. I'd already spent four months here, so I'd taken the time to go through the entire menu item by item.

It sounded like they were saying that if you just picked up a weapon at a shop then you could unlock the ability to use it.

"Naofumi, you mean to say that you didn't even know that? I'm impressed you've managed to stay alive for as long as you have!"

Ugh . . . now I was getting pissed. Really pissed! I'd just assumed that I could only use special shields I unlocked myself!

I'd only seen weird things like iron shields and round shields and book shields up until this point—I thought those were the only kinds available.

"You guys figured this out on your own?"

"Not really, we just went to buy weapons at the shop. That's a normal thing to do, right? Considering that the weapon you start out with is so weak."

I had tried to do the very same thing when I first got here. I'd wanted to give up on being a shielder, so I tried to use a sword I'd picked up at the weapon shop.

But when I did, a warning popped up that said, "You are unable to equip or carry a weapon other than the legendary weapon you have been assigned."

It meant that I couldn't use anything other than my shield in battle.

"The rules say that you can only use the weapon you've been assigned, but if you use the weapon copy system, you can pretty much equip anything."

"Yeah."

"That's right."

This was starting to give me a headache.

Besides, I was stuck with a shield. Attacking was the most important thing for me to focus on, so I had pretty much ignored the shields that were on sale at weapon shops.

I was already equipped with a shield that leveled up with me, so I had only been focused on trying to get a weapon, like a sword, into my other hand.

Maybe that's why I had never noticed?

"Alright, keep talking."

If they'd already covered such major things that I hadn't been able to figure out, I was nervous just thinking of how much else had been kept from me.

"When you kill a monster and it turns into materials that you absorb into your weapon, you can open the weapon menu at the same time to get the monster's dropped items."

Dropped items?

Hmm . . . I'd seen something like that in online RPGs before. Normally monsters would leave items behind once you defeated them.

They might leave behind something that had nothing to do with the sort of materials they were made from.

I'd been so stupid! I should have been able to figure something that simple out for myself!

"There are items that cost a lot of money at shops that get dropped pretty frequently. I have a bunch of rare stuff now, it really makes me feel like I'm in a whole new world."

"It does, doesn't it?"

"You're right. Sometimes the monsters leave really useful items behind."

They just kept on coming out with more and more important information. And on top of that, it seemed like they all already knew all of it.

They'd made me feel this way the first day I'd met them, but now I felt it again—that searing feeling that I was at a disadvantage.

"What else? Oh yeah, you can make tools."

"Tech skills, right? Yeah, we've had those from the very start."

"Keep going, I'm listening."

The information that they took for granted might all be

new to me. I needed to prepare myself to hear them out.

"If you have the tech skill and the recipe, then you can give the necessary materials to your weapon. It will absorb them, and after a certain amount of time the weapon will make what you want."

The weapons could systematize item production?! Were they joking? I couldn't bear to think back on all the time I'd spent crafting medicines.

Apparently the effectiveness of the item was the same whether the weapon made it automatically or if you stayed up all night working on it yourself—but if you had a recipe, and the weapon could do all the work for you, why go through all the trouble?

That must explain why Motoyasu had a stock of magic water—he wouldn't have gone through all the effort to make that on his own.

Maybe the materials needed to make it were easy to obtain from monsters?

"The only bad part is that you can't really use items aside from the drops you picked up or the ones you made yourself."

"That's right. You can't use them easily."

Apparently there were some issues with the item system. Not that I was concerned with that.

I couldn't believe there were so many empowering techniques I hadn't known about.

"As for efficient leveling areas, well, I don't think we can sum that up in a sentence or two."

"Right. We could make up a chart or something, listing good places and monsters depending on your level range. That way if you just stuck to the list appropriate for your level you wouldn't really run into any major problems."

"We have to make sure not to overlap though."

"Good point."

"Is there anything else you want to tell me about?"

I took mental notes of all the points they'd brought up and tried to keep the conversation moving.

"It seems like there is one major technique for getting stronger quickly that Naofumi doesn't know yet. I suppose I should tell him."

Itsuki stuck his chest out and spoke with an important air about him.

"In this world, the rarity of a weapon is very important. The abilities it comes with are just an afterthought. If the weapon itself isn't strong and rare, then it won't be worth very much."

"You mean unique weapons or legendary equipment?"

"Yes, something like that."

"Stop lying!"

"It's not right to start off telling the truth and then switch to lies halfway through."

Ren and Motoyasu both snapped and spat at Itsuki. Here come more lies.

"What? What are you saying? I'm telling the truth!"

"Nope. That was a lie."

"Yeah, you're a liar."

"I am not! I'm not lying!!"

What was going on? Itsuki had lost his cool. He really seemed to be angered by the other two.

Something strange was going on.

"Let's hear him out."

I waved off their little argument and signaled for Itsuki to continue.

"Right, well . . . . It depends on the type of weapon you're working with, obviously, but normally you can use ores to make them stronger."

It sounded like he was talking about some kind of refining system. I'd seen things like that in games before.

"Iron plates have the most amount of ore slots."

"I'm sure there's a risk of failure. You shouldn't tell such dangerous lies."

Motoyasu spoke out to silence Itsuki.

"No! It never fails!"

Wait, so there was no risk of failure? What was the truth?

"What are you talking about? You don't use ores to power up anything."

"You better stop calling me a liar! What about you, Ren? How do you power things up?"

"Me? Good question. I don't want to see Naofumi get all confused by your lies, so I guess I should step in and tell him the truth."

Why did he need to call me out by name? Whatever, he was right that I was getting confused.

"This world is all about your level. There might be other things to worry about, but in the end it all comes down to whether you have leveled up enough."

"Another liar."

"You! You think you can lie all you want if you keep your face all cool and aloof!"

What was going on here?

"Naofumi, apparently both of these guys are planning to lie their way to the end of this meeting. I guess it's up to me to tell you the truth. If you want to power up your weapon, it's all about skill mastery."

"Skill mastery?"

"Exactly. The more you use a weapon, the stronger that weapon will get. The important part is that when it's time to switch weapons, you have to turn that weapon's accumulated skill mastery into energy. Then you add that energy to your new weapon, and that will unlock the new weapon's hidden powers."

"That's one of the more impressive lies I've heard yet."

"Don't worry about him. You just need to keep increasing the rarity of your weapons. You may fail or you lose a weapon, but our legendary weapons are safe."

All of their stories made it sound so simple. But none of the things they mentioned could be found anywhere in the help menus.

I didn't know who to believe. Were Ren and Itsuki lying?

"Just listen to yourself, lying with a straight face like that. You're no better than Naofumi."

Motoyasu brushed Ren off.

"What was that?!"

"He's right, you shouldn't listen to him—he's lying."

"You're all crazy. Who is he supposed to believe? And I am NOT lying!"

"See for yourself. Open up your skill tree and look at a weapon you use a lot. You can check its skill mastery right there."

I did like Motoyasu said and opened my menu, then looked for the Chimera Shield.

But when I got the menu for the shield open, it just displayed the status like it always did.

He said I should check something? It was looking like a lie.

I reached a finger out to touch it but nothing happened.

"Nothing happened."

I should have known it was a lie. I knew enough not to believe them from the start of this, but I was surprised that they would lie to my face when I could check the veracity of their claims.

If that was a lie, then their claims about the weapon copy system were probably lies too.

"I am not lying! You're just trying to ruin my reputation!"

"I can't do it either."

"Me neither. That option just isn't in the help menu."

"Ugh! Whatever! I was stupid for trying to help you in the first place!"

Ren got very upset at each of Itsuki's and Motoyasu's explanations, sighing and crossing his arms angrily. He slumped down in his seat.

Ren was normally so cool and collected. In fact, I don't think I'd ever seen him so upset. Still, both of the other heroes insisted that he was lying, and a quick look through my own help menu seemed to verify as much.

"I wasn't finished. There is another way to power up your weapon. You have to take the energy out of another item and use it to enchant the weapon. If you do it will increase the power of the item by a certain percentage."

"You mean like raising the attack power by 10 percent?"

"Yes, but there is a significant risk. If you fail, then the value falls to zero."

"Another lie. Stop telling Naofumi about some other game."

"I'm telling the truth! This is how I've gotten stronger—by using the energy of different monsters and items to enchant my weapon. It works for all of my weapons. It's a parallel system to your current level—like having a job level."

Thinking over what he said, I realized I'd seen similar things in games I'd played in the past. You could level up your equipment to gain new abilities. It wasn't very exciting, but it worked. Still, I think I remembered learning some really powerful abilities that way.

"Okay, okay . . . Ren and Itsuki are getting a little out of control. Allow me . . . ."

"I'm not expecting much, but go ahead."

I was already expecting nothing but lies out of the whole group.

"I'm telling you, the most important thing to focus on is smelting weapons and status levels. The performance that you get out of status levels is way more important than what you get from your actual level. Even if you stick with the weakest weapon, the one you started with, if you smelt it properly, it can be really strong! I made all my equip bonuses work to raise my attack power."

"Now THAT'S a real lie!"

"It is. Naofumi, don't listen to him!"

Motoyasu brushed their protests aside and kept speaking directly to me.

"It's different for every weapon, but the first thing you need is to collect ores for smelting. Now, in *Emerald Online* you would lose your weapon if the smelting process failed. But that doesn't happen with our legendary weapons. Here, if you fail, the smelting value just falls to zero."

"That's not true!"

"Yeah!"

The argument was getting intense and out of control. The queen looked puzzled by all the disagreements.

Honestly, I was pretty confused myself.

Did they think they could get away with lying if they all lied?

"Anyway, then there are the eye spirits and the status enchantments. Depending on the piece of the monster soul you combine with the weapon, the effect will be different. The options vary by weapon, but let's say that you have a weapon for dueling. You can raise the damage the weapon does to other humans."

"Itsuki, didn't you say something similar to that?"

"There are only so many slots available on the weapon, and the percentages are fixed."

"Tell the truth!"

"Yeah, I'm tired of hearing about some other game."

Both Ren and Itsuki shouted to silence Motoyasu, who turned, frustrated, to face them both.

"Why do you all keep lying?"

"Why are YOU lying?"

"Both of you are lying!"

"Well I don't know who's lying and who's not . . . ."

The conversation had gone so well until we reached the end. Then apparently everyone had a different version of the truth.

The three of them all looked incensed—I don't think I'd ever seen them all in such blatant disagreement.

"Could it be that all of your weapons are powered up differently?"

"Let's just agree to disagree."

"It works as an explanation in the short run. Let's leave it at that."

"Fine—but so far none of your explanations have meshed with what I've seen going on."

And then, apparently, the conversation was over.

If all of them were as angry as they seemed to be, then they probably weren't lying.

Even if they were lying, their lies would only affect their own reputations.

"Fine. Well I guess it's my turn."

"Yes. We've all done our best to fill you in on what we

know, so you better come clean yourself."

"If you think I'm lying, I'm not going to take the blame."

This whole thing was getting more confusing by the minute.

"What do you want to know first?"

To tell the truth, these three approached everything as if it were a game. At the very least, I needed to find some way to make them take this seriously—or all our lives would be in danger. So I had better tell them the truth.

"Tell us why Raphtalia and Filo are as powerful as they are."

"That's easy enough. I have a Slave-User Shield and a Monster-User Shield, both of which have great equip bonuses that let me affect how they level up. There are effects like 'status adjustment' and other things. And Filo has one other bonus from my Filolial Shield."

Should I tell them about the floating cowlick during the class-up ceremony? I decided to wait and see how the rest of the meeting played out.

"The shield class in the game I know didn't have any skills that were that useful."

"I find that very difficult to believe. Such skills would break the game . . . . Where did you find a cheating shield?"

Cheating? Ha . . . whatever—there was no pleasing these guys.

"I got the Slave-User Shield from the ink that is used in the slave curse ceremony, and I got the Monster-User Shield from a piece of the egg that Filo hatched from."

"Well if he tells us where he got the shields, we might as well try for ourselves."

"You can try, but there's no guarantee that the same thing will happen for you."

"Sure, but you could be lying to us."

"Think whatever you want. What if it's a leveling system that's only available on the legendary shield?"

"Okay, let's just pretend you're telling the truth. It still doesn't explain why Filo is as strong as she is. Her power is remarkable. She'd been strong enough from the beginning, but now she's something else completely. How did that happen?"

"Oh—that. That happened when we were busy running away from you and Bitch. A nobleman that was under the employ of the Church of the Three Heroes removed the seal on a powerful monster."

"I heard about that—but I heard that you were the one that released the beast."

The queen leaned forward and interjected.

"Actually, I had an official investigation conducted concerning this matter. It seems the corrupt nobleman in the town refused to admit his defeat at Mr. Iwatani's hands, and then released the monster out of desperation."

I hadn't had a chance to go back and check on the area after we'd left. There was a really nice nobleman in the neighboring town. I privately called him Nice Guy. He'd made the local demi-human community into a priority of sorts. I wonder what ended up happening to him?

"Excuse me, your majesty. What happened to the nobility in the neighboring town?"

"After all that transpired, we have decided to have him brought back to his town. It's only been a short time, but he was very exhausted from the escape, and we have been seeing to his medical treatment in the meantime."

"Oh . . . ."

We'd also met someone from Raphtalia's village, and they'd escaped with Nice Guy. We could only hope that they'd all made it home safely.

"What sort of monster did the nobleman release?"

"We lured the beast away from any populated centers and attempted to fight it out in the wilderness. But just as the battle was starting, the queen of the filolials, Fitoria, appeared and defeated the monster. Then she used some sort of magic to transport us all to a safe place."

"Transport?"

"That's the only word I can think of. It was like I suddenly lost my footing. I don't really understand it."

"Don't you have any transport skills? When I saw you

running from Motoyasu before, I realized you didn't know any, but I figured you must have procured one or two by now."

Ren nodded along with Itsuki, and Motoyasu also nodded in agreement.

"There are skills like that?"

"Of course. Mine is a skill called Transport Bow. You can register places that you have already visited, and then instantly transport yourself and your party there at any time."

"Mine is called Transport Sword. It works the same way."

"Mine is Portal Spear. You really don't know about this stuff?"

"No! This is the first I've heard of it!"

What were they talking about? I sure wish I'd known that being a hero had such convenient benefits!

"To unlock it you have to be at level 50 though—a little high."

That would explain why I didn't have it. I was still at level 43.

Wait a second, did that mean that these clowns were all over level 50?

"What materials do you need?"

"The sand from the dragon hourglass."

"That's right . . . ."

The three of them nodded. But . . . .

"How did you get them to let you have any sand?!"

"We just asked for it and they gave it to us."

Dammit! I'd only run into those curmudgeon sisters when I was in the church—and they wouldn't let me have anything at all.

"Well? So what happened after the transport?"

"She spent some time teaching Filo how to battle effectively, and then she did . . . something . . . and Filo's stats shot way up. Then she sat me down and lectured me, saying that the heroes needed to work together. She said that if she didn't, she'd kill us all."

Ha! The three of them looked like they didn't believe a word that I was saying.

"If you think I'm lying, maybe you'd like to have a battle with Filo for yourselves? We just went through the class-up ceremony too, so she's even stronger now."

Didn't they realize that Filo's stats were nearly double my own?

Motoyasu had a hard enough time holding his own against me in a battle—he wouldn't stand a chance against Filo.

"No. That won't be necessary."

"Okay, I'll ask the next question. During the battle with the high priest, Naofumi commanded a lot of power. It was unnatural. It came from that ominous-looking shield of his. I never saw anything like that in the game I played."

Itsuki shot me a doubtful look and kept on talking.

"Where did you find a power like that? No, that's not quite right, let me rephrase: Where did you meet God?"

"What?"

"Did you meet God somewhere and receive a cheating shield from him? There's a web novel I read where the main character gets a special power like that and it enables him to pull ahead of the other characters. Tell me the truth."

Ha! I knew the story he was talking about, but nothing like that had happened here.

I'd been through a lot since showing up in this world, but few questions have irritated me the way that this one did.

"It's not cheating!"

"Oh, yes it is. A shielder shouldn't really be able to deal any damage at all!"

Ren and Motoyasu nodded.

"Where did you get it? If we were able to get our hands on a power like that then we would be unstoppable. You have to tell us."

These morons just spat nonsense on top of nonsense. It was starting to really piss me off.

"Maybe I just worked really hard for it?"

"Yeah right."

They were a bunch of brutes. They had already made up their minds about what a shielder could do.

But I had a feeling they were mistaken. I think that

shielders were stronger than they thought.

I saw it this way: I worked on getting more and better equip bonuses, and as a result I eventually got my hands on the curse series—that's how I ended up being stronger than any of them.

But they seemed to think that I had somehow figured out how to cheat so that I could be as powerful as they were.

"That shield is called the Shield of Rage. It's part of the curse series that is contained in the legendary shield. I don't know exactly what caused it to come out, but if I had to guess . . . I would say that it responded to my own anger. It first showed up when I was dueling with Motoyasu. I was very angry because I was tricked and cheated and everything was unfair."

I remembered when it happened. I was so angry and the anger had nowhere to go. I thought it was going to swallow me completely.

If Raphtalia hadn't been there to calm me down, who knows what would have happened?

"It's all right there in the help menu. It says you'll have to pay a price for using it. Could you three control it? By the way, I used it to defeat the high priest, but it attacked me too, and as a result my stats are still recovering."

Ren squinted and waved his finger through the air. He must have been looking through the help menus.

Then, as if it were the most obvious thing in the world, he said, "Nope. There's nothing like that in here."

Give me a break! It was right there in my menu. I'd been able to read about it from the moment the Shield of Rage was unlocked.

"It might not show up until you unlock the weapon."

"Do internet games tend to have lots of really powerful cursed weapons available?"

"Of course not. That growth adjusting shield seems pretty suspect too."

"If you're going to lie to us, you should think of better lies—just like Ren and Motoyasu here."

Ren completely lost his cool when he heard what Itsuki said. He leapt to his feet and jabbed his finger at Itsuki.

"Who the hell are you to talk?! You're the worst lying hypocrite here!"

"Is that so? What about you, always pretending to be so cool! You don't look so cool now, do you?!"

"Yeah, exactly."

Ren and Itsuki both turned and shouted together. "You're just a womanizing fool! Looking for another hussy yet?!"

"What was that?!"

"All of you! How long are you going to run around pretending this is a game? You need to act like actual heroes or we are all going to die!"

Honestly, I don't even want to remember what happened next. The room collapsed into vulgar name-calling.

The queen shouted in protest, saying whatever she could to try and get the room under control, but it was already too late. There was no stopping it.

The shouting and fighting continued until the door flew open, rattling on its hinges as a crowd of soldiers filed in.

"What happened?"

The sudden appearance of the soldiers somehow brought me back to reality, and my head cleared for a second.

"The heroes' party members have started to argue downstairs!"

"What?!"

Those idiots . . . what had they gotten themselves into now?

We all hurried out of the room and down the stairs.

"You better take that back!"

"I don't think so. That ugly thing—he's a scar on the world! My eyes don't lie."

"Are you sure you aren't talking about yourself?!"

"Ha! Like the servant of an arrogant fool like him would have any idea!"

By the time we arrived in the hall, Raphtalia was in a shouting match with Bitch and Armor, the flashy armor guy.

Ren's party, along with Filo and that Rishia girl, stood back and watched helplessly.

Raphtalia was furious. I'd never seen her so upset. What on earth had happened?

Bitch sure was looking energetic though. She'd just been poisoned and come back from the hospital, and she was already getting into fights?

Motoyasu's party, including Bitch, consisted of three people.

One of them was standing next to Bitch and participating in the argument. The other one was standing off at a distance, watching the battle unfold.

"Ha! How could anyone hope to survive with party members like dirty demi-humans and nasty monsters?"

"Oh just die and get it over with already! This is punishment for causing a ruckus."

The queen snapped her fingers and the slave curse activated.

"Kyaaaaaaaaa!"

A glowing seal appeared on Bitch's chest and she fell to the floor, writhing in pain.

Itsuki's teammate, the armor guy, was shocked at the queen's actions. He stood back and his face went pale as he watched.

"I swear . . . . Why do you have to do these things?"

The queen looked exhausted as she looked down on the writhing Bitch.

She wasn't going to kill her . . . was she?

"Raphtalia, what happened?"

"We were talking to the others about how to best cooperate from now on, when Bitch and the others came over and started saying that there was no need to team up with us, that only bad things could come of it. Then she started insulting my village and making fun of Filo . . . . Then she started insulting Melty, saying that she knew how to read her parents' faces so she could manipulate them. She was boasting of all the horrible things that she's done!"

I sighed and glared at Itsuki and Motoyasu.

"You mustn't! These two are friends of a hero, and they fight to save this world!"

Itsuki, sensing the direction things were going, turned to Armor and scolded him.

"But Master Itsuki . . . aren't these people wandering around and causing problems everywhere they go?"

That was rich. This coming from the guy who was causing a problem right here, right now.

"That has been shown to have been a misunderstanding. Please make your peace with them."

"Very well."

"Myn . . . I mean, Whore! Why are you treating her like this?"

Motoyasu cradled Bitch in his arms and glared at the queen.

"This is the punishment she receives for inciting disorder. It's as simple as that. From all that I've heard, the problem seems to lie with her and her alone."

The queen snapped open her fan and covered her mouth as she spoke. Motoyasu's displeasure was evident—he stared at her, hate burning in his eyes.

"Mr. Kitamura? Take the time to properly think this over. This girl just got back from her convalescence in the hospital, and this is the first thing she did."

"Urm . . . ."

"Did you hear what just happened here? Is it not obvious where the blame lies?"

Motoyasu, clearly sensing that he was over his head, said nothing else. He simply cradled Bitch in his arms and left the hall.

Itsuki had his hands full trying to calm down Armor.

The man was showing respect enough for Itsuki, but then he'd participate in actions like these.

"I think the feast has gone on long enough. Let's call it a day. Later, on another day when tempers are not so high, I'd like to attempt a conversation with you all once again, one with the heroes all present."

"Sure."

"Agreed."

Ren and I nodded.

Itsuki nodded his agreement and then left the room.

Give me a break . . . . Things were growing tenser by the minute. How were we supposed to learn to cooperate now?

The heroes had to cooperate, or else Fitoria would come and kill us all. We were already in dire straits, but our problems were continuing to multiply.

Chapter Three: Power Up

"Hmmm . . . ."

The hall was quiet now, and I was thinking over all they'd said. I'd already sent Raphtalia and Filo back to the room.

Thinking over it all with some silence, I realized I would just have to treat the heroes with suspicion.

I think I had already gotten all the information out of them that I could realistically hope for.

But I didn't know how to figure out what was actually true and what was just another elaborate lie.

There was one thing on which they had all agreed: when you absorbed a defeated monster, the monster released a drop item.

They had also all agreed on the weapon copy system.

The rest must have been differences between the games that they had all played back in their home worlds.

They said that if you held a weapon then you could make a copy of it, and that once you met the requirements you could equip it normally.

They'd also said that they weapon you used could perform certain tasks for you, like crafting.

Yeah, they'd all agreed on at least those points.

But they'd disagreed on how you were supposed to power up your items. I decided to try and figure out what their positions had been.

Let's say that everyone's weapons behaved differently—that's fine, except that I didn't know how my shield worked. Everyone else had experience with a game that reflected the way their weapons seemed to behave, but I didn't. Sure, I'd read a book about the heroes back in my world, but the section that was supposed to describe my own weapon was blank!

I took out a memo pad and tried to sum up what they'd all said about the power-up system.

★ Ren
Strength is basically determined by your level.

Mastery: using the same weapon would improve your proficiency with it.

Energy transfer: when you finished using a weapon, you could reset its mastery level and release the amount of energy you had invested in it. Finally, any items that you had absorbed into the weapon could also be turned into energy.

Increasing rarity: by imbuing a weapon with energy, you can increase its rarity level. This tends to increase the weapon's abilities.

★ Motoyasu

Everything is based on your weapon. The most important thing is spirit enchantment, and the original stats of your weapon are not very important. All you need is enough strength and experience to use the weapon.

Smelting: you can power up a piece of equipment using ores. There is a chance of failure.

Spirit enchantment: pieces of monsters' souls, or items, that have been absorbed into a weapon can be used to imbue the weapon with special powers. This has no chance of failure—maybe.

Status enchantment: stats can also be increased in the same way.

★ Itsuki

A weapon's rarity is the most important thing. The enchantments are just an extra boost. When you have something rare, it makes more sense to call it a rare weapon.

Power up: the power of a weapon can be raised by equipping it with certain ores. This never fails.

Item enchantment: items that have been absorbed into a weapon can be turned into energy, and that can be used to raise the percentage of various stats. The success is based on probability, and therefore there is a chance of failure.

Job level: you can increase your stats by using the energy contained in absorbed monsters or items.

That should be it.

They really had nothing to do with one another at all.

They all sort of involved energy power-ups, smelting, and rarity of some kind.

If I translated it into words I understood, it sounded like Itsuki was talking about unique weapons and rare weapons dropped by bosses.

Ren was talking about the rarity inherent in the actual weapon. Like a rare example of an iron sword or something.

As for enchanting, there were apparently three different versions.

The three of them were all familiar with this world from games that they had played, but those games must have been different from one another.

They'd called them VRMMO, then a normal MMO, and the last one was a consumer game.

I'd never heard of VRMMO, and MMO and consumer games certainly didn't sound like they were referring to the same system. If they had anything to do with one another, the consumer game might have been a fan-produced copy of an MMO.

Back in my own world, I'd played different games that had exhibited qualities similar to the systems the other three had all described.

It sort of made sense in a way. If they were all playing

different games, then their descriptions wouldn't match up, and of course they'd think the others were lying.

They'd all said that there was no such thing as the curse series.

When I'd first looked at my growth tree, I didn't see it either. In fact, that whole branch of the tree hadn't appeared until I thought Filo had died and I got really upset. This was just another instance of us all having different opinions on how the world worked.

But . . . what did it really mean?

I looked down at the shield on my arm.

Could it be that the legendary weapons somehow reflected the heart of its user?

The heart? What did that even mean?

Refusal . . . right. Somewhere deep inside, I was refusing.

Fitoria had warned me that the heroes had to work together. That must mean something.

Weapon copy . . . . The three of them had all agreed on it, so it couldn't have been a lie.

The drop items too.

But I hadn't known about those things, and they hadn't been listed in my help menu either.

I opened my weapon icon and looked through the options. Sure enough, those things weren't listed.

But now that I think about it, I think my menus had

included more options before I was framed and cast out of the castle. I wasn't imagining it. I was sure of it.

Alright! I had to try something.

There MUST be a section on item drops! There MUST be a section on weapon copying!

All three of them had confirmed those items simultaneously, so they had to be listed in their menus.

I tried to imagine a screen that listed all the dropped items I'd acquired up until this point. What would it look like?

I opened up the shield menu. There was a soft beep as the window opened before me.

There it was, with a flash—a long list of all the items dropped by monsters I'd defeated up until that point.

"What the hell?!"

You had to believe in it for it to appear. By guarding myself from others to keep myself safe, I'd limited my options.

It looked like there was an item box, and it was filled with monsters. When I clicked on the monster, the item it dropped would show up.

Hey, there were some medicinal herbs that you needed to make magic water. And there were lots of materials for making soul-healing water too.

And there was a lot of . . . garbage. And there were plenty of monster organs and guts too.

I'd been so angry, but they'd had no reason to lie. If I just thought that and opened the shield menu, but nothing showed up.

That meant that I was refusing it somehow.

I'd really never thought that those liars could be telling the truth.

Did I just not believe enough? Ha! This was starting to sound like a kid's show. But it was true. I believed it.

"Mr. Iwatani?"

The queen was calling for me. I decided that if I wanted to survive, I had to believe. I'd have to have a staring contest with the shield.

This is the legendary shield. What did it matter if they'd lied to me before?

Belief is another kind of power. What did I have to lose? I had to remember what I'd learned from my merchant life.

If you're too afraid of being tricked, then you'll miss your chance to really make a big deal.

I had to BELIEVE! Itsuki was right about powering up. There really WERE item enchantments.

If there weren't, then we would be just like other adventurers.

I believed it, and I pushed the shield icon. ZizZap—for a second, the icon flickered.

A moment later there was a soft beep, and a new menu item appeared. "Power up."

"Yes!"

I'd use the ore that was set in the shield, I just needed to find a shield that was compatible with it.

Bee Needle Shield 0/20: ability unlocked: equip bonus: attack 1: special effect: needle (small): bee poison (paralysis)

To try it out, I attempted to power up the Bee Needle Shield. There was a soft beep, and the displayed denominator changed to one.

I was starting to get it. It was easy enough to power up, and the numerator was 20. Back in my world, this power up system was used in a game where you hunted monsters.

While I was at it, I decided to try turning absorbed items into energy.

It looked like there were a whole bunch of different possible effects.

I found one that looked interesting. It would cut damage received from usapil-type monsters. I decided to give it a try.

The probability of success appeared to be 100 percent for the first attempt.

Bee Needle Shield 1/20: ability unlocked: equip bonus: attack 1: special effect: needle (small): bee poison

(paralysis): item enchantment level 1. usapil-type monster damage down 2%

I still had more energy to work with, so I decided to try again.

Damn! I failed. And the number dropped to zero. I decided to try again.

The counter moved up to two.

I kept trying again and again, and eventually the number rose to seven. The chance of success when moving up to level eight was very low.

Bee Needle Shield 1/20: ability unlocked: equip bonus: attack 1: special effect: needle (small): bee poison (paralysis): item enchantment level 7. usapil-type monster damage down 16%

I felt like I could take on usapil-type monsters by myself now, if I needed to.

But there was another gauge that hadn't moved.

Itsuki had said something about a "job level." I decided to try experimenting with that next.

Out of a large number of status, I decided to focus on my defense—considering my class, that only made sense.

defense job level 1
defense gauge 0/5

I'd apparently acquired a lot of monster bits and organs when I broke them down following battle, so I chose some of them and kept entering them in the available slots.

The gauge filled slowly though, and by the time it reached one, I'd used a number of different items.

defense gauge 5/5
gauge up! "defense +1"
defense job level 2

Then the defense gauge changed to say 0/6.

I was about to try adding more items, but a cool-down timer appeared.

Apparently you could only raise the gauge a certain amount over as set period.

It wasn't so impressive. But if you filled the gauge time and time again, it would probably end up being a force to reckon with. I wonder if I could learn skills this way too?

Regardless, I'd learned some important stuff here. I'd have to talk it over with the others.

I decided to try Ren's system next. Just like I had with Itsuki's system, I made sure that I really believed in the idea, and then opened the menu for my favorite weapon, the Chimera Viper Shield.

Chimera Viper Shield 0/30: ability unlocked: equip bonus: skill "change shield" antidote co: pounding up, poison resistance (medium): special effect "snake fang (medium)," "hook": mastery level: 100

Apparently the stats were already really high. Maybe they were 1.5 times higher than they had been?

The defense rating was particularly high. As for the mastery level, apparently 100 was the maximum value.

I pressed my finger against the menu option, and then . . .

Reset mastery level?

A system message popped up.

I hesitated for a moment before clicking "yes." The stat values then all returned to what they had always been.

Received 2000 mastery level energy points.

I went ahead and assigned them to the chimera viper. Damn, there weren't enough. I needed 4000 points.

I quickly went through the shields I don't use as often and turned their mastery level into energy points.

I heard a chime indicating that something had happened.

Chimera Viper Shield (awakened) 0/30 C: ability unlocked: equip bonus: skill "change shield," antidote compounding up, poison resistance (medium): special effect "snake fang (large)," "long hook": mastery level: 0

The basic ability had grown by quite a lot.

What the hell?!

What was left? Rarity? "C" probably meant common.

Of course I didn't have enough energy to change it, so I went through my other shields, collected the energy, and tried again.

Success!

Chimera Viper Shield (awakened) 0/30 UC: ability unlocked: equip bonus: skill "change shield,": antidote compounding up, poison resistance (medium): special effect "snake fang (large)," "long hook": mastery level: 0

"UC" must have meant "uncommon." The abilities looked to be about 1.2 times higher than they had been.

I tried a few more times until I'd raised the weapon to "R," which stood for rare. By that point, the abilities had grown substantially.

It had become . . . whoa, it had become way more powerful! If I added the stats from the mastery level then . . . WOW.

I decided to try Motoyasu's system next. I just had to throw my whole being into believing—I had to be a holy fool!

Dammit! I didn't have enough ore to try Motoyasu's growth system.

I'd have to ask the queen for some help on that one. If all the other systems had been a success, then I could probably count on Motoyasu's being true as well. But it would take time to procure the necessary materials. For the time being, I'd better just focused on what I could do now.

I wanted to try the spirit enchantments too, but I didn't have those materials either. I could try the status enchantment though. I could do it with materials . . . . I guess the outcome was random anyway.

In the end, the magic power was increased.

Chimera Viper Shield (awakened) 0/30 R: ability unlocked: equip bonus: skill "change shield,": antidote compounding up, poison resistance (medium): special effect "snake fang (large)," "long hook": mastery level: 0: status enchantment: magic power 20+

That was a serious boost!

Oh look, I can reset it. But I didn't have many materials left, so I decided to leave it as it was for now.

The shield even looked more powerful to my eye. All the stats and systems were a little confusing, so I didn't have it all worked out yet—but this was obviously something beneficial for me.

I read through the help menu one last time.

" . . . ."

Everything they had told me about appeared in the menus now.

If the system responded to my beliefs then maybe I could use a growth system from a game I used to play back in my own world?

"Huh?"

No matter how deeply I believed or fiddled with the menus, nothing changed. Sure, the shield was already substantially powered up, but I couldn't understand the mechanism at work.

"Queen . . . ."

"What is it?"

"Notify the other heroes. Everything they said was true. There wasn't a liar in the room. Tell them you have to believe what the others say for it to work."

I couldn't believe the way this was turning out. It

reminded me of something the queen had said.

She's said that the replica weapon the high priest had been using was only one quarter as powerful as the real article.

With what I knew now, that made sense. Actually, I'd now pulled ahead of the others.

I could have been happy that I'd pulled ahead of the others, but if all this was true, then in the worst case . . . .

The next morning, after breakfast, I went to visit the queen in her audience chamber.

I'd expected Ren, Motoyasu, and Itsuki to be there, but there was no sign that they had showed up.

"Where are the others?"

"They left early in the morning."

"What's the rush? Did they take a boat?"

"Yes. And I have prepared a boat for you as well. It is waiting in the harbor. Please hurry."

"Got it. Were you thinking of providing any funds for the journey?"

"I have provided for everything. If there is anything else you need, please just let me know."

"Alright then . . . ."

I took out a sheet of paper and scribbled the ores and materials I would need to power up the shield further, then passed it to the queen.

"Will you have these things sent to me?"

"Very well. If the other heroes come to understand how powerful you really are, perhaps they will come around?"

That would certainly be nice.

I ran a quick estimation of how much the further enhancements would power up my shield—it was significant.

Filo's stats had shot through the roof after her class-up ceremony, but it looked like I'd be in another league altogether after this.

"Alright. I'm off then."

"Travel safely."

"Here we goooooo! Mel-chan! We'll see you later!!!!"

Filo waved to Mel enthusiastically as we filed out of the castle.

Oh, I forgot to mention that last night, Filo and Melty slept together. Those two sure were close.

Chapter Four: Weapon Copy

We left the castle, but I decided to swing by the weapon shop before going to the harbor.

The old guy that ran the place had really stuck his neck out for me when everyone had framed and betrayed me. I felt like I owed the guy a lot.

He'd made Raphtalia's magic sword and the power gloves that Filo used when she was in human form.

"Hey old man—it's been a while."

"Well look who it is. The day after you left, the whole town was covered in posters saying there was a bounty on your head. I could hardly believe it."

"Tell me about it. Rough times."

"Well it looks like you convinced everyone of your innocence."

"Sure—a lot of that is thanks to you. Those tools you gave us ended up being a real help. Thank you."

"Yes, thank you very much."

"Thanks!"

Raphtalia and Filo both chimed in. They tried to return the tools to the old guy, but he turned them down.

"You stop that now. Makes me nervous, people trying to

give me things. Those were just an experiment of mine. You can keep 'em."

"That thing that you added to my shield helped us out once too. It formed a sort of force field that saved us, but then it broke."

"Don't worry about that. That thing was an experiment of mine too. I wanted to see if I could understand the legendary shield a little better—sure enough, that thing is mysterious."

"It's thanks to you that we got out of that alive. I don't know how to thank you enough."

"I told you to stop all of that. What can I do for you today, kid?"

"Could you show me some shields?"

"I don't think I have any that would be of much use to you . . . or is it for the young lass here?"

"No . . . actually, I guess I can tell you."

I told him what I'd heard about the weapon copy system. As expected, he looked a little disturbed by the idea.

"You know I'm the owner of this business. What you're talking about basically amounts to stealing from me."

"Would you rather I didn't tell you? I'll make sure the crown supports you, but in the meantime just let me try it."

"Well it sounds like the other heroes have been doing it in secret anyway . . . . . Fine, whatever. Besides, you're a good kid. Go ahead and grab anything you like."

There was a shield hanging on the wall, so I reached up and took it down from the hook it was hanging from. A vibratory rush shot through my arm, and an icon appeared to flash in my periphery.

Weapon copy system activated.

Iron Shield conditions unlocked.
Red Iron Shield conditions unlocked.
Pink Iron Shield conditions unlocked.
White Iron Shield conditions unlocked.
Brown Iron Shield conditions unlocked.
Blue Iron Shield conditions unlocked.
Sky Iron Shield conditions unlocked.
Etc . . . .

It unlocked every color variation of the Iron Shield!

When I just started out in Melromarc, I'd unlocked a few color variations of my Small Shield. The equip bonuses had all been boring stat bumps, so I hadn't paid much attention to them at the time.

But . . . if the weapon copy system worked the way it seemed to, I had an idea.

Was there a Balloon Shield? That was one of the monsters that had never unlocked a monster-based shield.

I knew there were red and orange balloons. Could there have been normal, uncolored balloons too?

Anyway, I went through the shop touching and unlocking all the shields.

There were round shields, bucklers, night shields, bronze shields, copper shields, steel shields, and silver shields. There were even leather shields—ones I hadn't been able to unlock from absorbing scraps of tanned leather earlier.

It seemed like most of the shields available for sale unlocked different color variations of the materials they were made from.

I went on copying a few more shields, like the magic silver shield, the heavy shield, the iron armor shield, and a magic shield.

The iron shield and the iron armor shield were technically different, I guess. As for the magic shield, it was more of a small device with a switch on it. When you flicked the switch it would turn the user's magic power into a shield. So it was basically something akin to Raphtalia's magic sword.

"Oh hey, hold on a second there, kid."

The old guy said, waving a hand as he snuck off to a back room.

I heard the sound of his heavy footsteps climbing a flight of stairs, and then a cacophony of clangs as he hammered on something metallic.

A minute later and he reemerged into the showroom.

"Sorry for the wait—this shield is pretty rare around these parts."

He came back brandishing a rugged-looking thing. But it was somehow glossy as well, catching the light in an odd way.

It was formed from some kind of metal. I assumed iron. But it felt different somehow.

I opened up a window to analyze it.

Siderite Shield quality: normal

"Siderite?"

"Yeah, it's a name for those strange stones that rain down from the sky sometimes. It's one of the most impressive display products to come out of Zeltbul. It's part of their siderite series of weapons."

"Really? A display product, eh? Why do you have it?"

"Back in the day, well . . . you know."

"Heh."

Whatever that meant, he probably had a good reason for not selling it.

Motoyasu had mentioned that the best weapon shop was in Zeltbul. I wonder if he'd gone there and copied it.

"Here, take it."

"Right."

The old guy handed me the Siderite Shield. I reached for it.

Weapon copy system activated!

Siderite Shield 0/20 C: ability locked: equip bonus: skill "shooting star": mastery level: 0

Now we're talking! The other heroes had all been using the shooting star skills, and now I'd found the shield version.

The copy system also unlocked a number of color variations, but they only had boring skill bumps for bonuses.

Was I part of the bumbling shooting star crowd now? I guess that would depend on how useful the skill actually was. I changed my shield in to the Siderite Shield.

"Whoa!"

The old guy gasped in surprise.

"This thing comes with a weird skill. Do you mind if I try it out?"

"I dunno about . . . ."

"Shooting star shield!"

I shouted the skill name, and I was suddenly enveloped in a sphere of pale light.

It extended about two meters in all directions, with me at the center. As for SP usage, it apparently used about five percent of my max value. The cool-down time was also really short—about 15 seconds.

Judging from what I knew about gaming, it seemed to be some kind of defensive barrier skill.

It might have behaved similarly to the magic shield that the old guy had just shown off.

If it worked the way I thought it did, then it was sure to come in handy.

"What kind of skill is it?"

"I think it forms a kind of defensive barrier."

Raphtalia reached out her hand and brushed her fingers against the sphere of light. They slipped right through it.

"Maybe not?"

"Hmmm . . . ."

Filo jumped through it once too. Then, realizing that it didn't affect her, she entertained herself by jumping back and forth through the barrier.

The shooting star series of skills that the other heroes used were probably pretty high-level skills. If that were the case, then it didn't make sense that the shield version would be useless.

"What the hell are you doing this in my store for? I swear you ki . . . ow!"

The old guy was waving his hand in a mock lecture, when he walked forward and slammed into the wall of light.

"Ah . . . I guess only your party members can pass through it."

I didn't have a way to test the durability of the sphere for now, but it apparently really was some kind of defensive force field. If I could learn to use it effectively, it would be a big help in battle.

It looked like the field would remain in place for about five minutes. With such a short cool-down time in comparison to its efficacy, the skill was looking exceptionally useful.

"Damn . . . I wish you'd think before you acted, kid."

"Sorry. I wanted to show you what it could do, since you've held on to the shield for so long."

"When you put it that way, I guess I don't have much to complain about."

"I guess that's just about enough experimenting for today. We're all about to head for the Cal Mira islands."

"Oh yeah, I hear the activation phenomenon is happening now. If you're going to go, now's the time."

"I think you're right, old man. I'll pay you another visit when we get back from the islands."

"Excellent! But are you sure you want to keep using my shop?"

"Of course. I come here because I see how talented you are. I trust you more than anyone in the country—more than the country itself."

"Kid . . . ."

The old guy seemed nearly overcome with emotion for a second.

Pretty much all the equipment I'd used up until now had come out of his shop. I felt safe there.

"Then I'll do what I can to make sure I stay useful to ya, kid."

"Great. I'll see you later then."

So we left the shop, having tested out the weapon copy system, and prepared to leave for the islands.

Chapter Five: Gravestones

"We're about to arrive at the harbor town."

Everyone was supposed to meet in a nearby harbor town to board the ship.

The other heroes had left before me, in carriages provided by the crown.

I wondered why they didn't just use the teleport skills they'd bragged about before.

Filo was enjoying the slow carriage journey—she loved that kind of travel, and it had been a while.

"Excuse me, Mr. Naofumi. Would you mind if we took a short detour on the way?"

"Huh?"

Raphtalia indicated that she would like to stop by somewhere. It was rare for her to speak out like that. The place she indicated wasn't very far at all from our course.

"Sure."

"Wonderful. Filo, will you please follow this road inland when in splits?"

"Okay!"

Soon enough we arrived at the spot she'd requested. It was the ruins of a village.

We passed by the debris. There were wells that nobody drank from, buildings without roofs, and the burned-out shells of family homes. The remaining, ruined structures scattered through the field all indicated that a village once stood there.

Everything was destroyed and rotten, but it probably hadn't been that way for all too long. Still, it wasn't anything very recent.

I looked around and tried to judge how long it had been abandoned.

I suspected that it was probably the remains of Raphtalia's village.

" . . . ."

We rolled through the ruins, and Raphtalia was silent the whole time.

I kept inspecting what was left, and before long I noticed the whole landscape was dotted with gravestones.

I'd heard that the village was wiped out when the first wave came to Melromarc. This was apparently all that was left.

More than three months had passed since I first arrived in this world.

I'd heard about what had happened before the heroes were summoned and estimated that the village had been destroyed about four months ago.

Imagining that this had been a bustling demi-human village only four months ago made me realize, once again, how severe the threat of the waves really was.

"Raphtalia, big sis, how far do you want to go?"

"Just to that cliff that overlooks the sea."

"Okay!"

The carriage rattled over the uneven remains of the road, and I looked out on the village that Raphtalia had been raised in.

We made it to the cliff by the sea, and Raphtalia climbed down from the carriage.

At the lip of the cliff stood a pile of stacked stones. I suddenly realized I was looking at a grave.

She knelt down next to them and started to dig another spot to the side. I didn't say anything, but I knelt too and helped her dig.

I had no idea what she was doing.

When we were on the run, we met the nobleman that had kidnapped and tortured Raphtalia, and there had been corpses in his basement of people from her village.

Maybe she wanted to give them a funeral.

She had taken some of the bones with her when she left. Now she removed them from her bag and put them in ground. She covered them over with dirt and clasped her hands in prayer.

Raphtalia had told me that they were the remains of a child, a friend of hers that had always wanted to meet the Shield Hero.

At least the child could rest here now and not in that dark, damp basement.

Maybe that was just an example of the tyranny of the living.

But even if it was, I prayed that the owner of those bones would find rest and peace here on the cliff by the sea.

. . . .

I realized again—had I forgotten? I realized that Raphtalia had lost her family only four months ago.

She was strong. Stronger, maybe, than I'd realized.

She lost her family, but survived. She told me that she'd had a very trying time before she met me.

When I eventually left and returned to my own world, what would Raphtalia do?

Filo had Melty, but Raphtalia had no one.

Sometimes she asked me why I wanted to return to my old world. Maybe she was worried about the same thing—about what would happen when all this was over. Maybe she was afraid that I would leave her alone.

"I . . . ."

Raphtalia's voice came soft. It was barely a whisper. I listened in silence.

"I . . . I'll live enough for all of them. I want to save everyone from the misery of the waves. Coming here now, I feel that even stronger than I had before."

"I know. And now we have the country's support. We can save more of them now."

People had refused to cooperate with me because I was the Shield Hero, and because of that, more people had died than necessary.

But now I had support. Now we could fight the waves together. I hoped to save more people than we'd been able to before.

"I'm sorry for all the trouble."

"Stop that. The important thing is that . . . well . . . let's get going."

"You're right. I'm going! Father . . . Mother . . . Rifana . . . ."

Raphtalia waved to the graves and climbed back into the carriage.

When the next wave was over, I'd have to think more about Raphtalia.

It was my responsibility to ensure her happiness.

What about her village and all that she'd lost? Was there a way to bring it all back?

When we defeated the nobleman that had tortured her, Raphtalia had said, "I'll get back the flag I saw that day. I'll get it back."

I couldn't bring the dead back—but there must have been survivors.

We'd found a child that was still alive in the nobleman's

basement. I'm pretty sure his name had been Keel.

Couldn't I bring the survivors together and find a place for them to start over?

Yes, I nodded to myself. When I had the chance to do it, I'd search them out. I had to do it for Raphtalia.

If I didn't I wasn't sure I'd be able to forgive myself.

The plan was for all the heroes to meet in the harbor town and ride on the same ship. Obviously, the ship's departure time was set in advance, so even though the other heroes had left before we had, that didn't get them to the islands any faster. When we arrived, they all looked grumpy and irritated by the wait.

After all that we'd been through and all that we'd discussed, why were they all still competing to be the best? A bunch of idiots—that's what they were.

There was still time to kill before the ship's scheduled departure time. Everyone was lined up along the seawall, waiting to board the ship.

The guy in front of me in line seemed to have too much spare time on his hands. He was fidgeting, like he didn't know what to do with himself.

"L'Arc, calm down, will you?"

"I know, I know! But I can't help it. Ships get me so excited."

Sigh. This guy sounded like he had the maturity of a kindergartener.

Apparently hearing my sigh, he spun on his heels and faced me.

"What's the matter, kiddo?"

"Kiddo?"

I was 20. I didn't like being called kiddo.

I sized him up. His hair was cropped short and stood up in styled spikes.

He must have held it up with some sort of hair band. Or maybe that's just how his hair was naturally?

You didn't normally run into people with a hairstyle like that. Maybe it was normal in this world—but it wasn't normal in mine.

He was handsome enough. The girls probably liked him.

His eyes showed confidence. He looked like the sort of person you could depend on.

His muscles stood out from his body, clearly built through battle. His shoulders were massive. I bet he could handle himself in a fight.

It was hard to judge his age. If I had to guess, I'd say he was probably in his late 20s.

All in all, he gave the impression of a cool, experienced adventurer. For some reason, a large scythe hung from his waist.

"I'm no kiddo. I'm 20."

"Oh, forgive me then. I didn't mean anything by it. It just pops out of my mouth when I meet people younger than myself."

I looked to the woman that had told him to calm down. I figured it was safe to assume they were traveling together.

The first thing you noticed about her was her beautiful white skin—it looked like ivory.

Her hair was strange—it was bluish-green and sparkled when it caught the light. But then again, so did Raphtalia's.

Her hair was pulled back into a braid of three thick strands, and it draped elegantly over her shoulder.

Her eyes made her look kind, but you could tell she had a rigid core that wouldn't bend. Again, something about her reminded me of Raphtalia.

She had wide bangles on both arms, both inset with massive jewels, and a tiara sat daintily on her forehead.

She was probably one of the most beautiful women I'd ever seen.

The sparkling jewels only made her look more beautiful. It was like she sparkled all over—a jewel of a woman.

There was one other impression that reminded me of Raphtalia. She was somehow . . . serious.

"L'Arc, please calm down. Can't you see you're bothering the other people?"

"I'm sorry, I'm sorry."

"I'm not upset. It does look like it's almost time to board though."

I pointed to the ship, and sure enough, the line lurched forward as the first customers stomped their way up the ramp.

At the very front of the line, looking very pompous and self-satisfied, were Ren, Itsuki, and Motoyasu. So they'd been waiting a while to board. The poor things.

"Hey!"

The line had started moving now, and so the guy in front of me finally started walking.

"Master!

Why was Filo already boarding the ship and waving to me?

Filo was supposed to be waiting for the carriage to be loaded, but she was already on the gangplank.

We'd managed to secure special permission to load the carriage even though we wouldn't be using it in Cal Mira.

I waved back to her, and Raphtalia and I proceeded to board the ship.

I decided to stop by our room first. All of the heroes were supposed to have rooms set aside for them and their parties, but for whatever reason, my room was down with all the other average guest rooms.

A crowd of staff members came running up to us.

"We apologize for the inconvenience!"

Did they think that they'd all get fired if I got upset with them? That I'd separate their heads from their necks?

"The heroes that boarded earlier took over all the prepared rooms, and they even occupied the captain's chambers. We tried to do something about it, but it seems that all the rooms are full, and . . . ."

The heroes that boarded earlier? Seriously? They took over the captain's room? Who did they think they were?

Well, I guess they all had pretty large parties. They probably gave the men and women separate rooms.

I'd also made an odd request—that they allow us to bring Filo's new carriage. Nothing good would come from complaining at this point.

Still, I'd make sure the queen heard about it later.

"We have compensated the other guests for breaking our agreement with them and are having them leave the ship to make more room for you. Please just wait a little while longer."

"Really? What sort of normal adventurers could afford to go to Cal Mira at a time like this?"

I asked the staff what the average price of a ticket was.

"Yes, well normally they are quite expensive. But this time the country has commissioned the trip and printed the tickets, so they are being sold directly at a lower price than normal. Still, the journey is sold out."

Apparently the country would occasionally commandeer the islands for the leveling of country loyalists—the army, loyal adventurers, and so on. It was possible for people to sneak over to the islands on their own, but the waters were typically too treacherous for small boats.

It was like trying to get a ticket to a pop star's concert.

The crown was covering the cost of my trip there, which meant . . . wait a second—were the islands part of Melromarc?

I felt bad for the poor adventurers getting kicked off of the boat, only to be compensated with a small breach of contract fee.

"You don't have to do all that. If I can just have a room to stay in, we'll all just share it so there's no problem."

I would have considered asking if there was any more space in the rooms the other heroes had taken, but I had to think about Raphtalia and Filo too—they probably wouldn't want to stay with the others.

I couldn't forget that we had all just collapsed into shouting and fighting when we tried to have a simple conversation back at the castle.

Ren's party might not be so bad. But there had been quite a lot of them, so I was sure they had no space in the room.

There might have been space in Itsuki or Motoyasu's room, but there would probably be issues if we tried to stay with them.

Itsuki's "bodyguard" had started a fight with Raphtalia, and Motoyasu was traveling with Bitch.

There was no getting around it—I had to give up. And so we accepted a normal room down in the bowels of the ship.

"Not a good sign, is it?"

"Sure isn't."

We finished talking with the staff, and we were led to our room. We stood outside, paused, and opened the door to find . . . .

"Oh HEY, kiddo!"

I quickly shut the door again. It was the giant kindergartener from before.

"Raphtalia, I'm sorry, but go ask the staff if we can still change rooms."

"Why? What's the problem?"

"Hey now, kiddo—what's the matter?"

The guy opened the door from the other side and stuck his head out.

"I told you not to call me 'kiddo.' I'm not much younger than you."

"I guess you're right. Anyway, what's the problem?"

"Oh nothing. Looks like we have to share a room."

"Oh yeah? Well if we're going to share a room we might as well be friends! Come on in! Don't stand out in that cold hallway."

He flashed a warm smile and waved us into the room.

Something about his manic energy annoyed me. He was like the weapon shop owner sped up—I thought I might go crazy dealing with him.

"Allow me to introduce myself first. My name is L'Arc Berg—call me L'Arc."

"Pleasure. My name's . . . ."

"I'm an adventurer. And this over here is Therese."

Oh boy . . . . He spoke right over me. Sure enough, we were sharing a room with a seriously annoying guy.

"Pleased to meet you. My name is Therese Alexanderite."

"My name is Raphtalia."

"And myyyyy name's Filo!"

"Great to meet you guys!"

"Um, pardon me, but is Therese from another country? I had trouble understanding her."

"Huh? Oh . . . yeah. Therese?"

L'Arc called Therese over.

She reached over and brushed her fingertips against the scythe hanging at L'Arc's waist. Suddenly, a magic ball came floating into view.

"Can you understand me now?"

"Oh, yes, actually. I can understand you just fine now."

"Tee-hee. I'm sorry for forgetting. I will use magic to make myself understood, so please bear with me."

Wow . . . I never knew there was magic like that.

But actually, I guess my shield had been doing that for me since I got here. No one else had a legendary weapon handy though, did they?

I realized that I was the only one who had yet to introduce myself. Oh well.

The room was organized with three beds, stacked vertically as bunks, on each side of the room—it was an arrangement that would allow six people to share one room.

Raphtalia, Filo, and I would take one side of the room. The other two would use the other side, but that would leave one bed free.

The staff was considerate enough to not try and fill the last bed, so the five of us ended up sharing the room.

"Huh? Looks like the ship has set sail."

With the rocking of the ship pulling away from the pier, I felt my anger subside. The rocking grew a little more noticeable, and finally the scene viewed through the window of the room began to move.

And so our anxiety-filled, worrisome journey began. Maybe I was just imagining it.

"So, kiddo, what's your name?"

If I didn't tell him, I'd have to sit through being called "kiddo" for the rest of the trip.

If Ren, Itsuki, or Motoyasu overheard my new nickname,

there's no telling what they would do with that. I decided it wasn't worth allowing that possibility.

"It's Naofumi."

"Naofumi?"

I nodded, and L'Arc let out a raucous peel of laughter.

"Hahaha! What are you talking about? That's the Shield Hero's name. If you're gonna use an alias, you might want to come up with a better one."

"I AM the Shield Hero."

"I don't think so. The Shield Hero isn't some kiddo."

"Excuse me?"

"Listen up. The Shield Hero is a cheater. He steals from the pockets of the people he defeats. He's no good."

I guess I couldn't call him a liar.

When Glass defeated Bitch, I did reach into her pockets and took some magic water and soul-healing water.

Even so, what kind of person would say that about someone they had just met?

Humans can do the most evil things with a smile. It's crazy.

Just like Bitch!

"An immoral creature like that wouldn't look so nice—would he?"

"People often tell me I don't look so nice."

"Oh stop that. You're not so bad, kiddo. You just have an attitude."

We kept going back and forth like that, and Raphtalia eventually held her head in her hands and started moaning.

Whatever—I guess if you were objective about it, I probably wasn't the most moral guy around.

"I don't even know what to say to that . . . ," Raphtalia muttered.

"That's what I'm saying! Kiddo here doesn't seem like such a suspicious guy to me."

Guess he wouldn't believe me.

But still, I couldn't stand to let him go on calling me kiddo.

"Fine, how about this . . . ."

I held up my shield and changed it into different shapes, one after the other, in front of him.

"Does that convince you that I'm the Shield Hero?"

"Not really. You know I just hunted down an imposter Shield Hero a while back, and he was doing the same thing the whole time."

"What?"

"A little while ago we had a problem with a whole crowd of imposters of the Shield Hero. They were showing up left and right. Hunting them down and catching them was basically a full time job. Kiddo—honestly you do look a bit like the wanted posters. Those things aren't up anymore, though. I suggest you stop lying, before someone throws you off of the boat."

People pretending to be the Shield Hero? That's right, members of the church had claimed to be the Shield Hero while they committed crimes. It had been an overwrought effort to trash my reputation.

Meanwhile, I'd been pretending to be a saint of the bird god and had left the castle town far behind me while I traveled around the fringes of the country peddling wares. So I'd been able to stay out of the church's clutches for a while.

Now that I think about it, the high priest had been using a replica of a legendary weapon. It had been very powerful, but what stood out to me the most now was that it had been able to change forms just like my shield. So, at the very least, it must have been possible for them to duplicate the *appearance* of a legendary weapon.

Well damn. If my shield wouldn't convince him of my authenticity, then I didn't really have any other ideas.

I figured he'd believe me just because I looked like the picture in the posters—but apparently he was set on doubting me.

Sure, a Japanese-looking face was relatively rare here, but you saw people like that from time to time. What was the deal with that?

Heroes had been summoned before—in fact they were summoned periodically. Some of them must have left descendants behind. That would explain it.

If there were other people out there pretending to be the Shield Hero—and if they looked like they might be Japanese too—then how was I supposed to prove who I was?

Maybe I could get an official form from the queen. I'd think Filo would be enough proof for any skeptic out there.

Raphtalia too . . . . The public had probably heard about the pretty raccoon-type demi-human traveling with the Shield Hero.

I can't really explain why, but I felt like he wouldn't believe me even if I showed him Filo's monster form. If he had seen the wanted posters, and if he'd seen that crystal ball that had a video of me inside, and he STILL didn't believe me then he was probably just an idiot.

I'd had to learn to read people when I was a merchant of sorts, and that intuition was telling me that this guy was just a little slow on the uptake. So I just gave up.

"Sure. Fine. I don't care. Call me whatever you like."

"Lazy, aren't ya, kiddo?"

"Nothing I do or say is changing your mind. So I gave up."

"Mr. Naofumi, be careful with your phrasing."

"No thanks. I don't have the energy."

"Okay, well—fine. Nice to meet you, Shield Kiddo."

Either way, we'd only have to entertain this jerk for the length of the journey—it wasn't that important that I corrected him.

And so we ended up sharing a room with some unknown adventurers, as our ship slowly made its way to the Cal Mira islands.

Chapter Six: Cal Mira

The staff on the boat had implied that they wanted the heroes to gather and introduce themselves, so I was prepared to run to the meeting place.

But then it turned out that the other three heroes were all seasick.

"Seasick . . . ?"

I'd never gotten motion sickness of any kind, but it sure seemed like a lot of people around me got sick on any sort of vehicle.

Did they have any idea what sort of situation they had stuck me with by commandeering all the good rooms?

"Naofumi, how can you stand this rocking?

"I dunno—it's never bothered me."

Honestly, I didn't feel like sitting around and being friendly with them. That would be their punishment for stealing the private rooms.

"Kyahoooo!"

Filo let out a triumphant shout and jumped from the deck into the water. She swam through the waves below like a fish.

"Ah . . . ."

I saw a large silhouette below the surface. It was catching up on Filo from behind.

"Filo! You better watch out!"

"Hmmm?"

Filo took her sweet time turning around to look, and by the time she did, a large, shark-like monster was bearing down on her. Its mouth opened wide—its teeth flashing.

"Take that!"

She did a quick flip and kicked the shark-like monster in the chin. The beast flew out of the water and flipped through the air.

Then she jumped and delivered another swift kick. The shark flew towards the boat and crashed on the deck. The staff and customers all screamed.

The large creature was thrashing about on the deck, so Filo jumped in and finished it off.

"If you think you can make a meal out of me that easily, you better think again!"

She stuck a claw out and slit the beast's stomach open, spilling its guts out onto the deck.

"Stop making a mess."

"I think I'm going to be sick."

Itsuki whispered. He was white as a sheet. I guess by most standards, Filo's behavior was strange. But for Filo, all this was pretty normal.

By the way, this was the second shark she'd done this to. I broke down the first one and absorbed it into my shield.

And I unlocked something pretty interesting.

Blue Shark Shield conditions met.
Shark Bite Shield conditions met.

Blue Shark Shield: ability locked: equip bonus: swimming skill 1

Shark Bite Shield: ability locked: equip bonus: naval combat skill 1: special effect: shark tooth

Swimming ability, huh? I could already swim well enough.

As for naval combat, would that somehow affect the movement of the ship?

If we ran into a situation that required combat, it might prove useful. If I had any spare time, I figured I might as well unlock it.

I'd already gotten the abilities I could from other sharks she'd killed, so I let Filo eat the new one.

"Are you really THAT sick? Just from riding on a boat?"

"You're the weird one, Naofumi."

"Oh hey, Shield Kiddo. What's going on?"

"What?"

L'Arc came sauntering over. Raphtalia followed behind him.

"What's going on? Nothing, I'm just talking with these people."

"Those seasick losers over there? Give me break. We've only been at sea for a few hours."

"Even though we'll be arriving tomorrow morning. Seems a shame."

Apparently L'Arc and Therese didn't get seasick.

I sat down near the bow and watched the ocean. The waves were growing taller.

Raphtalia and the staff were whispering that it might turn into a storm.

"Hey, kiddo. What are you guys doing when we get to the island?"

"If Cal Mira is in the middle of an activation event, there's really only one thing worth doing."

Obviously, I was going there to level.

And of course I was also going to explore and look into any new items and monster drops that I encountered along the way.

"I figured as much."

Also . . . I'd heard there were hot springs on the island. Apparently they were considered restorative for cursed people.

If that were true, I'd definitely stop by for a soak.

"Well if you're going to be leveling, want to team up with us?"

"Huh? What are you after?"

"I figure there's a reason we ended up roomies on the boat. Besides, Therese and I leveling alone gets a little lonely. I was thinking we could all team up."

Hm . . . . Honestly, I didn't really care one way or the other.

It sounded like L'Arc still didn't believe I was the Shield Hero. So he wanted to team up with just any old adventurer that he thought was pretending to be the Shield Hero.

That was enough reason to trust his intentions.

I wonder what he was thinking? I looked over to Raphtalia.

"What do you think?"

"I don't have a problem with it. Do we have anything to lose by letting them come along?"

If this world was like an MMO, I wondered if there was an upper limit on the number of party members that you could have at once.

It was possible to set reserve troops for assistance under the formation menu, but that was limited to the waves of destruction.

I had played games before that would let you form parties of up to 20 members, but I wasn't sure what the rules were here.

I was ruminating over the issue when I suddenly remembered Itsuki's party.

There were a whole bunch of them. I counted six members, and with Itsuki that made seven.

If he was able to have seven people in his party, then me, Raphtalia, Filo, L'Arc, and Therese made five. That shouldn't be a problem.

"Sure, but try not to hold the rest of us back, will you?"

"Haha, I'd like to say the same thing."

L'Arc kept his cool and laughed off my insult.

I didn't really have any problem with people like him, but he did cause a ruckus.

"I don't really know what's up with that bird of yours, but once we figure her out I'm sure we will all get along fine."

"I'm sure we will.

So I ended up agreeing to go hunting and leveling with two adventurers I knew nothing about.

If I was able to do that, I guess I'd done a lot of personal introspection and healing since the days of being tricked and framed by Trash and Bitch.

I started to wonder what the other heroes' party members were doing, but I had my answer within a second or two: they were all relaxing in the captain's chambers.

Night fell, and we sailed through of storm of some kind—the boat rocked pretty aggressively in every direction you could imagine. But everything had cleared up by morning, and we arrived right on schedule.

Our room was small enough that we didn't get thrown around too much. Filo was freaking out the whole time though, and Raphtalia was feeling pretty seasick.

Any adventurer that wasn't a crew member . . . . Well, you can imagine how sick they all were.

Cal Mira was much larger than I had anticipated. It rose tall from the sea, a massive volcanic island.

I didn't know if I could trust the measurements on the map I'd been given, but if I had to compare it to something back in my own world, Hawaii was probably pretty close.

It was an archipelago, of which Cal Mira was the largest island, so sometimes people just talked about the area as if it were only Cal Mira.

As you might expect from a tropical archipelago, I could see a number of other islands offshore.

The interior of the atoll was protected from the deep ocean, and so the waves were small and peaceful. When the tide was out, they say you could walk to some of the other islands. We'll have to see about that.

I wondered if could I ride Filo to another island.

"Alright, kiddo, what do you say we head out in two days or so?"

"Sure. Whatever."

We didn't go through the formalities of figuring out how

we were going to meet back up, but nevertheless we parted ways with L'Arc.

"Well, we made it to Cal Mira."

I turned and saw the other heroes. They were clearly elated to be back on solid ground.

Having spent the night being flung around their stately room, the other heroes apparently hadn't been able to get much sleep. They were dragging their feet down the pier, looking groggy and worn.

Bitch was pale and disheveled. She seemed right on the verge of throwing up.

"Aren't you guys playing this up a little much? It was just a little boat ride."

"Naofumi . . . you're the weird one here."

"I thought we were going to sink!"

Granted, there had been a few times throughout the night where it seemed like the ship really had slipped under the waves. But you couldn't just keep freaking out about it.

I had gotten a little tired of being tossed about the room, though.

By the way, apparently storms very rarely got that big in these parts. I wondered if the strange weather was somehow related to the waves of destruction. Had we been back in my world, I'd have said that the storm was big enough to tip most ships of average size.

"I was a little worried that we'd have to start a new life on a deserted island. I'm glad we made it."

"What are you blathering about?"

"I'm not kidding!"

"Anyway, let's get to bed early tonight. We need to make the most of our time here."

The queen had recommended an inn to us, but I recalled that before we retired for the day, we had to go introduce ourselves to the nobles in charge of governing the islands.

We might have been in the middle of nowhere, but the place attracted a lot of travelers, so there were certain to be all sorts of people around.

"Welcome! Welcome! The Legendary Heroes and their retinues!"

I was waiting for the other heroes to recover from their seasickness down at the harbor, when someone who seemed to be leading a tour group (based on the little flag they were carrying) came running over.

He was dressed in a Melromarc military uniform and seemed to be just on the cusp of old age—the little flag didn't suit him at all.

"I am the Earl of Habenburg, and the care of these islands has been entrusted to me."

I was the only hero that wasn't sick, so I stepped forward and met the visitor.

"Very pleased to make your acquaintance."

"Oh, um . . . . Yes. Pleasure."

The other heroes all nodded to the Earl of Habenburg.

"Please allow me to tell you all a little bit about our lovely islands."

Oh come on—he really WAS a tour guide? I hated sitting through this kind of thing.

"You know we really didn't come as tourists . . . ."

We'd come to get our hands on the extra experience points and loot available during the activation event. And now we had to sit through a lecture on the oral traditions of the islanders? I wasn't in the mood to play tourist.

"Yes, well—these oral traditions speak of Cal Mira long being a place special to the four heroes—for aeons they have trained here."

He started his tour at the market and gesticulated and described the scene as we walked through it.

Halfway through the market I spotted something strange. It was a statue, something like a totem pole, and it consisted of a penguin, rabbit, squirrel, and dog stacked one on top of the other. All of the animals were wearing Santa hats.

The penguin held a fishing-pole, the rabbit held a hoe, the squirrel a saw, and the dog a rope.

What was it supposed to mean?

"You have a sharp eye, Shield Hero. These are the four

pioneers that brought prosperity to our island: Pekkul, Usauni, Risuka, and Inult."

Those names all sounded Japanese. I wonder if previous heroes had named them.

"Just so you know, these were all named by a previous group of heroes. They named them after what these animals were called in their own language, in the land from which they came."

Whatever their motivation had been—those were some ugly names. They could have tried a little harder.

"Are there animals like that on this island?"

"No. After developing the island, they moved on to other, unknown lands. They have not been seen since."

So I guess they had died somewhere else. There wasn't even a good reason to suspect that they had been historical figures. I mean, what sort of penguins and rabbits turn into frontier pioneers?

"Oh wow . . . . They look yummy!"

A thread of saliva dangled from Filo's beak as she looked at the animal statues.

Come to think of it, here was a monster I knew personally that loved to pull carriages as a hobby. Maybe pioneering monsters weren't such an oddity after all?

There was another strange object next to the statue of the animals. It was a stone pillar of some sort.

"What is that thing?"

"It is an inscription left to us from the Four Legendary Heroes."

"Really . . . ."

There was a very good chance that the other heroes, like the four of us, had been Japanese.

Could they have left their phrase in Japanese?

It said something like . . . .

"Hey! This thing is fake!"

The other heroes came close to see if they could read it.

"Well that is strange . . . . It is said they left it here to guide the heroes that would come after them."

"Is this some kind of joke? What is the deal with the magical writing of this world?"

Magical letters . . . those things were really starting to get annoying.

They weren't the sort of writing that you could just learn how to read.

I'm not sure how to explain it. They sort of changed what they said based on the person reading them.

I'll try to explain further. Raphtalia was skilled with light and shadow magic, so she could read books that were written about that magic because they shared an affinity—but if I tried to read the same book it wouldn't say anything. If I translated what was written it was just gibberish. But Raphtalia could read it, understand it, and then perform magical spells based on what she'd read.

There were magical letters that were made for everyone to read too, but if you weren't about to use the information written there, then it would become illegible. It was like they reacted to your innate magical ability. Of course you'd have to be able to read the letters they used in this world anyway.

"Hey, can you read that?"

"Well you guys were depending on that crystal ball, so I know that you can't read it. I, on the other hand, had to make due for myself in the wake of all the trouble Trash put me through. If I didn't learn to read, I would never have been able to use any magic."

You could learn magic in one of two ways: either you had to read it out of a book, or you could automatically learn the spell through a magical crystal ball. If you learned from a ball then the spell was easy to learn but difficult to power up. Learning from a book took longer but was easier to adjust along the way.

"What's it say?"

"Um . . . ."

I focused my magic and tried to read what was on the stone. It was written in simple language.

"I am the source of all power. The Shield Hero commands you. He has understood this inscription. Support him!"

"Zweite Aura . . . ."

I could choose a target for the spell. I guess I might as well start with Filo.

I held out my hand in Filo's direction and a soft, transparent magic field appeared around her.

"Oh wow! I feel like I'm full of power!"

Filo started jumping up and down in place. She was in human form, but she could still jump pretty high.

I checked her stats and found that most of them had increased.

"Aura . . . . It's a spell that only the legendary heroes can use. It raises the target's stats."

One of Itsuki's teammates whispered. It was that Rishia girl.

"Awesome! Let's all learn it!"

The prospect of learning ancient magic really excited the others, as it fit in perfectly with their game-like attitude. They all tried reading the words.

But . . . .

"Damn . . . I can't read it."

"Maybe that's because you guys never learned how to read the magic letters?"

Sure, they'd learned their magic easily enough with the crystal balls, but if they never learned to read, they'd never be able to learn aura.

"Naofumi."

Itsuki turned to me and spoke.

"What?"

"Where did you get the shield that taught you to read magic letters?"

"I learned to read it myself! The weapon can't do everything for you!"

"Don't be like that!"

"Yeah! Teach us!"

They had no shame at all. Soon they'd want me to teach them the whole language.

They must have thought that their weapons had absolved them of the need to make any sort of effort.

"I learned a spell from this called 'Aura,' but that doesn't mean that you guys are going to learn the same thing."

"That might be true. We might learn something even better."

Their condescension was becoming even more apparent. I couldn't stand being talked down to like that.

They couldn't even hold their own against the high priest. I caught myself getting upset and tried to calm down.

"Let's move on. Is there anything else you wanted to show us?"

"Very well then, we will head for the inn—but I will make sure to introduce you to items and places of interest along the way."

The earl interjected short explanations now and again as we walked to the inn.

The areas of Cal Mira that were filled with wildlife were in a veritable uproar now, thanks to the activation event. The life cycles of the monsters had all been accelerated.

The monsters would go on reproducing exponentially, and the island would find itself in dire straits if adventurers and heroes didn't come to help cull the exploding population. Our immediate goal was to help beat back the monsters—and to level up substantially in the process.

The earl explained that it would help the island most if we completely eradicated any group of monsters we chanced upon.

There was no need for us to defer to other adventurers that were leveling there, but if we came across a battle under-way, they asked that we avoid unnecessary conflict by not jumping in and taking other adventurers' kills.

It sounded a lot like typical manners in an MMORPG.

If we wanted to move between the islands, there were small boats that we could use—but they wouldn't shuttle us around. In the worst case, the earl said, it was possible to swim.

The inn that the queen had reserved from us was the nic-est building on the island. In my world, it would have been equivalent to a high-class hotel.

I wondered if it used to be a castle or something.

Anyway, it was a huge, ornate place that felt very clean. The walls were formed of something like marble and were polished so they reflected the light.

There was a fountain that included statues of Pekkul and Risuka. All in all, the place made me feel like I was back in my own world, in a strange sort of way.

Had I just gone to a trip to the southern islands? Maybe I was back in Hawaii?

We were led down a hallway to our rooms, and there was a thick, plush carpet running the length of it.

The hotel insisted that they would see to our luggage, so we'd given them our things, as well as Filo's carriage.

Opening the door to our room, we found that our luggage had already arrived, so we decided to head right out again and start hunting monsters.

We jumped in a small boat, picked another island at random, and shoved off.

"It's been a while since we could battle monsters just to level up."

"I guess you're right."

Once Filo had hatched we'd turned our attention to our merchant work. During that time we'd only really fought monsters that we happened to come across on the way, and not many people specifically asked that we battle for them.

Then we realized we couldn't participate in the class-up ceremony, so we decided to head to another country—but then the crown put a bounty on my head.

Once we defeated the high priest, we ended up stuck on a long journey back to the castle, then we jumped right on the ship to Cal Mira. Sure, Filo had killed a few monsters on the way, but nothing that would count as intentional leveling.

Thinking back on it all, Raphtalia was right. It really had been a while.

When we were on the run, we didn't have the time to be systematic about it—and instead of using them for materials, we'd had to eat most of them.

"We'll be leveling up from now until the time we leave Cal Mira. Good luck everyone."

"Yeah!"

"Yes."

We climbed out of the small boat and stepped into the wild.

The area was infested with Bio Red Blobs, Magenta Frogs, Yellow Beetles, and Cactus Worms.

None of those monsters sounded very strong to me. I was thinking over the names when a Magenta Frog came flying at us from some nearby bushes.

"Hey!"

I held my shield to block it, and its belly crashed into the shield.

There was a sucking and popping sound. I looked down to find the frog stuck to the outer edge of my shield.

"Haaa!"

Raphtalia flashed her sword at the frog.

Yes, she moved very quickly.

EXP 95

Hey, that was more experience points than I would have expected to get from such a weak monster.

Raphtalia had defeated it with one swing of her sword. Raphtalia was looking down at her sword, surprised.

"The monster was very weak, but we received quite a bit of experience points from it."

"I wonder if that's because of the activation event?"

"I hope so. Well, there's no need to hold back."

"Just make sure you don't steal another adventurer's mark."

"I'll be careful! Hya!"

"Take that!"

Raphtalia sliced a monster in two. Another monster was minced by Filo's furious claws. If I wanted to absorb anything into the shield, they'd have to leave some scraps behind.

I realized that I was now powerful enough to take on a number of monsters at once. Actually, they weren't damaging me at all, so eventually the monsters started to ignore me.

You had to give the monsters that much—they weren't stupid. Something like a balloon might have just gone on attacking me forever. But these monsters were smarter. They realized they didn't have a chance of injuring me, so they directed their attention at Raphtalia and Filo.

I tried to stand at the front of the party, defend against the attacks, and find openings in the monster's defenses. But there were so many of them that I wasn't doing much good. Luckily Raphtalia and Filo were quick and powerful enough to dodge the monsters' attacks that had gotten past me.

But there was still a problem. If I wasn't the one stopping their attacks, then there wasn't really a need for me to be there.

"Mr. Naofumi, I feel like the monsters are a little too weak for us. Perhaps we should move on?"

"Hmm . . . ."

There must have been some way around the problem.

Maybe I could switch to a weaker shield.

Maybe they would realize that the shield was weaker, and so they would focus more of their attention on me—thinking that they stood a chance—and stop attacking Raphtalia and Filo. Besides, I could unlock a few shields in the process.

There was a limited amount of time until the next wave arrived. I wanted to use the time we had in the most efficient way possible.

Yes, for the time being, I'd go with that plan.

Even still, Raphtalia and Filo were probably powerful enough to make it to the center of this particular island without too much help from me. They were defeating all the monsters with one hit.

We battled on like that for a short while, when I suddenly realized that I wasn't receiving experience points any longer.

"Why?"

"What happened?"

"I stopped receiving experience points. What about you, Raphtalia?"

"I'm still getting points just like normal."

I double-checked their points in my menu. Sure enough, they were both still getting experience—I was the only one who'd stopped accumulating points.

I was wondering what was going on, then it happened.

"You bastard! You stole my kill! Someone should kill you next!"

"What?!"

Itsuki, Armor, and their friends killed a monster that another adventurer had been battling.

Come on now! Hadn't we JUST been warned not to steal other people's kills?

I shot them all an annoyed glance, but then Itsuki looked confused, realizing that he wasn't receiving experience, and he looked at me for help.

"Oh, Naofumi. I didn't realize you were here. That probably explains why I'm not getting experience."

"You mean because our weapons are interfering with each other?"

"Yes. If it's not too much trouble, do you think you could go to another island?"

The idiot . . . . Why did I have to move? Was he incapable of moving himself? Was he incapable of considering the feelings of others?

I swear . . . everything Itsuki did these days irritated me.

"Yeah! Yeah! The Shield Hero is going to another island!"

"Oh SHUT UP already!"

Armor was getting really annoying.

What did he have against me? What did I do to make him think I was his enemy?

"Itsuki . . . . What was that all about?"

"What do you mean?"

"Did you hear what the earl said? About not stealing other adventurers' kills?"

"What do you mean? That was my kill. I started that battle."

His eyes wandered off in the distance. Quite far away an adventurer was battling a monster. Itsuki drew his bow back and fired a killing shot.

"Um . . . ."

"What is it? We got the first attack."

The adventurer and I clearly had the same concerns, but Itsuki didn't seem worried by them. He answered like it was the most obvious thing in the world.

Maybe he wasn't technically breaking the rules, but there was something wrong with that kind of behavior.

If this were an MMORPG, that was called target stealing, or fishing.

The behavior was prohibited or permitted depending on the game, so I couldn't be sure what the rules were here. But it was clearly annoying. It clearly bothered the other adventurers. And we'd been warned about it, in a way, so why behave that way?

That reminded me. Itsuki had said that this world reminded him of a consumer game that he'd played.

"Itsuki, you realize that behavior like that would get you in trouble if this were an online game."

"What? Oh stop that now. We scored the first hit!"

"Only because you have a ranged weapon. Does that mean that only you have the right to hunt here?"

Itsuki was troubled by the question, but he slowly nodded. It gave me a headache to figure him out, but I was starting to understand.

In a consumer game, there was no need to worry about stuff like this.

The other characters weren't really people, and so they weren't actually in competition for the monsters. They didn't steal from each other.

So I had to find the right way to approach the issue.

"Go ask Ren and Motoyasu about it. Or go ask the earl of the island. I think you'll find that everyone is against disruptive behavior like that."

"What are you talking about?"

"Alright . . . see ya!"

I signaled to Filo with my eyes.

Itsuki had already leveled his bow at a monster that was poking around in the weeds.

"First wind!"

Filo sent a torrent of wind magic to hit the monster first. A second later, Itsuki's arrow connected, and the monster died.

"You stole our kill! We were hunting that monster, and you stole it! How could you?!"

I shoved an accusatory finger at Itsuki and shouted to make my point.

When I did, Armor looked very upset, and he stepped forward.

"You fool! Despite being a hero yourself, you'd turn on Master Itsuki?!"

Itsuki looked troubled for a moment, then upset. I

realized he had come to understand the situation.

"Please calm down. I understand what you mean now."

He smiled peacefully, but his eyes were not smiling at all. He could hide his discomfort with a mask of smiles, but I saw right through it.

We left. I don't know if he continued to "understand" after we were gone though. I figured it was best to try our luck at another island.

"Should we have some lunch while we wait for my experience points to become available again?"

Itsuki signaled to his party that it was time to take a break.

I wasn't very invested in his party members or their lunches, until . . . .

"Rishia! It's lunchtime!"

"Oh . . . okay!"

Armor and the other party members all yelled at Rishia to get their meals ready.

They certainly thought highly of themselves, didn't they? Who did they think they were? Why did she have to make their lunches?

"Why not make your own lunches?"

I whispered it to myself, but Armor heard me and came running over.

"What was that?! Rishia is the newest recruit here! These chores are her responsibility!"

"What?!"

I didn't know what to say. Recruit?

What was this? Did he think he was running a company or something?

Rishia prepared to hand out the lunches. But apparently there was a prescribed order that they had to be handed out in. She looked carefully at each lunch, confirmed the name, then softly called the name out.

As she got further down in the list, the lunches became less impressive-looking.

Was Itsuki's his own homemade lunch? She passed him a lunch box.

Armor was next. His lunch was a large piece of meat on the bone, plus a sandwich stacked high with meats.

Then came the soldiers. They got a sandwich and grilled fish. The next up was . . . . Well, it went on and on like that until only Rishia was left. Then she reached into a bag and pulled out one piece of fruit, which she began to eat in silence.

What was all that about? Why didn't they eat the same things?

"What's going on? You have different ranks in your party?"

"What are you watching us for? Naofumi, you're becoming a bother, so please move on to the next island."

"Are you kidding me? Itsuki, are you all right in the head?"

It might have made me a hypocrite to say so, but he was treating this girl, Rishia, like a slave!

Actually, Raphtalia and I ate the same meals. Itsuki was worse than that. He was treating her worse than a slave!

"Master, I'm hungry!"

"Filo! Shut up for a second!"

She'd been overtaken by hunger watching Itsuki and his party chow down. Now all she could think about was food.

Armor looked over at us triumphantly. He smiled and opened his mouth wide.

"Our rank is decided upon by the amount that Master Itsuki trusts us and by how much we have contributed to the group. What is the problem with that? Should we have a nice long chat? I could tell you all about Master Itsuki's most impressive characteristics."

"No thanks, I think I've heard enough."

"Well I'll tell you anyway. When I first met Master Itsuki, he opened my eyes to justice."

Armor went on talking, then the rest of the party joined in. They recounted all of Itsuki's most impressive achievements.

I'd rather not go over the crap they said. Most of the stories involved Itsuki hiding out, and then taking down bad guys in secret. From the way they talked about him, they really did seem to think that he was the sole hero in charge of saving the world.

It was like a religion of some kind. They were devotees of Itsuki, practitioners of Itsuki-ism.

Finally Itsuki was watching over us all, an expression of deep satisfaction plastered over his face.

That was it exactly—he was using them to brag about himself.

My analysis is as follows. Itsuki was always dealing with bad people in secret. Therefore Itsuki must be a savior of justice.

I'm pretty sure there was some kind of name for a disorder like that.

I'd seen an old movie about it. There was a police officer in some other country who fought for justice. He became stimulated by the fight against evil. They'd named a disorder after him. It was a disorder that often affected police officers.

I couldn't remember what it was called, but they'd taken the name from the title of the movie. The character said that those that served evil had no right to live, and would punish all transgressions, regardless of their severity, with death. If someone tried to avoid punishment, they would be punished for that too with death.

The actual policeman in the movie never went quite that far, but the concept remained, an indelible portrait of the psychosis.

Anyway, I couldn't help but bring that character to mind when I thought of Itsuki.

I wanted to shake him and ask if he was really so confident that he was right. What if he was just imagining all this justice?

The Records of the Four Holy Weapons had said that the Bow Hero had a strong sense of justice.

But Itsuki has misunderstood what justice was. Being "correct" and doing the right thing were not always the same.

Anyway, I don't think Itsuki would hear me out if I tried to explain it all to him.

Besides, I didn't expect very much from Itsuki to begin with—much less expect that he would be open to persuasion.

"We're going deeper into the island. Naofumi, we'll see you later."

"Right, later. Try not to annoy the other adventurers."

Itsuki's party quickly packed up their lunches and left the area.

"I'd realized this when I tried speaking to them back at the castle, but they really are a difficult bunch, aren't they?"

"Sure are."

I'd rather not run into Itsuki again.

Moving between the islands was a little annoying, so if there were going to be four heroes here at the same time, it would have been smart to agree to level in different places before we set out.

Regardless, we couldn't level on that island anymore. We made our way back to the main island.

"Hey, hey . . . if it isn't Shield Kiddo? From the look of it, the monsters were too tough for you, so you came running back. Am I right?"

We got off the boat at the main island harbor and ran into L'Arc and Therese on the dock.

"The monsters were weak. No trouble at all. We do have our reasons for coming back so soon though."

The real reason was that the heroes were not able to accumulate experience points when leveling in the same place because their weapons interfered with one another. But it would be a pain to try and explain that to him.

"What's the matter?"

"It's lunchtime. That, and another hero showed up so we need to move to another island."

We'd wasted plenty of time already, about two hours. Why did we have to sit and listen to Itsuki's party brag about their master's valorous deeds?

We could head out to another island now, but by the time we got there it would be getting late, and we'd just have to turn around and come right back.

The first step was to find out where the other heroes were leveling. Then I could make sure to avoid them.

"Well look at you! You're really taking this hero-impersonation scheme of yours all the way, aren't you? You mean about how their weapons interfere?"

"Yeah, something like that."

"Are you and Therese heading out hunting now?" asked Raphtalia.

"Yeah. We just want to go and see what sort of monsters we'll be dealing with. What was it like for you kiddos?"

"The monsters were not very strong, but they gave quite a lot of experience."

"Pretty good."

We were chatting about the monsters when Therese came over and spoke to me.

"May I call you Mr. Naofumi? Raphtalia was kind enough to tell me your name."

"Huh? What now?"

"I hear that you are quite skilled with crafting?"

That came out of the blue.

L'Arc hadn't shut up from the minute I met him, but Therese tended to keep quiet. I wasn't really sure how to speak to her yet.

"I wouldn't say I'm really skilled, but I learned from an expert and managed to get the basics under my belt."

"If I provided the materials and the funds, could you make an item for me?"

"Probably . . . that is, if I had the time."

"I'd love to purchase one."

"Sure."

I wasn't about to turn down a job. I'd make sure I was paid well.

"So what kind of item were you thinking about?"

"I'd love a bracelet. I'll let you pick the type and design."

Those types of requests were the worst. I wished she would just make up her mind.

I decided to wait and see what materials she provided me with. Then I would just make whatever I could from them.

"Well, I can't make anything without any materials."

"Okay. L'Arc!"

"What's up?"

She reached over and pointed to a small pouch synched at L'Arc's waist. He opened it to show off a number of different ore fragments that were inside.

Many of them seemed to be rough gemstones.

"So what do you want?"

"Just pick the best thing out of that pouch and make a bracelet from it."

"Fine."

L'Arc passed me the pouch. I'd have to think of it as a side quest.

"Alright. I'll bill you for the bracelet when it's finished."

"Awesome! Thanks, Shield Kiddo."

"Whatever."

I was starting to understand how the old guy must feel

running that weapon shop. He must have felt this way when I stopped by and asked him to make me things.

Well, I'd accepted the job, so I was determined to make something good.

"Alright, we're heading out."

"Good luck, L'Arc. And you too, Therese."

"Bye now!"

"Raphtalia and Filo waved them off. They climbed into small boat and rowed away from the dock.

It was so much easier to get along with these normal adventurers than it was to tolerate Itsuki. Something about that felt a little sad.

We hunted down a shadow and the earl, who had both come from the castle, and asked them to tell us where the other heroes were leveling.

The other heroes, Ren and Motoyasu, had planned where they were going and made sure not to overlap.

So they were all on different islands.

This was all turning into such a pain. Why did the legendary weapons have to interfere with each other like this? Up until now we'd only fought in the same place during the waves of destruction, so I hadn't really been bothered by it.

I felt like I was losing valuable time. I had to think of something.

"Raphtalia."

"What is it?"

"Want to do some leveling at night? Then we could make up for lost time."

She rubbed her chin and seriously considered it.

"Good idea. It might be a little dangerous, but we could use the leveling time."

"Are we fighting at nighty-night?"

"Yeah."

I could have used a soak in those curse-curing hot springs, but after all the time at sea I kind of wanted the exercise.

If we were going to make up for lost time, leveling at night would be our best bet.

Besides, who knew what time the next wave would come? There was no guarantee that they only occurred during the day.

And besides, Filo was like a wild animal, and we'd fought during the night plenty of times when we were on the run from that bounty.

And so we decided to go to an island where there were no other heroes and battle through the night.

"Whew . . . ."

"That should do it."

"Yeah."

We landed at the island and continued to battle monsters after the sun had dipped below the waves.

I soon discovered that the monsters in the Cal Mira islands dropped all sorts of items. They dropped plenty of medicinal herbs, but also magic waters and the materials you needed to make soul-healing water.

Once night fell, and it was dark, the monsters started to appear with greater frequency.

The more monsters we fought, the more experience points we were going to get. So by my estimation, we were accumulating a lot of points.

We eventually grew tired and built a bonfire. We needed a rest.

Filo's eyes kept darting around the camp though. It didn't look like she was ready to fall asleep.

There were a lot of different islands in the Cal Mira archipelago. Some were steep mountains, others were heavily forested, others were like jungles.

"There are so many monsters out tonight."

"I know."

The island we were camping on was more like a giant mountain.

I looked up to the peak. It stood out ruddy against the sky, a stark silhouette.

I wondered if the color had something to do with the activation event.

I think we were getting more experience points for battling at night. We had all managed to level up a bit.

When we'd arrived on the island I'd been at level 43, while Raphtalia was at level 40. Now I was at level 48, and Raphtalia and Filo had reached levels 50 and 51.

Raphtalia almost seemed bored. The monsters were not presenting much of a challenge for her.

Another thing I noticed was that the monsters had the same names, but some were bigger than others, and some gave more points than others.

We'd even run into a Magenta Frog that was as large as I was. Despite being so large, Filo had taken the beast down with a single kick.

They weren't so strong. But they really were rewarding us with a lot of experience points, and they were appearing very frequently. All in all, it was good for us.

We'd managed to level up quite a lot in just a single day.

Raphtalia and Filo's stats were rising quickly too. I was focused on trying to power up my shield—but I think I'd done all I could with the materials I currently had.

I'd managed to power up the Chimera Viper Shield pretty well, but it wasn't like I didn't use other shields. I didn't want to have to depend on the dangerous Shield of Wrath either. So I wanted to find a weaker shield that I could power up.

"Hm . . . ."

"Mr. Naofumi, I worry that you might be pushing yourself too hard. I know you would have a hard time saying so yourself, but you must me tired. Your curse still has not healed. Why don't you rest a little?"

My body did feel heavy. I don't think I could make it through any long, drawn-out battles at this point.

Still, I'd hoped I could power up a shield to the point where it was so powerful that it didn't really matter whether I was cursed or not.

"The monsters here hadn't been able to damage me at all, so I figured it would be okay to keep going."

I took her invitation to relax though. I stretched my legs out and started to recline when I heard footsteps approaching.

Who was it?

I was about to jump to my feet, when I realized it was L'Arc and Therese.

"Everyone is freaking out that you guys haven't come back yet, so we decided to come looking for you!"

"What?"

"The boat manager at the docks was getting worried about you kiddos. He said that you left forever ago and hadn't come back."

"I'm sure adventurers die on the islands all the time. There's no need to freak out over us."

He thought that I was just a normal adventurer pretending

to be the Shield Hero. Wouldn't it be normal for a new adventurer to overestimate their abilities, run off into the wilderness, and end up dead?

Honestly I hadn't spent much time speaking with other adventurers, so I didn't really know for sure what they considered normal.

"That might be true. But we got a little worried."

Hmm . . . so they were worried about us and took a boat out to an island in the middle of the night?

A part of me was thankful for that. A little part of me felt some affection for them.

The two of them must have been real worrywarts. They were less like adventurers and more like paladins, or something.

Even though the knights and paladins of Melromarc were a bunch of jerks.

"We wanted to make up for lost time, so we decided to battle through the night."

"Anyway, come back to the hotel with us. You have everyone worried."

"Fine."

I had to take care of my curse anyway. That was probably enough night battling for today.

"Alright, let's head back."

"Yes, let's. And we're sorry to have worried you."

"We're going back?!"

Filo cocked her head to the side.

"Yeah."

"Okaaaay! Let's go go!"

We packed up our camp and went back to the main island.

The random people we met on the docks were becoming more entangled in our lives by the day.

Chapter Seven: The Tavern

"Sorry for the trouble."

"It's no trouble at all, kiddo."

We climbed back into our boats and returned to the main island.

It was very dark now, and all the lights had been lit in town. The businesses that had all been bustling during the day had all been shuttered.

All of them, that is, except for the tavern.

"Hey, kiddo! Why don't we celebrate your safe return with a trip to the tavern?"

"I'd really been planning on hitting the hot springs and then getting to bed early . . . ."

"You're no fun at all, are you?"

These two had worried about us and come looking for us. I guess it wouldn't hurt to stick around a little while longer.

"Fine. But just for a little."

"Yeah!"

The tavern was cheerful and there was quite a raucous inside—adventurers were really cutting loose.

It sounded like most of them were discussing the best places to level.

It turned out that the queen had already arranged to cover the bar tabs of the heroes. I was planning on using the money that had been set aside for another purpose.

We found a table large enough to accommodate us all.

The old guy working the counter came over and started pouring us drinks.

"Filo, what will you do?"

"Huh?"

Filo hated the smell of alcohol. She wrinkled up her human nose and looked around at the loud tavern.

"It looks so fun, but it smells weird."

"Well said."

Filo was clearly too young to enjoy the bar.

She was just a child. Besides, who knew what would happen if you gave alcohol to a filolial? I didn't want to be held accountable if anything crazy happened.

"So who's going to win?"

Someone was shouting at a table across the room. A man clearly impressed with the size of his biceps was looking for arm wrestling challengers.

Another person sat down. They clapped their hands together and started pushing and straining to wrench the other's arm down.

A crowd formed behind them and started betting on the outcome. I looked around the crowd and spotted Motoyasu leaning in on a girl, giving her more to drink. He never changed. He'd turn into a monster on the way home—no doubt about it.

A girl danced provocatively behind them. A group of musicians lined the wall next to her, plucking strings and singing. Looking over the scene, it really felt like a different world.

"Heeey! That looks fun!"

Filo was a bird monster, so she got really excited about music and songs.

"Go check it out then—but don't bother anyone."

"Okay!"

Filo tottered over in the direction of the dancing and song.

At the same time, our drinks arrived. I took a small sip.

Yup, alcohol tasted pretty much the same in this world.

"So THIS is alcohol . . . ."

Raphtalia was carefully inspecting her glass.

"Oh that's right. You shouldn't drink any of that."

"Hm? Why not?"

I suddenly realized that Raphtalia was still a child.

But hadn't her body already matured? In that case, was it technically okay to drink or not?

"Fine. Just don't drink too much."

"Okay!"

She looked like a child tiptoeing into a pool—she

approached the glass slowly and deliberately.

"It's a little bitter."

"Yeah, it is."

"Ahaha! Maybe Raphtalia-chan isn't quite ready for it."

L'Arc raised a huge stein and started chugging it.

Therese was slowly sipping her drink. The way they both drank seemed in encapsulate their personalities.

I didn't think it was very different from drinking water or soda. I guess it's because I don't get drunk.

"Mr. Naofumi, what do you think about alcohol?"

"I don't really think anything. It's not a pastime of mine. Sometimes I drink with other people."

"Oh, okay."

"There are plenty of people back in my world that don't drink—but that might be more rare here."

Ren and Itsuki were underage back home, but they might have been drinking age in this world.

I spotted Itsuki. He was sitting outside of the tavern, part of some kind of party. He was definitely under age.

But I guess this was a different world. It wasn't against the law here. If Itsuki was drinking, then Ren probably was too.

"It might be a good idea to keep an eye on how much you are drinking."

"Oh . . . ."

Raphtalia held her cup up and downed it in one gulp.

"You mean like that?"

"Hey yeah! Look at her go!"

"Sure."

It reminded me of parties back in my own world.

I certainly didn't have a problem with girls drinking.

Since ancient times, people have used alcohol to relax after a hard day of work. If people had been doing it for so long, then it was safe to assume it was effective.

Raphtalia always behaved herself and acted proper. I kind of wondered what she would be like if she let her guard down.

"No need to be scared of it. Drink up."

"Okay."

I slid another cup over to Raphtalia, and as I did some sort of disturbance erupted over by the musicians.

I looked over to find Filo singing along with the group. She was kind of good at it.

At first the musicians were surprised and worried, but they quickly realized that she was actually pretty talented, and now they were all excited.

What's that? Motoyasu had noticed Filo's singing.

"Filo! Bravo! Bravo!"

What had happened to the girl that was with him?

"Yaaaah!"

The tavern was getting wild.

Thirty minutes passed.

"How much leveling can we do on this island? If we go further in will the monsters be stronger?"

"Ha . . . kiddo . . . . This girl is tough!"

Raphtalia had downed 15 bottles of booze. She turned to me and started talking.

Apparently, she could really hold her liquor.

"Buzatt . . . zat's uat am sajin . . . ."

L'Arc, on the other hand, had clearly overdone it. He was as drunk as drunk gets. All his words were jumbled together.

"Come on L'Arc, we need to get back to our room soon."

Therese climbed under his arm and hoisted him up by the shoulder.

I was impressed with how much weight she could handle, but then I noticed she was using magic.

"That's just about enough for tonight, isn't it? We'll be heading back to our room now."

"Sure. We'll see you tomorrow."

"You two can certainly handle your liquor, especially you, Mr. Naofumi. It's like you're completely unaffected."

"Yeah well . . . I've always been like this."

"I've never scene anything like it."

Therese smiled, shifted L'Arc's weight onto her shoulder, and left the tavern.

"Mr. Naofumi?" Raphtalia said. "Let's drink a little more."

"Are you sure you want to drink so much?"

The barkeeper couldn't hide his surprise either. Raphtalia was really holding out. I wondered if maybe alcohol affected demi-humans differently. I couldn't help but think of the Shigaraki Tanuki statues and the massive tokkuri they carried.

The loser of the latest batch of arm wrestling came stumbling over and tripped, collapsing onto our table.

"Excuse you! We're having a discussion here, so please don't bother us!"

Raphtalia shouted at the drunk man.

Normally she wouldn't be so brash. Maybe the alcohol was affecting her?

I thought back on the last few months we'd spent together. We were always traveling, selling things, fighting in the waves, and running from the crown. We hadn't ever really stopped to catch out breath.

Maybe she needed to blow off some steam.

"Ha! If you got a problem with me, let's settle it with an arm wrestle!"

"If that's what you want, then fine. I'll be your opponent."

Raphtalia announced that she would be participating in the arm wrestling match.

She'd be fine, right? Our whole leveling campaign would collapse if she got hurt now.

I was worried about her, but I moved over to the bar and decided to watch from a distance.

There was a bunch of fruit, something like grapes, hanging there next to me, so I reached out for one and popped it into my mouth.

"?!"

It was so delicious I couldn't believe it. It tasted like a very strong grape, but the aftertaste was clean, but it hung around, delicious as ever, encouraging me to take another. So I did.

"We have a winner!"

"This girl is STRONG!"

"I won! Whose next?!"

Raphtalia threw a fist into the air, triumphant. Maybe she was drunk after all.

Should I put a stop to this before it got out of hand?

"Excuse me . . . ."

The bartender came over to me, and he looked worried.

"Yes?"

"Is everything okay?"

"You worried about the shop? You might be right. I'll try and wrap things up."

"That's not what I meant . . . ."

"Huh?"

His face was pale. I looked him in the eyes and even more color drained from his face.

It was because Raphtalia was defeating these strong men in arm wrestling. He must have just been surprised by it all.

"Booze! We need more booze over here!"

A large man came lumbering in. He was holding a large barrel. Setting it in the corner, he picked one of the grape-like fruits and dropped it into the booze before stirring. I guess it was some kind of secret ingredient. Those things were really delicious.

The tavern continued to grow more and more lively.

Raphtalia continued to win her arm-wrestling matches, and the betting going on behind her was getting more intense.

"Can anyone beat this girl?!"

As for Filo, she had joined the other musicians in song, and they were all really into the performance.

Everyone looked happy and enlivened.

I picked another fruit and popped it into my mouth.

"Hey you! What are you doing?!"

A man screamed. He was pointing a finger at me. The whole room fell silent.

"What? What's the matter?"

I swallowed the fruit.

Maybe he was just drunk?

"You can't just EAT a rucolu! You'll die!"

"What? What are you getting at?"

There was another bunch nearby, so I picked another fruit and threw it into my mouth.

The whole tavern erupted in shocked murmurs. Was it so strange?

"Mr . . . Mr. Naofumi? Are you all right?"

Raphtalia seemed to have instantly sobered up.

"I'm fine. What's everyone freaking out about?"

They were so delicious. They were quickly becoming a favorite of mine. I wanted another.

I picked another one and threw it back.

"WHAT?! He ate ANOTHER one?!"

All the eyes in the room were fixed on me. Why did everything have to be such a big deal? Couldn't I just eat in peace?

What was so shocking about that?"

"What's the big deal?"

Motoyasu came sauntering over and shouted condescendingly at me.

"Nothing. I eat a grape and the whole room starts freaking out about it."

"Oh yeah? Maybe those things are really expensive?"

"Are they? If so, then I'm sorry. I'll pay for them, so just give it a rest."

The queen was going to cover our tabs anyway. I could really eat as much as I wanted.

"Well they are somewhat expensive, but that's not really the problem . . . ."

The barkeep started to explain. He was very cautious.

"What's the problem then?"

"Rucolu are, um . . . . Well that barrel is full of water. Dissolving a single fruit in all that water turns it into alcohol. If you eat one directly, well . . . ."

"What are you talking about? That can't be true! Stop with the jokes."

"I'm telling the truth."

"But Naofumi isn't drunk, so you have to be lying."

Motoyasu picked one of the fruits and popped it into this mouth.

"You know, they are really delicious, savory, in a way . . . ."

Before Motoyasu could finish his review, he clutched his stomach and fell forward, collapsing to the floor with a loud crash.

Haha! His eyes rolled back into his head! Hilarious. But were those fruits really so dangerous?

"Oh no! He ate a rucolu whole!"

"We have to make him throw it up!"

"Yeah!"

The whole tavern sprung into action. Men gathered around and lifted Motoyasu up, then carried him out of the room.

Well . . . so much for our fun night.

But I guess the fruits really were filled with strong alcohol. I had an idea.

"Raphtalia, you want one?"

"No . . . ."

"What about you Filo?"

Filo stopped singing and came running over. I held a fruit out to her and she came close to sniff it.

Then she covered her mouth with her hands and backed away quickly.

"No!"

"But you eat everything."

"I don't like that thing!"

Well that was a strong reaction—specially coming from Filo. I hadn't been expecting her to turn it down.

"We've got a real devil here!"

"A monster!"

"The alcohol gods have run away, their tails between their legs!"

The crowd was wild and raucous again.

I wondered if the fruit was some sort of prank they were all playing on me. Or maybe human biology was different in this world? Motoyasu and I might have had a lot in common, but we did come from different universes.

"Well I'm sorry for causing such a fuss. We'll be going back to our room now."

"Oh . . . alright then."

The tavern was still in an uproar as we collected our things and left for the night.

Chapter Eight: Karma

The next morning, we left to go leveling once the sun had climbed over the horizon.

We'd agreed to go out hunting with L'Arc and Therese the day after that.

It's not like I felt like we needed to be prepared for leveling with them, just that I wanted to work on leveling anyway—while we had the time.

Besides, leveling was fun.

Oh yeah, that's right. When I'd been trying out the weapon copy system at the old guy's shop, I'd learned a pretty neat skill.

It was called Hate Reaction.

"Hate Reaction!"

Nothing seemed to happen. I turned my head in confusion. Filo blinked.

"Master! There's some kind of nastiness coming from you. It's flying out in all directions."

That was Filo's assessment. At first I hadn't understood what was happening, but now I was starting to get it.

All the monsters in the area had turned their eyes on me and were creeping in my direction.

Even the ones that other adventurers had been battling with.

The skill seemed to affect an area extending about 15 meters in all directions.

Even the monsters that had learned to stay away from us on the previous day were now creeping in my direction.

It was the sort of skill that would be a burden on everyone if I used it in a populated area. But what if we were deeper inland . . . ?

If we went into an area that was off-limits to all but the most advanced adventurers, I could probably put the skill to better use.

I doubt that any normal adventurers would bother to brave the interior of the island.

Normal people had their level capped at 40. Unless you were a hero, areas like that were likely to be too dangerous.

It wasn't like we were sure we could be alone there, but I think that the further inland we went, the less likely we were to run into anyone else.

I came across something like . . . like skin stretched taught over bones, dried till it was stiff. The further inland we went, the more it felt like a Darwinian battle to survive. I wondered how many adventurers had met their ends there.

To think that L'Arc and Therese had come looking for us in an environment like this. That must have been a real risk for a normal adventurer.

So we went on cutting our way through the forest, until we were very deep in the center of the island, when we ran into a new monster, the Karma Dog Familia. It was a very large, black dog.

It reminded me of the large, two-headed black dog that Raphtalia and I had fought a while back. The dog looked like a Doberman.

This one only had one head, but its fur was rough and kind of intimidating. As you might expect, Raphtalia looked a little uncomfortable.

"You alright?"

"Yes. There's no problem."

She arranged her fingers and gripped her sword tightly, readying it for battle.

Slowly, inch by inch, Filo moved in closer to the Karma Dog Familia.

There was nothing left to do but fight.

I stood at the front of the group, readied my shield, and dashed at the dog.

"Gah!"

The dog opened its mouth wide and clamped its jaws down on my shoulder.

But I'd powered up recently, and my stats were too high for the dog to deal any damage.

I ducked my head down and threw my weight forward, pushing the dog back.

"Ha!"

"Take that!"

Raphtalia and Filo didn't miss the opportunity. They rushed in and attacked.

"This thing is tough!"

Raphtalia sunk her sword deep into the dog's belly, and Filo delivered a brutal kick, tearing the dog's hind leg clean off.

" . . . ?!"

The dog let out an ear-splitting squeal.

But it didn't give up. It kept coming at us—at me. Screaming until its last breath, it bit at me.

I had to admire its tenacity. It was fighting as if it didn't care for its own life at all.

It was strong, but it probably had to be to survive deep in the island's interior.

"That was one persistent dog."

"Yes, it was."

"And its bite was really something to contend with."

Filo tottered over to the corpse and started snacking on it.

"Stop that."

"Fiiiine."

Stupid bird . . . . I knelt down by the dog and absorbed it into my shield.

Karma Dog Familia Shield conditions met.

Karma Dog Familia Shield: ability locked: equip bonus: sense of smell up (low): inult status adjustment (small)

There were a number of other items that appeared in the menu, but I was most drawn to the unlock conditions and the equip bonus.

Sense of smell up seemed self-explanatory enough.

If I kept increasing my sense stats like this, I wondered if I would turn into a feral creature like Filo.

Inult . . . . Wasn't that the name of the monster that had pioneered civilization in the islands? Where was I going to find one of those?!

The drop item was actually bad luck. There wasn't one.

If we met another one I would break it down a bit before absorbing its parts.

As for experience points, we'd gotten quite a lot when we won. I think it had been worth about 800 points.

The monsters on the perimeter of the island had been giving us around 90, so this was a big step up.

"Gah!"

Huh? Another one appeared. We defeated it, then came across another. And on and on we moved deeper into the island's interior.

"Is this the end of the line?"

"Who knows?"

We kept on going in the same direction, and the monster's strength, as well as the points they were worth, continued to rise.

But our own levels were rising rapidly too.

I'd reached level 57, Raphtalia was at 59, and Filo was at level 61.

We were leveling so fast that all our time up until then felt like it had been a waste. Raphtalia and Filo's stats were also rising quickly.

"Ugh . . . ."

Raphtalia was closely inspecting her sword. Then she started moaning.

"What is it?"

"Nothing. It feels like my sword has lost its core . . . ."

Raphtalia forcefully swung her sword a few times to check. I couldn't really tell, but it looked like the blade was bending. The sword itself wasn't very old. What did it mean?

"You've probably outgrown it."

If she kept using it like she was, it looked like it might bend or break.

I looked over to Filo, only to find that her metal claws were chipped too—the points had nearly broken off completely.

"What's happening master?"

"I don't know."

I had a hunch that Raphtalia and Filo's power levels had outgrown the durability of their equipment.

If we were preparing for the next wave, I'd have to give priority to their weapons. If I didn't we might end up in real trouble.

For the time being, I had a couple iron swords that had been item drops, so we could use those if there was an emergency—not that they would really be much help.

It was probably time for us to start relying on custom equipment. We were going to need powerful weapons from this point on.

"Should I switch to the magic sword?"

Raphtalia sheathed her sword and switched to the magic sword.

The sword worked against disembodied enemies, but against normal enemies it only cut through their magic power. It couldn't actually kill a normal enemy, but it could cause them to lose consciousness.

And there was little chance of it breaking. Raphtalia summoned the magic blade, and it appeared there now, extending from the hilt.

It seemed to be outputting more power than it had before. It was a large blade, and it was crackling with energy.

"Ah . . . ."

Raphtalia hurried to switch it off.

"What happened?"

"I can't use it. There's too much power. The hilt gets too hot to hold.

"If you're not careful, you might break it."

"Understood."

We moved on, deeper into the woods. When we finally arrived at what seemed to be the center, we found a large structure there, a temple of some kind. It reminded me of Stonehenge. It appeared to be ruins.

In the center of the circle was some kind of sphere. It was like a magic lens.

"What is this thing?"

"Who knows?"

It reminded me of the rifts that appeared in the sky during the waves. I could tell that it wasn't quite the same thing though.

"Filo, will you try attacking it for me?"

"Sure!"

She jumped forward and kicked the black sphere.

For a moment, it looked like the whole object warped and bent—but a second later it was back to its original shape.

What could it mean? If it functioned anything like objects in the games that I had played, it would probably only become functional if certain conditions were met.

Suddenly, a very large dog appeared—and it was covered in black feathers. It was huge, probably five meters from head to tail.

It was shaped something like a golden retriever. It was large and clumsy looking, but it was still a vicious monster.

I checked the beast's name in the menu. It was called a Karma Dog.

Was it the boss monster of the island?

It seemed like a reasonable assumption. The Karma Dog Familias that we'd met up until now were probably its underlings.

"Raphtalia, Filo, let's go! First Aura!"

I cast the support magic on them and the battle began in earnest.

The huge dog lunged at me, its fangs bared.

"Hya!"

It opened its mouth wider to bite me, but I threw out my arm and grabbed it by the teeth, pushing the beast back.

There was a loud, clanging sound, but I'd managed to stop the monster in its tracks.

Slowly, the fangs sunk into my skin, and peels of pain shot up my arm.

This beast was clearly much stronger than the other dogs had been. If it could get through my defenses then it must have been pretty damn powerful.

Granted, I hadn't finished powering up. Still, I thought that my stats had really improved—and they had—but it still wasn't enough.

"Hya!"

"Whoop!"

Raphtalia's sword and Filo's claws bit into the underbelly of the beast. But it wasn't enough to stop the monster. I couldn't control its claws, and it turned them on the girls.

"You won't get me that easily!"

"Ha!"

I hadn't been able to stop the monster, but I'd apparently slowed it down enough. They dodged its attack easily.

"WAOOOOOOOOOO!"

The dog howled. As the beast's voice died down, two Karma Dog Famlilas suddenly appeared from the mysterious sphere!

Damn. This wasn't looking good.

"Raphtalia, Filo! Can you keep this up?!"

"Yeah!"

"Not a problem!"

"Great! Let's use a combination skill. Filo, watch me!"

"Okay!"

I'd seen Motoyasu and the others use combination skills before. It was when you combined magic and a skill to form a stronger attack.

They normally had better secondary effects than other skills.

"Filo, are you watching? I'm going to use air strike shield, so you need to use some wind attack magic at the same time!"

"Okay!"

Filo closed her eyes and started to concentrate.

"I'm the source of all power. Hear my words and heed them! Wrap them in a fierce tornado!"

"Zweite Tornado!"

As she cast the spell, a list of compatible skills appeared before me.

"Tornado Shield!"

A Karma Dog Familia was rushing to attack us, but before it could a massive shield formed of wind appeared in the air before the beast.

The dog slammed into the shield and was forced to stop. When it did, a huge tornado, one bigger than Filo's magic could normally produce, shot from the center of the shield and carried the two Karma Dog Familias up into the air.

Hey now, that was a pretty useful combination! If we could coordinate our attacks like this, we were even stronger than I had thought.

As for Raphtalia, her magic was normally illusion-based, so it wouldn't work so well as an attack medium.

We wouldn't be able to do the same thing, but we might

be able to trick the monsters. It would depend on how the combination skill worked.

"Raphtalia!"

"I'm on it!"

"I am the source of all power. Hear my words and heed them! Confuse the enemy!"

"First Mirage!"

"Mirage Shield!"

I used second shield and was able to use another skill while the first was still deployed.

The tornado disappeared, and the two dogs plummeted to the ground. Before they hit though, another shield appeared beneath them, and they slammed into that shield instead.

This shield was flexible though. The minute they connected with it, it expanded in a quick puff, completely enclosing them.

"Kyan!"

The shield disappeared, and the two dogs fell to the ground again, but this time they were upside down, and they landed on their backs. They tottered around, unable to regain their bearings.

And then . . . .

"Gah!"

The two of them barked and growled and started to fight one another!

Both of them had probably become confused as to who the enemy was, so they just attacked whatever creature was nearest to them.

It looked like the Mirage Shield had an interesting effect on the enemy.

"Great! Now's our chance! Finish them!"

"I'm on it!"

We tightened our grip on our weapons and turned to face the Karma Dog.

"Whew."

We defeated the monster. It kept calling for reinforcements, which caused the fight to drag on a little.

Luckily we were always able to get the reinforcements to fight among themselves. Raphtalia and Filo had become really powerful in the last few days as well, so eventually we were able to win the battle without too much trouble.

When the main beast was gone, we took out the remaining reinforcements. Once I was sure that the coast was clear, I absorbed the Karma Dog into the shield and received its drop item.

I used to be a pretty avid gamer, and those gamer instincts were still alive and kicking inside me. I figured that the Karma Dog had been a boss monster, and boss monsters were sure to leave behind really good drop items.

For gamers, few things were more coveted than the drop items from bosses. There was a chance it would leave behind a unique, rare, or powerful weapon.

So I was excited to check out the Karma Dog's drop.

Oreikul Ore? I assumed it was something you could use to power up. I felt like I'd seen it somewhere before.

Huh?

"Karma Dog Claw?"

Judging by the name, maybe it was some sort of weapon? I quickly opened the menu to check it out.

There was a heavy clang, and two black claws jutted out of my shield.

"What's that?"

"I already explained it, remember? It's something the legendary shield can do."

"I understand that, but I've never seen the shield grow claws like that. I was just surprised."

I couldn't fault her for that.

I examined the claws closer. They were about the size of my palm, so I don't think they would fit onto Filo's feet. Again, I opened a menu to read about the item.

Karma Dog Claw: quality: excellent: additional effects: agility up, magic down, attack up, defense down.

The stat increases were nothing to turn your nose up at.

But unfortunately they didn't seem to have a blood clean coating on them. So if we used them, we'd have to make sure they stayed sharpened.

Besides, I was concerned about the stat decreases too.

"Claws?"

Filo cocked her head to the side. She was intrigued.

"That's what it looks like, but . . . ."

They wouldn't fit on Filo's feet.

"I want to try them out!"

"I think you'll have to be in human form."

Filo had made a point of staying in filolial form when we were fighting monsters. Fitoria had made a point of telling her that battles went smoothly when you matched the size of your enemy.

"Okay! Them I'm going to try fighting as a human!"

She turned into her human form and slipped the claws over her hands.

"Well, if that's what you want to do, then I don't have a problem with it. Let's see if we can find a monster to try them out on."

So we walked around in the woods for a short while until we found a monster to fight.

"Tornado Claw!"

The second we spotted a monster Filo shouted the attack

and started spinning in tight circles in the direction of the Karma Dog Familia.

"Gah?!"

The second she made contact, the beast went flying through the air. A moment later, it fell to the ground, shredded into ribbons.

"Wow Master! These things are SHARP!"

But the shredded beast didn't just lie there. Large scars appeared on the body, a black curse of some kind.

The corpse started to smell, and Filo scrunched her nose up.

"If I kill the monster with these, then I can't eat it."

"You're right."

They must have been dark-elemental weapons. Either that or they had been cursed.

"Filo? Can you take those claws off? Do they feel normal?"

"Huh? What do you mean?"

She slipped the claws off of her hands like any other weapon. Apparently they weren't cursed.

And the status decreases didn't seem to bother Filo much at all.

They seemed safe enough to use, at least until we were able to meet with the old guy at the weapon shop again.

"Should we have Filo act as the main attacker from now on?"

"Sure, why not?"

We finished our little meeting about the claws and spent another two hours in the area. The mysterious sphere in the center of the stone ruins continued to warp and release Karma Dogs.

It seemed like the monsters were being emitted from the sphere on a set interval. They were reappearing approximately every 30 minutes or so.

But now that Filo had such a powerful weapon equipped, the fights were even easier than they had been. We were defeating the dogs without much effort.

We were also getting plenty of experience points, so I'd say we were having a pretty successful day leveling.

By the way, as we continued to defeat the Karma Dogs I noticed that they were leaving behind claws of all different sizes. With some simple crafting, I was able to make a pair large enough for Filo to wear when she was in filolial form.

Now she could use the Karma Dog Gloves in whatever form she was in.

The sun was slanting down in the sky when we made it back to the main island.

I had reached level 63. Raphtalia was at level 65, and Filo was at 67.

How much further could we level up in the islands?

Not that you could ever be over-leveled . . . .

"Hey! How are you all doing?"

I was mulling over our leveling progress when L'Arc and Therese came walking over.

"We're doing well. Leveling really fast. What about you two?"

"Same. I feel like we're really sinking our teeth into the monsters out there."

"Great to hear."

"You know what I heard? I heard that the four heroes are in the islands right now! Everyone is gossiping about it."

" . . . ."

I didn't feel like I needed to rehash all this with him. I didn't want to reiterate that he was standing in front of one of those heroes.

And besides, L'Arc had already made up his mind that I was pretending to be a hero. He wasn't going to listen to me no matter what I said.

"Oh really?"

I just wanted him to change the subject, so I tried to make it clear that I wasn't really listening.

"What sort of gossip?"

Raphtalia jumped in and took over the conversation. I wasn't too excited about talking it over with him, so I decided to leave it up to her.

"Well I heard that the Sword Hero was leveling by himself, and that the Spear Hero was walking around the marketplace trying to pick up girls in the street."

Well at least he was talking about the same people that I knew.

"What about the Bow Hero?"

Raphtalia chimed, but L'Arc and Therese suddenly looked uncomfortable. They averted their eyes when they answered.

"Everyone is pissed off, because apparently he's claimed ownership of some hunting grounds."

I figured as much. I shouldn't have expected him to listen to us. Everything was turning out pretty much as I imagined it would.

Regardless, none of the gossip was particularly positive. I wondered what a normal adventurer would think when they heard it.

We were talking it over, when—speak of the devil—the other heroes came walking up.

"Alright! Let's head back to the room, shall we?"

"I guess."

"Yes! Let's rest up and get ready for tomorrow!"

All three of them were walking together in the direction of the inn.

"I wonder where the heroes are?"

"Right? If they're as crazy as everyone says they are, I'd like to meet them at least once."

Didn't he realize that they were walking right under his nose at that very moment? There was no saving these two—they were as dull as rocks.

Still, they were friendly enough to hang around with, and peaceful too. I could ignore their faults on account of their strengths. I had sort of started to like them.

They really were dull as rocks though.

"Is that so? And what sort of gossip have you heard about the Shield Hero?"

"I hear he's a real lush."

"Like he's fancy?"

"No, like he drinks a lot, Therese. Get with the program, will ya?"

"One of us needs to get with the program. But which one?"

"Oh please . . . ."

A drinker, am I? Was this all because of those little fruits I ate?

"Besides, the Shield Hero isn't known for the deeds in the islands. They've been talking about him everywhere else!"

"What have they been saying?"

"I think we talking about it on the boat ride over here, didn't we? That he's a liar, a thief, a conman, a rapist, a demon . . . . I heard he kills anyone that gets in his way."

Is that what I looked like to the rest of the world?

Well, I guess I couldn't say they were wrong.

Still, at least half of that stuff was lies the church had spread about me. The rest were probably from Bitch and Trash.

Raphtalia slapped her hand to her head and sighed.

"It's a shame we can't make the rumors stop."

"Raphtalia, sticking up for me are you? I haven't given up on my more notorious pursuits yet!"

"What are you bragging about?!"

"Haha!"

"This is not a joke. This is your reputation we're talking about here."

People had been talking about me that way from the minute I stepped foot in this world. I was getting used to it.

Still, little by little the rumors were being addressed. Eventually they would die down.

Only a week or so had passed since our battle with the high priest. I couldn't expect the whole country to have a change of heart overnight.

"Ha! Kiddo, are you still pretending to be the Shield Hero? You'd better cut that out."

"Oh, right. Sure thing."

These two sure were an optimistic bunch, weren't they?

"So what are you kiddos going to do next?"

"I'll tell you this—we're not leveling through the night

this time. We'll head back to the inn and try to rest up. I was thinking I might get to work on Therese's item if I have the time."

"Really?"

"Good thinking, kiddo. So do you want to meet on the docks tomorrow morning?"

"Sounds good. See you then."

"Right on. Later."

Raphtalia and Filo waved to them as we parted ways.

"Alright, let's get some rest. You two head out on the town and enjoy yourselves."

"What about you?"

"I'm just going to rest in the room. I still have that curse to deal with, after all."

"Oh? Well then I guess I'll come with you."

"Imma go swimming!"

"Good idea. Have fun. Raphtalia, are you sure? This is the last vacation we'll have for a while."

"I'm a little worn out from all the battling we did today."

That made sense. We had been fighting for two days straight. It was important to get rest.

Filo went swimming in the ocean and didn't come back until pretty late. When she got back she was ebullient. The ocean, she said, was super pretty.

"So I guess this is the day we level up with L'Arc."

I had to think about what island we should head for—I didn't want to overlap with one of the other heroes.

I didn't know if it was a real strategy or not, but it sounded like they were moving through the islands in order. Apparently the shadows and envoys from Melromarc were following them and suggesting when it was time to move on.

That was better for them anyway—they would probably level up faster fighting a variety of monsters.

We walked to the docks and found L'Arc and Therese waiting for us there.

"Hey, kiddo! How are you all feeling today?"

"What does it matter, the day hasn't even started? Oh, Therese—I had a little free time last night, so I went ahead and made the item you requested."

I took out the item and tossed it to Therese.

There had been a mysterious, rough jewel in the pouch they had given me. It was called a starfire, and I couldn't suppress my curiosity.

I polished up the raw material and imbued it with magic, but it took me a little while to think of what sort of ore I should mount it to.

Eventually I settled on the ore I'd gotten yesterday, the Oreikul ore. I brought it to the island blacksmith and had him work it into a band.

So even though I had just sort of fumbled some materials together, it ended up being a pretty impressive piece.

Oreikul Starfire Bracelet: magic power up (max): quality: very good

"This . . . ."

Therese looked down at the item and appeared to be at a loss for words.

"Wow! The stone is overflowing with joy. I never expected so much."

Tears welled up in her eyes.

I didn't see what the big deal was—it was certainly nothing to cry over.

Maybe Therese was a little overemotional.

"H . . . hey!"

"It's amazing . . . I . . . I really never thought . . . ."

"Therese! Get a hold of yourself!"

"L'Arc, can't you tell? The jewel is overflowing with joy. Overflowing! This is like the door to a whole new world."

"Now you're exaggerating."

"This is very impressive work, Mr. Naofumi. You mustn't hide your talent! Please continue your crafting work."

She didn't realize I already had a job as the Shield Hero. I certainly was no item maker.

"So . . . about the payment I was promised . . . ."

Before I could finish the sentence Therese produced a bad of gold and tossed it to me.

"Hey! Therese! You can't . . . ."

"That doesn't even begin to cover it. L'Arc, give me your wallet."

"Therese! Get a hold of yourself!"

But she wouldn't be deterred. She started pulling his clothes off to get at the wallet. Pedestrians began to stop and take notice.

"Calm down! You can just pay me in installments."

"Excellent."

Therese backed away from L'Arc and nodded her approval.

I hated women that just took what they wanted from men.

Still, if she was that impressed with what I'd made I couldn't help but feel a little proud. Once again, I started to understand how the old guy at the weapon shop must feel.

"Shall we make our way to the hunting grounds?"

"You know, to get Therese that excited, kiddo, you must be a really impressive item-maker."

"I don't know about all that."

I think I'd just had access to good materials.

"Alright, should we get going?"

"Oh hey, I almost forgot to mention it—but guess what?

We found the Shield Hero."

"Oh yeah?"

L'Arc nodded a few times and went on.

"Yeah, I knew him the second I saw him. I thought it was pretty much obvious. He looked like the kind of guy that would do anything, if you know what I mean."

"You don't say? Where is he?"

What kind of person would measure up to the gossip that was out there? Depending on who the guy was, I might have to teach him a lesson.

"Look, he's over there."

L'Arc pointed over to some people preparing for the hunt. It was Itsuki's party and L'Arc was pointing to flashy Armor.

"See what I mean, kiddo? There's no mistaking him. See how he just oozes self-satisfaction? His face says he wouldn't mind killing anyone that got in his way. It's the kind of face that never doubts itself."

Give me a break! There WAS a hero there, but it was the wrong one.

"That guy is going to cause trouble at some point or another. Stay on your toes around him."

"Can't disagree with you there."

Come to think of it, Itsuki and his party had been causing trouble pretty much since we left the harbor in Melromarc.

The shadows and soldiers that had come with us all from

the castle looked like they were exhausted from dealing with it all.

"To think you'd be confused with someone like that . . . ."

Raphtalia looked almost sickened by the suggestion.

I wanted to tell him how disappointing it was to be put in the same category as Armor, but I was pretty sure L'Arc wasn't going to be convinced that easily.

"Well that's enough chitchat, isn't it? Should we get going?"

"Good thinking."

I sent them an invitation to join the party, and they accepted.

"We've already picked the island we want to head for, but did you have any other suggestions before we leave?"

I really hoped they were going to agree with my choice—if they didn't we might end up running into other heroes.

"No problem, Shield Kiddo. If you have a place picked out, then that should do fine. We can probably handle ourselves pretty much anywhere."

"Yes, I agree. The item you made me can't wait to get into battle."

The item wanted to fight? Uh . . . okay.

I was a little perturbed by how overly excited Therese was about the bracelet, but I didn't say anything about it. Instead, I pointed to the island I'd picked out.

"By the way, L'Arc, what level are you guys?"

If they had made it up to level 40 then there shouldn't be any problems. Actually we'd gone ahead and leveled up pretty far on our own, so even if they were lower than that, we should be able to make up for it."

But still, no matter how you looked at it, if he was a normal adventurer, then I don't see how they could have leveled past 40.

"I'm 56 and she's 52."

Huh? I guess they'd been through the class-up ceremony. If so, there shouldn't be any problem.

But they were pretty high level. In a good way, I sort of felt like I'd been betrayed. But it was the sort of betrayal I was happy to accept.

"What about you kiddos?"

"I'm at 63, Raphtalia is 65, Filo is 67."

"Ha! You guys don't mess around, do you?"

"Well we leveled a lot over the last two days."

Filo had shot up 27 levels in that time.

The leveling had been so fast it made my head spin. Sure, the shield helped by keeping the enemies at bay—but still.

"Let's talk strategy. What kind of fighting style do you use, kiddo?"

"A shield is only good for one thing. I stand at the front and block the monster's attacks. I keep them at bay. Then my friends jump in when they show their weak points."

"Ha! You're really into the Shield Hero thing, aren't ya? But that's okay, I like the simple folk."

"What about you?"

He had an absurdly large scythe hanging at his waist, but did he really fight with it?

What a strange weapon to use. I'd seen scythes in games before. They were normally used by death-type characters. I didn't really know why though. In the real world they were used for harvesting grain, or something like that.

"Who, me? I use this bad boy right here," he said, touching the scythe. "Therese mostly sticks to magic."

"That's right. I have to say that I'm really excited to see how this new item works in battle."

So I guess L'Arc was the offensive player while Therese backed him up with magic. We'd work together well—my party was pretty skewed towards offense, so I could use help with supporting the others.

There might be too many people at the front though. Maybe we needed more support in the center.

The center was basically a space between the frontline and the support group. It was populated by characters that could handle both offense and defense when the need arose.

The niche could also be filled by people with ranged weapons, so they could stay in the back line and still deal damage.

Among the four heroes, Motoyasu probably fit the bill most clearly.

If the four of us were fighting together, then Ren and I would be in the front, Motoyasu in the center, and Itsuki would be in the back.

The center was basically there to protect the back row from any enemies that made it through the first line of defense. Either that or it was there to help support the front when the back wasn't able to.

They could really do anything, which was both a blessing and a curse. Motoyasu's personality, however, pretty much put him at the front.

"Fine. I'll stand at the front to stop the enemy attacks. L'Arc and Therese, you help Raphtalia and Filo."

That pretty much summed it up.

If they came at me with weapons or magic though, it wasn't going to be pretty.

"Sounds good!"

L'Arc seemed to be in full support.

We climbed out of the boat and stepped out onto the shore before pushing for the interior of the island.

The monsters that we met along the way were not very strong at all, so Filo basically took them out with a single kick the moment that we encountered them.

For the moment, Filo was fighting in human form.

I got the feeling that she was practicing her human fighting tactics on purpose, to make sure that she was always prepared.

"Alright . . . ."

"What should we do with this monster?"

L'Arc was pointing to the corpse at our feet.

"Huh? We could break it down for materials."

Honestly, most of the monsters we'd run into on the islands were not great for materials. And that went double for all the weaklings we ran into on the path deeper into the island.

"I was actually wondering if I could take it."

"Hmm . . . ."

The drop would be some usable potion of something, which I guess might be a little useful.

I was considering it, when L'Arc lowered his weapon and pointed it at the corpse.

"We'll split it then."

And then, just like I did with my shield, he absorbed it into his scythe.

"What?"

"What's the matter, kiddo?"

He'd absorbed the corpse so naturally—I was speechless for a minute.

What was going on? I was pretty sure that was an ability

only possible with one of the heroes' legendary weapons.

But L'Arc wasn't a hero. I knew that he wasn't, because when we killed the monster I got experience points out of it.

What on earth was going on?"

"Alright, I'm next."

I held out my shield and absorbed the corpse.

I could barely believe it. The queen hadn't said anything about this either. This world was full of mysteries.

L'Arc had a weapon that processed abilities I'd thought were only available to the heroes and their legendary weapons.

Actually, now that I thought about it, I didn't really know very much about normal adventurers.

There was that transformation ability, I guess. I didn't know very much about it. Melty had said something about it before, something about the reappearance of the heroes' skills or something . . . .

I'd have to make a point to discuss it with the old guy at the weapon shop the next time I saw him.

If there were weapons that could do THAT, why hadn't he sold me one?

Anyway, it was clear that I didn't have enough information to figure out what was going on.

"I think we just met someone very interesting, don't you think?"

"Maybe so . . . ."

Raphtalia and I whispered. She was motioning towards L'Arc with her eyes.

"Filo, you sure are a tough girl!"

"Hehe! I know I am!"

L'Arc and Therese were talking to Filo, who had her chest puffed up with pride at her victory.

I wanted to find out just how powerful these two really were.

We pushed on further into the interior of the island and encountered a monster called the Karma Rabbit Familia. It was basically a giant black rabbit. If this island was anything like the last one, there would probably be a boss waiting at the end, the Karma Rabbit.

Should we bring L'Arc and Therese all the way back there?

Regardless, I needed to focus on the battles that were happening along the way.

I couldn't let myself be tricked by the appearance of the cute rabbit.

Rabbit-type enemies always appeared in games in a tricky way—they always sort of betrayed your expectations of them.

The first time you ran into them, they'd be one of the lower level monsters that you ran into at the start of the game—like the usapils back in Melromarc.

But once you got further along in the game, rabbit-type monsters would appear again, but they would normally be way stronger than you would expect from your previous experience.

I'd run into that in games before. They trick you by looking cute, and then when your guard is down they rush in with a killing move.

You'd let your guard down, and they'd kick your head from your shoulders.

The rabbit tensed its powerful hind legs and shot through the air at us.

I anticipated the attack and raised my shield to block my neck. The rabbit connected and produced a shower of sparks.

I figured it would do something like that.

I jumped back and caught the Karma Rabbit Familia as it tried to escape.

"Everyone watch out! These things are way stronger than they look! They're fast too!"

"Got it!"

"Understood."

L'Arc and Raphtalia signaled that they understood.

"I'm going in!"

Filo shot forward and ran for the rabbit.

Therese was still hanging back. What was she doing?

"All-encompassing power of the jewel, hear my plea and show yourself. My name is Therese Alexanderite. I am your friend. Lend me the power to destroy them!"

She was chanting a spell.

But it was a phrasing I'd never heard before. As she chanted, her hair began to turn red.

The bracelet on her wrist began to glow, and then a giant ball of flame appeared, hovering before her.

"Shining stone, ball of flame!"

Of all the magic attacks I'd seen before this one was the most beautiful. It shot toward the Karma Rabbit Familia.

But it sucked me into its path of destruction on the way.

"Mr. Naofumi!"

Hey! I'm standing here! Why did they have to hit ME with their magic?

Or so I was thinking, but then something mysterious happened.

The spell didn't hurt me. It only affected the rabbit, which burst into flames.

And when it passed me by unscathed, I heard a voice.

It was a voice I'd never heard before. I think it said "thank you."

By the time I realized what was happening, the rabbit was engulfed in flames.

I didn't even feel any heat. And it wasn't because of my defense level either. The flames didn't seem to have any effect on me at all.

To take it one step further, it was almost as if the flames

had protected me. The parts of my body that had felt sluggish since the curse suddenly felt lighter, as if they had been purified.

What a strange spell.

The flames finally burned out, and then L'Arc held his scythe aloft before bringing it down hard.

"Flying Circle!"

His scythe transformed into energy and spun rapidly, producing a circle of light that fell on the rabbit, slicing it in two.

The Karma Rabbit Familia was now definitely dead.

"Are you alright?"

"What was that spell you used?"

"Therese's magic doesn't hurt her allies!"

"Yeah . . . I'd figured that much out."

It was a form of magic I had never seen before.

"The bracelet you made me is very powerful, Mr. Naofumi."

"She's right. I could tell from the minute the spell activated. We could give you all the money we have and it wouldn't be enough. Thanks a bunch, kiddo."

"That's not really what I meant."

L'Arc finally seemed to understand what I was trying to ask. He rubbed his chin and answered.

"Therese's magic works by combining her magic with the power of the jewels she wears."

"Hm . . . ."

"I've never heard of such a thing."

"Oh well, it's a pretty common type of magic where I'm from."

"What are you saying Therese? Your magic is . . . ."

But before he could finish, Therese rushed over and clapped her hand down over L'Arc's mouth. Then she whispered something in his ear, and he nodded along.

What were they talking about?

"Oh . . . ."

To be fair, I guess we hadn't been completely upfront with them either, so I couldn't really blame them.

And besides, we were only going to be sticking around for the duration of the activation event. But if they were as powerful as they seemed to be, then it might be worth keeping them around.

"These things give tons of experience!"

"Yeah, they do."

For such a short battle, the rewards were great. Each time we defeated a monster, L'Arc and I split the drop items and the corpse.

I unlocked a few skills, but only one looked interesting.

Karma Rabbit Familia Shield: abilities locked: equip bonus: alert range (small): usauni status adjustment (small)

Alert range (small), huh? It was probably something similar to the ability I got from the dogs, the sense of smell up (small). Maybe this ability was even better?

"You kiddos sure are powerful."

"Well . . . ."

If the Shield Hero wasn't able to block the attacks of enemies, then he really wasn't good for anything, was he?

"Actually, L'Arc, I'm pretty surprised by how powerful you guys are."

L'Arc seemed to have just about as much attack power as Raphtalia. He was defeating enemies with one hit.

It seemed like the scythe was normally more portable, but it grew to be really large when it was time for battle.

It wasn't a hero weapon. And it wasn't a replica of a legendary weapon like the high priest had used. It must have just been something I'd never heard of, but what?

I recalled something the queen had said. She'd said that the heroes were weaker than she had been expecting.

Maybe this is just what powerful adventurers were like? If so, then what she'd said made sense.

Anyway, I never got an answer to my questions, and we all moved on deeper into the island.

As expected, we found a strange Stonehenge-like structure, and in the center was another mysterious sphere, just like the one we'd seen that was protected by the Karma Dog.

We approached the sphere, and it suddenly warped—just like last time—and a monster appeared. This time it was a Karma Rabbit.

Its ears were very long, and they moved almost as if they were hands.

From the look of it, I had an idea of how the battle was going to go. Just like we'd done when fighting the underlings, I'd have to block the sneak attack that it had—only this time I'd have to find some way to deal with those hand-like ears too.

"Boo!"

In my world, rabbits weren't known for their voices. But the Karma Rabbit opened its mouth and exhaled sharply, and it certainly seemed to be shouting at us.

At the same time, huge spikes shot up from the ground all around the Karma Rabbit.

So it had earth attacks. That wasn't good.

"Alright! I'm going to stop that thing in its tracks. Everyone, attack when you get the chance! Got it?!"

"Yes."

"Yeah!"

"Okay!"

"Let's do it!"

And so the battle with the Karma Rabbit began.

Throughout the battle, familias kept appearing. They weren't a significant threat though, and we cut through them pretty quickly.

The Karma Rabbit had a lot of different attacks at its disposal, and it was a violent and crazy thing. But I was able to restrict its movement enough that its agility didn't do it much good. We were able to defeat it easily compared to the boss we'd taken on the day before.

"Whew."

"I guess that's that."

Raphtalia flicked her sword to knock the blood off of it, but then she stopped to inspect the blade more carefully.

The blade itself was definitely starting to bend. It probably wouldn't be long before it broke.

"You kiddos are . . . ."

"Huh? What?"

I felt like he looked at me for a second, considering something carefully.

"Never mind, it's nothing. You kiddos sure are tough!"

"Well I'm pretty impressed with you two as well."

They were stronger than I'd expected. Suspiciously so.

If they hadn't been with us, that battle definitely would have been a little tougher.

"Well I'm glad we didn't disappoint you."

"Yeah, yeah . . . . Anyway, what should we do with this thing? Want me to take it?"

I wanted to see what sort of drop item the Karma Rabbit had been carrying. The Karma Dog's drop item had significantly increased Filo's attack power. And because of that, she had probably done the most damage out of anyone in the fight against the Karma Rabbit.

"Sure, it's all yours. You guys did most of the work anyway."

"Thanks."

I absorbed the corpse into my shield.

Then I checked the drop item.

"Karma Rabbit Sword?"

I pulled the sword out of my shield. The hilt was black, and it was engraved with a rabbit pattern. It looked like it was part of the same weapon series as Filo's claws had been.

Karma Rabbit Sword: quality: excellent: special effects: agility up, magic down, attack up, defense down

It seemed to be a very powerful weapon. It must have been just like Filo's new claws.

"Raphtalia, try this thing out."

"Oh, okay."

"What's up? You got a new weapon?"

"Yeah."

Raphtalia gripped the hilt and gave the sword a few light swings.

"It seems to be an excellent sword. I think I can use it for the time being."

We spent a little more time leveling up with L'Arc and Therese in the interior of the island.

By the time we thought about finishing up, we had all gained quite a few levels.

I had grown to level 70, Raphtalia was at 72, and Filo was at 73.

We'd leveled up, but it was definitely less efficient than it had been yesterday. I wonder why? Did it mean that we were approaching the appropriate level for where we were?

There was still so much I didn't understand about this world.

It seemed like you could power level if you wanted, but it also sort of seemed like there were level caps on areas.

Those sorts of systems were different depending on the game you were playing.

There were MMOs that made it so that you couldn't level past a certain point if you were battling weaker enemies.

They called it appropriate leveling, and basically you were only awarded experience points for the battle if your level and the enemy's level were within a certain range of one another.

If the system was set up that way, then you couldn't put characters in your party that were substantially weaker than you were and still expect to be able to level them in difficult areas.

But when we were raising Filo after she hatched, I never

got the feeling that there was a system like that in place here. Just what was going on?

"Raphtalia, how's that new sword working out for you?"

"It's very light and easy to wield, but I haven't gotten used to its nuances yet."

So apparently it was powerful, but nuanced, and easy to use.

I wondered if the old guy at the weapon shop could make something like it, if I mentioned that it was part of the "karma series" of weapons. I'm sure he'd need the materials though.

It seemed like I could count on the series for serious attack power though—which was great.

Still, they didn't have a blood clean coating, so we wouldn't be able to use them for very long, which was not so great.

I could always use the whetstone shield on them at night when we were back at the inn. But I had so many shield abilities that I still needed to unlock. I'd have to prioritize that over the sharpening. Maybe I could bring the weapons to the old guy in Melromarc and he could apply a coating to them. Regardless, I'd have to pay him a visit before the next wave.

Anyway, we leveled up so much so quickly that I hadn't really figured it all out yet.

It had all happened so fast that it almost made me anxious.

I was working to unlock the new shields the whole time, but there were still so many monsters that I hadn't collected yet, it made me anxious to think that I was going to miss out on something important.

I had to ignore that feeling. I would just have to wait until the next wave was over, then I could go out in search of new leveling grounds.

I could probably count on the queen for her assistance too, so I didn't think that money was going to be an issue.

But first things first, I'd have to power up as much as I could in the meantime—Raphtalia and Filo too.

"Had about enough for today?"

The sun had started to sink low when L'Arc suggested we head back.

"Huh? Yeah, I guess so. I think it was a pretty good day, all in all. What are you doing tomorrow?"

The Karma Rabbits were not offering us much in the way of a challenge anymore.

It would have been an easy enough area with just Raphtalia and Filo, never mind L'Arc and Therese.

I wanted to make sure that we weren't wasting their time.

"Oh boy, I think we've done just about enough, but it was a great time. I think you guys can handle yourselves tomorrow."

"Oh . . . ."

That was kind of a disappointment. But then again, adventurers typically valued their freedom.

When it was time to leave the island, I would have to think about inviting them to join the party.

"Let's head back then."

"Alright."

And so we left and went back to the main island. We arrived before sunset was over.

While we were still in the boat, there were moments of silence where L'Arc and Therese seemed to be ruminating over something.

What was it all about? Had they realized that I really was the Shield Hero, but they didn't want to say it?

I didn't think so. L'Arc didn't seem like the kind of guy to hold back from saying whatever he wants.

"Later, Shield Kiddo. Hope to fight with you again someday."

"Yeah. And if you run into any spare cash before you leave the islands, come pay me!"

We parted ways. It had been an enjoyable time we'd spent together.

"That's the first time we've fought on the same side with anyone since we were traveling with Melty."

"You're right."

"They were very experienced and powerful."

They were. I nodded.

They had been surprisingly strong. They were just as strong as we were.

If I got the chance, I wanted them in my party.

Chapter Nine: Island Days

We continued to level at different spots around the islands. We defeated a boss called the Karma Pengu. It was a monster that flew in the air and looked like a giant black penguin.

But we defeated it so easily it was almost boring. Just more of the same. It was all so easy and so expected—I figured that was probably why the other heroes hadn't abandoned the idea that it was all just a game.

Karma Pengu Shield: ability locked: equip bonus: swimming skill 2, fishing skill 3, pekkul status adjustment (medium): special effect: underwater swimming time increased

Karma Pengu Familia Shield: ability locked: equip bonus, swimming skill 1, fishing skill 2, penkul status adjustment (small)

Pekkul . . . I thought those had gone extinct?

I'd gotten pretty similar shields out of the other karma series monsters that we had been fighting since we got here.

I think they were called usaunis and inults.

It was great that I could use them if I wanted to, but they were extinct—so it wasn't going to do me much good, was it? I was complaining to myself while I checked the monster's drop item.

Pekkul Kigurimi?
"Is it some kind of sleeping bag?"
It was a soft costume of a penguin wearing a Santa hat. I checked out the stats.

Pekkul Kigurimi: defense up, attack resistance (small), water resistance (large), shadow resistance (small), HP recovery (low), magic up (medium): automatic recovery function, underwater swimming time increased, size adjustment, skill adjustment (small): type alteration, monster equip time, no alterations other than type

Wow! It had a lot of great effects. It was at least as powerful as the barbarian armor +1 that I was using. If it would increase underwater swimming time, did that mean that it was for diving or something?
"It looks like it's a really good piece of equipment. Raphtalia, why don't you . . . ."
"No thank you! I don't care how good it is, I'm not fighting in that!"

I thought she might say that. I felt the same way.

"Alright then. You try it on, Filo."

"I thought she hated clothes?"

"Looks fun!"

Filo turned into her giant filolial queen form, and when she went to try it on the kigurumi grew to her massive size!

Maybe that's what size adjustment meant? That was pretty neat!"

"I'm gonna wear it!"

Filo clucked her approval as she slipped into the giant kigurumi. Then the kigurumi seemed to glow for a second before melting into her feathers?"

Then Filo was standing there as normal, but her coloring had changed to look more like a penguin, and she was wearing a Santa hat.

"Urm . . . . It feels kinda scratchy!"

"Really?"

"Yeah . . . and I feel sort of . . . sort of like I can't flex my muscles?"

"Then take it off."

It probably had something to do with the type adjustment effect. Its magical effects would make her into something other than a filolial, so my monster status adjustment probably stopped working. That effectively meant that monsters couldn't use the equipment—which limited its use for me.

"But I kind of want to wear it when I sleep back at the inn!"

"Yeah, that seems to be what it's for."

It was probably most useful as a type of pajama. I wondered if she could just take it off so easily? But there was nothing to worry about, her coloring returned to normal, and the kigurumi appeared in her hands. What a weird piece of equipment.

"Mr. Naofumi, if I wear your armor, you could wear the kigurumi, and then it wouldn't go to waste. "

"Raphtalia, are you seriously suggesting I wear that thing?"

Still, its effects were nothing to scoff at.

Because of my shield, the monsters weren't able to damage me anyway. And I was getting concerned about Raphtalia and Filo's equipment too.

"Um . . . uh . . . ."

"Fine then, let's draw straws to see who wears it. After how it melted onto Filo, it's probably safe to assume that it doesn't restrict movement."

"Oh . . . okay then . . . ."

Oh boy. It was looking like I was going to have start measuring efficiency and power next to looks and fashion. It was going to be a tough choice.

"Master, you're so cuuuute!"

"Shut up! I'm taking it off the second we start heading back!"

I was mortified at the thought of being seen in it. And it wasn't acting the way it had when Filo had worn it.

It hung off of me, baggy, just like a normal kigurumi.

I really didn't want anyone to see me wearing it!

It mostly hid my face though, so unless they saw my shield they'd have no way of knowing that it was me. That's right, I looked like a pekkul.

And it raised my stats while I had it on. But when I wore it the type adjustment didn't activate.

Raphtalia wore my armor, and we pressed on. The Karma Pengu Familias we ran into along the way didn't pose any threat to us at all.

"Raphtalia . . . ."

"What?! Why are you looking at me like that? I'm not going to wear that thing."

I held out a cup of straws to her.

"You're wearing this thing tomorrow. I swear it. Better make your peace with that now."

"Hmph!"

As for Filo . . . well, she better just be happy that she was born a filolial.

"Well that ended up being a pretty good day."

"Yes, you're right."

We were in the boat on the way back to the main island, and Raphtalia seemed concerned.

I could sort of see where she was coming from. It was the way our leveling had dropped off that had her upset.

I made it to level 73, she was at 75, and Filo was at 76.

According to the earl, it was basically impossible to level past 80 there.

When things seemed too good to be true, they were. That's what people say anyway.

Right about the time we started approaching level 70, I'd noticed the leveling efficiency dropping off. If we didn't push really hard to keep leveling, I didn't see how we were going to make it to level 80.

It was still fun and interesting to collect drop items, but if the leveling efficiency wasn't worth it, then it might be smart to start looking for another way to level. The wave would be upon us pretty soon.

"But we still leveled up, isn't that good enough?"

"Yeah!"

Filo apparently still felt like she hadn't done enough swimming. She was in the water next to the boat.

"Filo, I wasn't talking to you."

"Oh . . . ."

"Back to what I was saying, we've still gone up over 30 levels since we got here."

"I know that . . . but . . . the monsters are just too weak . .
. and I'm starting to wonder if it's going to be good enough."

"I know how you feel."

With how things were now, the Karma series bosses barely
caused us to break a sweat, and as for the rest of the monsters
we encountered, they all went down with a single hit. Raphtalia
and Filo had powered up very dramatically though, so I suppose that was enough to be grateful for.

There were still a ton of shields that had equip bonuses I'd
yet to unlock.

We'd been leveling really efficiently since we got to the
islands, but I think we were all realizing that getting more powerful wasn't going to be quite that simple.

The levels had . . . well they possessed some sort of magical meaning, but they didn't directly translate into confidence.

We were going to have to raise our confidence, and our
morale, if we wanted to stand a hope of facing the injustices
that surely awaited us in the future. There was no avoiding
that.

In the online games I'd played, there were lots of players
that had leveled up quickly but didn't have the skills or the
knowledge to handle themselves. They were powerful enough,
but too ignorant and weak-willed to really be of use to anyone.

And there were plenty of them that made the mistake of
thinking their high levels automatically made them impressive
and respectable.

It was a real danger, one we'd have to watch out for. And that all went double for Itsuki and his party.

Chapter Ten: The Water Temple

We ended up spending a few peaceful days on the islands.

Filo was pretty obsessed with swimming the whole time.

We'd been on the islands for five days or so when Filo said it:

"Hey master! There's a thing. It's like another island! It's red! It's at the bottom of the ocean!"

"What?"

What was she talking about? It sounded pretty interesting though.

I suddenly recalled the red outline of the island that I'd seen against the sky. It had seemed to be glowing.

I'd just assumed it had been related to the activation event. I'd seen it pretty much every day since we'd arrived.

"Yeah! If you go out into the ocean at night, you can see it at the bottom!"

Hm . . . another island?

"Well, our leveling has pretty much stopped anyway. We might as well go check it out."

"Are you sure?"

"We've got that new equipment that let's us swim, don't we?"

Raphtalia scrunched her nose up. She'd worn the kigurumi the previous day and hadn't been happy about it.

The thing sure made you look like a fool, but I couldn't argue with the stat boosts.

The drop item wasn't all that common, but by the time the day was done we'd ended up with three of them.

So if we wanted to, we could all wear one and swim. It didn't help Filo though.

"The bottom of the ocean . . . ?"

"What, you can't swim?"

Big sister can swim just as well as I can!"

"Well, isn't that something?"

I'd watched Filo swim for a few days now. She could stay underwater for quite a while. She could really hold her breath.

If Raphtalia could match that, then it was pretty impressive.

"Well I am from a fishing village, so I'm a pretty decent swimmer."

"I guess that settles it then. Let's go check this place out."

"I wonder what the monsters in the ocean are like?"

"We're pretty strong now. I'm sure we'll be alright."

"I hope so."

We had never fought in the water before. Eventually we were going to have to learn how to do it.

"Ride on my back!"

Filo turned into her filolial queen form and jumped into the water.

We could climb on her back and go wherever we wanted. I guess we never really needed to use a boat.

We climbed onto her back, and she lunged forward into the surf.

"It's down there."

We had left the island pretty far behind and were getting out into deeper water when Filo indicated the location.

"Let's change into the kigurumi and swim down there then."

Fumbling on Filo's back, we pulled the kigurumi on.

Raphtalia still wasn't thrilled about the idea, but eventually we had the new equipment on and were ready,

"Alright, let's dive."

"Okay."

"This looks so strange."

"Too bad. This is the only equipment we have that will let us swim to the bottom."

We grumbled about it, but a second later and we were diving below the waves.

Wow! It was incredible! We could swim with so little effort, we didn't really need to try to hold our breath, and the littlest kick sent us moving swiftly through the water. I didn't care how it looked. I could get used to this.

Filo pointed the way and kept on swimming downwards.

We followed her, and soon enough we saw something that appeared to be an island rising from the ocean floor below.

Had it sunk or something? It was glowing red, just like the island had been when we first approached.

We dove towards it.

Ten minutes had elapsed since we started to dive.

It was amazing that we were able to stay underwater for that long. This world really was like a game—if you had the right equipment you could basically do anything.

Even still, I felt like I was starting to approach my limit. I don't think we'd be able to stay under for more than 20 minutes.

Luckily, we didn't run into any monsters while we were swimming.

If we had gotten in a fight, I wasn't totally sure what we were going to do. Could Raphtalia swing her sword under water? Before I had to worry about it any more, we arrived at the island.

It didn't seem like there were any monsters lurking about. Besides, if we wasted time with a battle we were sure to run out of air. I looked around the island and quickly spotted something artificial. It looked like a building.

We swam over to get a better look. It seemed to be a temple of some kind.

Was it a water temple? The door was shut tight.

I reached out to touch it. When I did, the jewel in the center of my shield started to glow, and the heavy door creaked open on its own. I looked over to Raphtalia.

We were going to run out of breath soon. Should we go to the surface?

A bubble of air plopped out of the opening door. Was there air inside? I swam to the bottom and looked up, into the temple.

The surface of the water broke soon after the entrance, and it looked like we could climb into the temple to get out of the water.

I motioned for Raphtalia and Filo to follow me.

"Ha!"

"Where are we?"

"I don't know . . . ."

We all took deep breaths and looked around to get a sense of the place. It was pretty dark, but our eyes soon adjusted. We were in a large room built from stone. The interior of the building looked dry, and the water was only there in the entrance. We walked deeper into the temple.

"It's so dark."

"Should I use some of my light magic?"

"Yeah."

Raphtalia chanted a spell and the room lit up. When the room came into view, I could hardly believe my eyes.

"What the . . . ."

Large and looming in the center of the room stood a giant dragon hourglass.

To make matters even more mysterious, the top portion seemed to be nearly empty. Like it had been counting down to our entry.

What was a dragon hourglass doing in a place like this?

I remember that Fitoria had mentioned it. She'd said that waves occurred in other places too, places without people.

This must have been one of those places.

What should we do? The area might have been under Fitoria's control, but it didn't seem wise to just ignore it either.

The islands were full of adventurers and tourists. If a wave happened now, the destruction would be immense.

The wave wouldn't be confined to the island either.

The ocean all around would overflow with monsters. It would be exceedingly dangerous.

"We need to hurry back and report this to the soldiers."

"Yes, you're right."

I held my shield up to the hourglass.

A light flashed from the hourglass and entered the jewel in my shield. The remaining time appeared in my field of view.

48:21

There were two days left before the countdown ended.

"There's a dragon hourglass in the underwater temple?"

When we have back to the main island, I called an emergency meeting of the heroes.

"But that . . . ."

"If you don't believe me, I'll take you there right now."

"I'm not calling you a liar."

"At the bottom of the ocean? I remember a really rare quest like that in my game."

Itsuki responded exactly how I assumed he would.

"So what do you want to do? Ignore it?"

If we ignored it, a wave of monsters would wash over the islands.

At the very least, we needed to evacuate the islands. That would do a lot to prevent loss of life.

But if what Fitoria has said was true, then the heroes had a responsibility to do something about it.

I thought that if the heroes ignored the hourglass, Fitoria might show up and kill us all.

"It's a good chance to put our new powers to the test. I'm not against it."

"Me neither. It'll be a good challenge if Naofumi is telling the truth."

"I'm not lying. I'll take you there."

Both Motoyasu and Itsuki were on board with going because they wanted to put there new, higher level parties to the test.

"Huh? Give me a break, who cares?"

But one hero didn't seem interested.

It was the Sword Hero, Ren. He'd been quiet for the whole conversation. Now he said he didn't care and acted like he was about to leave.

"Hey, haven't we been charged with protecting the world? Are you going to turn your back on it?"

I thought that he LIKED fighting. Was he saying that he didn't care what happened to the world one way or another? He was starting to piss me off.

I grabbed his hand before he could leave. He shook me off.

"Don't touch me. I didn't come here to make friends with you all. If you three think you can handle it on your own, then I'm going to leave the islands."

That struck me as strange. Why was he acting like that?

I slipped my arms under his and grabbed him, to keep him from leaving.

I wondered if I was breaking a rule of some sort by restraining a hero.

But nothing happened. As long as I wasn't attacking him

directly I guess it was okay to restrain him.

"Let me go!"

Ren started violently writhing and tried to throw me off. What was it with him?

"Motoyasu! Itsuki! Make Naofumi stop this! I'm not going to let you force me to fight!"

Haha! I suddenly understood what was going on. It seemed like Motoyasu and Itsuki figured it out too.

"Ren, you don't know how to swim, do you?"

"What? No! That's not it! Fine. If you want me to come so badly, I will. I'll do it for you. Be grateful."

He couldn't swim, so of course he didn't want to go to an underwater temple. And if a wave of destruction was going to come to the islands, he wanted to make sure that he was somewhere else.

That had to be it.

Ren was still refusing, and it looked like he was preparing to fight back in earnest.

"Naofumi, you better let me go before you get hurt. "

"Go ahead and try."

"ARRRRRGGGGH!"

He thrashed violently and tried to throw me off, but I had him from behind and he couldn't get at me.

Was he really that scared of the water?

"What are you going to do?"

"Are you really afraid of the water? Naofumi, just drag him into the ocean and let's go."

"Sure."

I couldn't believe I was agreeing with Motoyasu, but I was. We had to see if Ren was lying.

If he tried to look cool and pretend that he could swim when he really couldn't we'd end up in deep trouble by the time we got to the water temple.

"Hey! Stop it! I can swim, so just let me go!"

"Fine."

I dragged Ren over to the docks.

"Itsuki, you can swim, right?"

"Yes."

"And you wouldn't lie like Ren here, would you? You'll have to prove it eventually."

"That's fine."

"Let me goooooo!"

"Ren is always acting so cool. How lame is it that he can't swim?!"

Motoyasu was gloating and laughing at Ren.

"I . . . I CAN swim."

"Then show us."

I loosened my grip on him, and Motoyasu kicked Ren off the pier and into the water.

"?!"

With a pathetic look on his face, Ren fell straight into the water, headfirst.

Bubbles came floating to the surface behind him, but Ren went on sinking.

" . . . ."

" . . . ."

"He's not coming up, is he?"

"Oh well."

I jumped into the water after him. The water wasn't deep at all, but Ren was randomly struggling at the bottom.

I slipped my arms around him and pulled him up. The idiot. He'd drown in four feet of water!

"Upah! You idiots! Why are you doing this!?"

Ren was furious, but not intimidating at all.

"You didn't waste a minute drowning."

He hadn't even been in the water 30 seconds.

He could have just stood up, but he just let himself sink— it was a scene I wouldn't soon forget.

"Doesn't look like Ren is going to be much help."

"That's not good for the rest of us."

It was a serious loss to lose one of our main offensive heroes.

"I can swim!"

"You still say that after what we all just saw?

We weren't going to be able to take him with us, which

meant that we were going to have to think about another strategy.

"When the waves come, we'll have to be in a boat or something. Then we can leave Ren in the boat any time we have to be in the water."

He was going to be a burden, but if we were in a boat, then he wouldn't be completely useless.

"Who knows what's going to happen. But let's plan on using the boat."

"Good idea."

"What about the rest of you. I hope you've realized that you can add support troops to your party during the waves."

Motoyasu and Itsuki both winced.

I wasn't making fun of them or anything. I was just telling them the truth.

"Yes, we understand."

"Of course we know that!"

"Then let's talk strategy. What sort of formation are you thinking of using? It will depend on the situation, but what sort of patterns do you have in mind?"

"Naofumi, you sound like you know your stuff."

"Are you three still thinking of these huge scale battles as if they were the exact same thing you've encountered in the games you know?"

If I was being honest, I was an *otaku* myself.

So I had a ton of knowledge about event battles in MMOs.

It's not like I was the strongest player, or that I'd maxed out my stats or anything like that, but I did really enjoy these exciting events when they happened online.

I used to make my own guilds and teams. I recruited all the players by myself. I really enjoyed those sorts of events, and so I felt like I knew how to play them most effectively. They were one of my favorite parts of online games.

The waves of destruction did seem to have a lot in common with those sorts of events.

"I have experience with things like this from games I've played, but the mechanics are not the exact same. It sounds like these sorts of events were part of the games that you all are used to."

"I already told you that I have experience with this stuff."

Motoyasu disagreed—not that I really cared.

Motoyasu might have had experience of a sort, but it sounded like he had never been in charge. He's always let the other players figure things out.

He might as well have not known anything at all.

"Motoyasu, your experience was always just as a participator, right? Have you ever fought in a guild of like 50, or a hundred people?"

"No . . . are you saying that you have?"

"Yeah."

I had once set up and run the third most powerful guild on a server.

"Really?"

"If you think I'm lying, just try to remember what happened during the last wave. Pretty much all the villagers escaped unharmed."

Itsuki and Motoyasu shot me some disgruntled looks. Whatever, I was only stating the facts.

They both knew plenty about the world, but that didn't mean that they were experienced.

Diplomacy was necessary, even in games. Equipment and leveling could only take you so far. You needed an instinct for command.

"I can figure out the basics and tell people what to do. But I think that there are people in this world that know better than we do, so I'd rather just leave it up to them."

They were still thinking of it as a game. How much use were they going to be in a real battle? At the end of the day, a game is just a game.

Once formations were formed, we'd have to deal with offense, retreats, and holding patterns. Just getting an army together wasn't the end of the job. People that played these games were not natural soldiers.

There was no guarantee that the people you played with

would respect your commands, so there was always an element of unpredictability due to the individual players. All you could really do was point out weaknesses and time your attacks.

But in this world, there were actual soldiers.

If you tried to utilize actual troops the same way that you used online gamers, you weren't going to get the same result.

And besides, there were rules that governed behavior in games that weren't applicable here. In this world, you could do anything.

But in this case, the waves of destruction were a mystery—you never knew quite what to expect when the time came.

Furthermore, there were way more classes and jobs here than there were in games. So the possibilities were far more varied. For example, I was used to online battle events where large armies tried to control the opposing team's fort. The walls around the fort were indestructible, so you couldn't destroy the fort by breaking down its defenses.

But here, I was sure that you could break down a wall if you were strong enough. If so, then it would require a different strategy all together.

"We should call for reinforcements from Melromarc. We'll have to use the formation function to get them to participate in the battle. They will be really useful because they understand how to fight in this world."

"Alright. I'm starting to understand."

"That's a very roundabout way of saying that you want to depend on the castle troops."

He wasn't wrong. But it's not like I could hope to depend on the other heroes. Hadn't they realized yet that they weren't going to be able to face down the waves on their own?

"Anyway, here's how I see it. We call for reinforcements, but we have to act as the high level players in the battle. We have to lead the charge and break through the defenses. We need to assume that we are the secret weapon here. You got that?"

"Yes."

"I hate to admit it, but you're right."

"I can swim!"

"Ren, are you still harping on that? Regardless, we are going to the water temple, so we'll find out soon enough how well you can swim."

"What? You want me to come with you? I thought I was supposed to go call for reinforcements?!"

"Nope, here's a kigurumi. Wear it. I've got three."

"What is that thing?!"

Motoyasu burst out laughing when he saw the pekkul kigurumi.

"I know it looks stupid, but it gives you great abilities when you're in the water. Didn't you guys get the drop items from the island bosses?"

"Yes, but I received a risuka kigurumi."

"Yeah, and I got a usauni kigurumi."

"Mine was an inult kigurumi."

There was no overlap at all. I wanted to laugh. I pictured us all wearing the different kigurumi and it was hard not to smile.

The fact that they were actually good pieces of equipment only made it worse somehow. Raphtalia had really resisted wearing one too.

"Anyway, we all received the drops, but I certainly didn't end up with THREE of them."

"Sure, the bosses didn't appear all that frequently, but they were just weaklings, so eventually I ended up with three."

"Weren't they sort of strong though? I mean, they WERE the island bosses."

"Really?"

What was that supposed to mean. They'd thought those monsters were strong? That didn't bode well.

"Anyway, let's go."

In the end, we all jumped into the water to go to the water temple, but when Ren tried to swim a clanging sound indicated that he wasn't able to. He finally admitted that he didn't know how. Luckily enough there was a convenient magic spell that enabled him to breath underwater for an hour, so we were able to get him down to the temple in the end.

One of the magic-using castle soldiers came with us just to confirm the existence of the hourglass.

Unfortunately the magic wasn't for use in battle, so it wasn't effective if you moved too quickly. That meant it didn't work where the current was strong or when the water got too deep.

The spell stopped working pretty much immediately when we got down to the temple. Had it cut out any earlier, Ren would have drowned.

Motoyasu and Itsuki had a blast laughing at the pekkul kigurumi, but Ren didn't make any jokes about them at all.

So we began to prepare for the approaching wave.

"So there aren't any sailors?'

"Not really."

We were talking strategy with the earl and the soldiers the castle had sent, and there weren't any sailors in the bunch."

I didn't think that the heroes were going to be very much help during the battle this time, so I was going to be acting as commander of the troops. I was hoping that some actual commanders of actual wars would be around to help.

"There are a number of sailors here on the islands that can help, but it doesn't look like the castle is going to be able to send us much more support. The army commander has agreed to help, but they were hoping that a hero would come to the castle as a representative."

"Heh. I'll see what I can do."

A hero could go back to the castle and still be transported here for the wave as long as they had registered the location.

But who knew if they would be able to prepare the boats and troops in time.

"If the battle will be on the ocean, then we won't be able to evacuate, which means we won't need troops for that job."

"We are planning on the battle taking place on the sea."

"I'll leave that up to you then. Who knows what sort of monsters will come out of the water though, so make sure you stay on your toes."

"Very well. We also have rucolu explosive barrels prepared. Normally they are banned due to fishing laws."

"Rucolu barrels?"

"Yes. Barrels filled with rucolu that we detonate in the water. It turns the water into alcohol and kills any monsters in the area."

Heh. I wasn't able to attack myself, so it was always interesting to hear the sorts of offensive measures that people came up with.

That was one that I'd never considered.

If that worked, it sounded like it would probably come in handy.

"What about the adventurers in town? Some of them are probably itching for a battle anyway."

"Huh? Oh yeah, good idea. Just make sure you pick good ones."

There was no reason to try and fight the battle with soldiers alone. When I had been in the first wave, a lot of adventurers had helped out. We needed to use whatever resources we had if we wanted to survive.

The fact that the islands were in the middle of an activation event was sort of good news for us, because it meant there would be more high-level adventurers in town.

"The orders have already been sent out."

"Thanks."

I thought back about the last wave we'd fought it. If this one was anything like the last time, there was a good chance we would run into Glass again.

We'd leveled up a lot in the interim though.

I really wanted to think that we were powerful enough to win this time, but I couldn't pretend that was a done deal. She'd been very powerful.

That evening, we went around the island and posted flyers to recruit adventurers.

We appealed to people that wanted to level up in the wave and test themselves.

I was waiting at the dock for a ship to arrive with supplies when L'Arc and Therese showed up.

"Hey, Shield Kiddo. Where are you off to?"

"Nowhere fun. Unfortunately this is all work."

In the end, I'd been chosen to go back to the castle and register the queen and her troops for teleportation. We'd discussed just sending for more troops, but there wasn't enough time for them all to get here. So we would have to use the teleport skill at the hourglass.

Dragon Hourglass Sand Shield conditions met!

Dragon Hourglass Sand Shield: ability locked: equip bonus: skill "Portal Shield."

The problem was that the activation event had rendered the teleportation impossible.

According the Motoyasu and the others, the first teleportation point was the room where we were first summoned. So if I left the range of the activation event, I'd be transported to the castle to add the queen to our formation.

"Still, I'll be fighting in the wave."

I sighed. I really didn't want to fight if I didn't have to, but I didn't really have a choice.

"Oh hey, now that you mention it, we signed up to battle in the wave too!"

"Oh yeah?"

I knew I could depend on them. They were powerful enough to take out the waves of lesser monsters on their own.

I was glad to hear they were going to help. It would make it all a little easier.

"The bracelet that you made me can shoot fire!"

Therese was clearly still excited by it all.

"She still hasn't calmed down about it."

I was glad that she liked it, but if she didn't take the battle seriously she'd end up dead—and that wouldn't help any of us.

"I'll see you in the wave then."

"Glad to fight with you again, kiddo."

"We're counting on you."

"No problem!"

We boarded a boat headed for Melromarc harbor and set off into the night.

The ship was actually really crowded. Apparently there were plenty of people that had heard the wave was coming, and they were trying to get off the islands before they got mixed up in the chaos.

Still, at least we'd been given a private room this time, so it was an easier journey than the trip over had been.

Every once and a while I would try to use the Portal

Shield skill, but it wasn't working yet.

The sun had sunk long ago, and we were getting into the later hours of the evening when...

"Portal Shield!"

This time, the icon indicating that it wasn't going to work vanished, and I was able to shout out a destination or choose from a list of registered places.

Teleport ↑
Teleport location memory.

Be conscious of teleportation.

Melromarc, Summoning Room.

I assumed it was the room I'd originally been summoned to—what else could it mean?

A circle appeared around me on the ground, indicating the range of the spell.

I could select who else would be teleported with me. Which meant I could also select who DIDN'T get teleported.

But the range of the skill was actually really big. Why couldn't it just be people I was touching, or something like that? It was probably so that the spell could be used as an emergency escape measure.

When the high priest had trapped the other heroes, why hadn't they used it?

"Alright, I'm using the teleport skill."

"Okay!"

The words "Melromarc, Summoning Room" appeared in the air before me, and the same time a ghostly, half transparent view of the room also came into view.

I recognized it as the room I'd been summoned to all those months ago.

"Alright!"

I pulled Raphtalia and Filo over to where I was standing and activated the skill on the deck of the boat.

There was a swift rush of wind, and the scenery around us instantly changed. We were in a dark room that smelled of dirt.

I remembered having stood in that same place.

The room was empty. I guess they weren't in the middle of a ceremony though, so I should have expected that.

"Amazing. That was instantaneous."

"Wow! We're back at the castle!"

"It sure looks like it."

"Mel-chan!"

Filo skipped merrily out of the room.

We called to some soldiers that had been posted in the hallway and requested an audience with the queen.

They had already received word from the islands, and the queen had been waiting for us.

We spent the night at the castle, and when morning came we immediately began preparing for the wave.

The queen had prepared a whole warehouse full of the materials I'd requested before leaving for the islands. She said she would continue to have more sent to us for the duration of our stay on Cal Mira.

"Then I won't hold back in using them."

I'd been thinking that I hadn't powered up enough anyway.

Still, I hadn't run into any real trouble while we'd been leveling up, which made me think that my previous power up session had been very useful.

I picked out the shield I wanted to use during the wave.

Soul Eater Shield (awakened) +6 35/35 SR: abilities locked: equip bonus: skill "second shield" spirit resistance (medium), spirit attack resistance (medium) SP up: special effect soul eat SP recovery (weak), drain null, wall escape, undead control: mastery level 60: item enchantment level 7 SP 10% up: porcupine spirit counter efficacy up defense 50: status enchantment strength 30+

After powering up the shield I could hardly believe how

powerful it had become. It was now even stronger than the Chimera Viper Shield.

Maybe it's because I got the shield from the last wave boss, but it seemed to respond more dramatically to powering up.

The special effects drain null, wall escape, and undead control all appeared once the shield was awakened.

Wall escape meant that you could pass through solid objects, but to pass through a single wall would use the entirety of your SP points. I'd also only tried it on a very thin wall, and I'd barely made it through, so I was a little worried about what would happen were I to try using it on a thicker wall. Undead control, I assumed, would allow the user to control undead-type monsters. I'd have to try it out to be sure though.

According to the numbers, my defense stat was now four times higher than it had been.

Finally, even though I would only use it if I were absolutely forced to, I decided to try powering up the Wrath Shield.

I really wanted to avoid using it if possible, since I was still cursed from the last time.

I'd healed a lot since then, but I still wasn't back to normal.

Wrath Shield III (Awakened) +7 50/50 SR: abilities locked: equip bonus: skill "change shield (attack)", "iron

maiden", "blood sacrifice": special effect: dark curse burning S, strength up, dragon rage, howl, familial rage, magic sharing, robe of rage (medium): mastery Level 0

Apparently you could use items or spirit enchantments on shields that hadn't been unlocked yet. It was the same for the mastery level. I don't think it was even possible to unlock the Wrath Shield.

But the stat books were impressive.

If I switched to it in battle, I felt like it would completely take over my consciousness, which scared me.

Morning came, and the timer flashing in my periphery was much lower than it had been.

00:20

I think I'd done all I could by way of preparation.

The other heroes should be waiting on the boat. The only question left was where we would be teleported to.

Just to be safe I had a boat prepared for us and ordered it set aside in a nearby river. It was a small thing, only useful in a river, and it wasn't outfitted with sails.

But that just meant that we could shave off all the time it would take to load a larger boat.

"Mr. Naofumi?"

Raphtalia came walking over with the queen.

"Mr. Iwatani, the preparations are complete."

"Is this your first time participating in a wave battle?"

"I have participated in a battle before, but it was in a different country. I have a basic understanding of the battle strategy."

"Great."

"Yes. While it is still a little early for this type of thing, perhaps we should do something to raise the morale of the gathered troops?"

She was right.

If the soldiers weren't fully motivated, then there would be more casualties than necessary.

"Everyone! We must keep the destruction to an absolute minimum during the battle!"

"Yes my queen!"

The gathered crowd snapped to attention when the queen spoke.

I hoped the other heroes were doing something similar.

00:10

There were ten minutes left.

"Now it comes down to location. Will we be on the ocean or on an island?"

We didn't know exactly what we were going to be facing. That was why we needed to prepare for all possibilities.

"Fighting on the sea may prove difficult."

"I know."

We didn't really have any experience fighting on the water yet.

I imagined that simply swinging a sword through the water would be more difficult than we might expect. If so, we'd have to try using other weapons.

As for Filo, I'd seen her take out monsters in the water before, so I was pretty confident about her abilities.

If we were in the water, then we didn't even have the ground to depend on. An attack could come from any direction.

I was hoping that I could use shooting star shield to buy us some time, but I didn't know if it would be effective against the powerful monsters that tended to appear during the waves.

"Raphtalia's right. This might be a really tough battle."

"If only Sadeena were here. She'd know what to do."

"Who's that?"

"She fished for my village. She was like an older sister to me."

"Oh yeah? Was she a good swimmer?"

"She was the best in the village."

"Was she the same type of demi-human as you?"

"No . . . she was an aquatic type."

I could picture it now. She would have had unique swimming skills. Raphtalia was right. I wished Sadeena were here.

But this was no time for daydreaming.

"I hope she's still alive."

"Me too."

I forced the thought out of my mind. We had other things to focus on now.

The time was almost here. I raised my hand and made an announcement.

"If we end up on land then your priority is to split up and protect the civilians. If we end up on the ocean, then we need to get to the larger ships and support the heroes!"

"Yes sir!"

I turned to Raphtalia and Filo.

"This is the third wave we've fought in. Let's power through! Everything will be fine!"

"Yes! And we'll keep the casualties to an absolute minimum!"

"Imma do my best!"

Chapter Eleven: Inter-dimensional Whale

00:00

The timer ran out.

At the same time, our surroundings all disappeared, and for a second it was like I was floating in the air.

A clanging sound came from the boat.

A second later and my periphery was filled with other boats, many of them, and we were floating in the ocean.

So it would be an ocean battle. I looked towards the rifts that had appeared in the sky. They marked the presence of the wave of destruction.

The sky was violet, and warped, and covered with fine cracks.

"Hurry! We have to get to the larger ships!"

The queen shouted the order, and the knights and soldiers on board began rowing furiously, bringing us up to the side of a larger ship nearby. We all climbed out and boarded.

Filo was in her filolial form, and Raphtalia and I climbed on to her back, then she jumped up on to the deck, delivering us to the ship in one fell swoop.

The heroes where standing on the deck and staring off in the direction of the rifts.

I could hardly believe my eyes. One of Itsuki's party members was standing there in a risuka kigurumi, a different colored Santa hat on his head.

I knew I shouldn't worry about it, but I couldn't stop staring!

"Fueee . . . ."

Large, intimidated eyes gazed out from the kigurumi. But, which one of his party members had eyes like that? It must have been that Rishia girl.

Anyway, the pekkul kigurumi had come with great stat boosts and abilities, so the risuka version probably did too. It wasn't so strange to imagine her wearing it for a major battle. At first glance it looked like they weren't taking it seriously though.

"What's happening?"

"It just started so we don't really know yet, but I've seen monsters start to come out of the rifts."

Itsuki said and pointed to the rifts in the sky.

It looked like giant fish, or something like fish, were streaming from the rifts.

I had expected birds or something like that. So I guess this was better in a way.

"How should we fight?"

At least we had sailors now, thanks to my Melromarc detour.

"The best swimmers are all already in the water, fighting the monsters there."

The queen was acting as the high commander. She came running over and reported on the plan.

"Water-type demi-humans led the charge. Many adventurers joined them, trusting their knowledge of the sea. They are already swimming and battling."

"Good thing we recruited those adventurers around town."

Melromarc was a human supremacist country, and so there weren't many demi-humans in the army.

As a consequence, most of the soldiers that could fight in the wave, or that we could organize to fight in the wave, were humans. And humans could really only fight from the deck of a ship—with cannons.

That meant it was going to be our job, the heroes' job, to get out on the front lines.

"Let's get going."

"Mr. Iwatani, wait just a moment."

"What is it?"

"There are a great number of smaller monsters to deal with, but I think we can handle them. I would like the heroes to focus on the larger threats that come from the wave."

"I understand. But how are we supposed to find the larger threats?"

I sort of imagined they would be concentrated at the foot of the wave, where the rifts in the sky met the surface of the water.

The surface of the ocean was white and frothy. You could see that it was writhing with creatures moving towards the ships. We were going to have to dive into the water to fight them.

I spotted a swiftly moving shadow under the water. A second later the beast had flung itself up onto the deck. It was an inter-dimensional sahuagin shadow.

It looked like a half fish, half man-type creature. As for the shadow, I wasn't sure, but it might have been a type of demi-human.

"Shooting Star Spear!"

Motoyasu stabbed at the saguahin with his spear.

"This thing is tougher than it looks!"

"Hya!"

Bitch and her retinue, Ren and his party, Itsuki and his party, all of them ran to attack the line of monsters that was threatening to overtake the boat.

"Hya!"

Filo flew forward and spun, kicking one of the monsters high into the air and off of the boat.

But there were more monsters. A lot more.

I looked around. There were ten ships or so. How were we supposed to protect ten ships?

The troops were made up of the strongest adventurers on Cal Mira and experienced soldiers from Melromarc. I hoped they could stand their ground.

But the battle line was getting chaotic. Should I use the shooting star shield?

It would be impenetrable to anyone not in my party though and it wasn't large enough to protect the entire ship.

I saw a crowd of monsters fly off the ship.

"Full Moon Army!"

It was L'Arc.

He was swinging his giant scythe.

Wow, with so many monsters swarming the deck it looked like a scene from that Dynasty battle game. He seemed to be having a good time.

Therese was behind him, casting a spell.

"Shining stone, showering thunder!"

A sharp crack of lightning shot out of the sky and killed a monster in front of her.

Those two were really something. I had to find some way to get them into my party.

"We're dropping a rucolu explosive barrel into the sea! Warn the adventurers!"

The queen shouted the order and another soldier blew into a conch—the sound resounded and echoed over the ships and water.

The adventurers and demi-humans in the water all came swimming back to the ship. One second later, and a number of barrels were pushed overboard.

"The explosive barrels . . . ."

I looked over the side of the ship to see what happened.

The barrels slowly sunk. How effective would they be?

The second I though it, the barrels exploded dramatically, sending up a geyser of bubbles into the air. The sea itself slowly turned red.

Whoa! Slowly, the corpses of fish and monsters came floating to the surface. There were tons of them.

I guess the whole sea really had turned into alcohol.

Of course it was only effective in the immediate area, so over time the water would mix with the rest of the ocean and the effect would diminish. But in the interim, it seemed to have a deadly effect on the monsters there.

It was amazing. I never would have thought those little fruits were so powerful.

"Don't get too comfortable!"

"Right!"

"Where's the boss?!"

That reminded me. I'd actually never seen the arrival of a boss monster before.

I'd only seen the other heroes battling the boss from far off in the distance.

"Should we jump in and swim out to find it?"

I think that maybe you had to attack the rifts directly to get the boss to appear.

I wasn't going to be able to do that by myself, but with Raphtalia and Filo it wouldn't be impossible.

And we didn't really have another option. The monsters had not stopped coming out of the rifts.

There was no point to stay on the ship and keep fighting these minor monsters.

"But if we don't kill the boss first, it will take a long time."

Damn.

That was why they'd dedicated all the energies to defeating the boss during the last wave. I guess.

We were talking over our plan when one of the neighboring ships flew into the air and broke apart.

There must have been a huge monster below it.

The sailors and soldiers all started to scream.

"What was that?!"

I spun on my heels to look. There was a massive whale falling back into the ocean from where it had jumped. It had massive horns growing out of its head.

Its name appeared in my menu screen.

Inter-dimensional whale.

How big was that thing? Judging the best I could, it looked like it was over 150 meters long. It looked like a sperm whale with a twisting horn like a drill, and the whole beast was unnaturally white.

In a few places there were large bumps that seemed to be jewels. They made the whole thing look like it had an undefined shape.

All in all, it didn't really seem right to call it a whale—it was too different.

It also seemed safe to assume that we were looking at this wave's boss monster.

I pointed to it and made sure that Ren, Motoyasu, and Itsuki were looking at the same thing that I was.

Ren was shaking his head, Itsuki was nodding, and Motoyasu was pointing.

"That must be it."

"It can't be!"

"You can wait here, Ren. Deal with all the minor monsters while we're gone!"

"Dammit! Hundred Sword!"

He held his sword a loft and it shattered into hundreds of smaller swords that flew into the air and rained down on the weaker monsters in the ocean.

What could he do if he couldn't swim? He'd have to do what the other adventurers were doing—shoot cannons and stuff like that.

Itsuki had turned his bow into a giant ballista and was shooing arrow after arrow.

Was there no job left for a shielder like me?

"Motoyasu! You're the Spear Hero, aren't you? That's the same as a harpoon! Go kill that thing!"

Isn't there some story about a captain who wants revenge? Channel that energy and kill that thing!

"Motoyasu! Do a kamikaze run at the thing!"

"Naofumi! You bastard!"

"Stop arguing!"

Raphtalia snapped at me like I was the bad guy or something.

"Mr. Naofumi, we need to think of a plan instead of arguing."

"You're right. Motoyasu?"

"What?"

I motioned for him to come over to the edge of the deck. He came over suspiciously, wondering if I really had a plan.

"You're weapon is the best suited for a battle at sea, so you need to get closer and lead the charge!"

And I pushed him over the edge.

"What?! AHHHHHH!"

That was easier than I had expected. He just fell right over the side.

He fell heavily in the water, sending up a spray of foam behind him.

"Oh nooooo! Mr. Motoyasu!"

Bitch and her friends all screamed.

"The Shield Hero is trying to kill the Spear Hero!"

Bitch raised her hand to point and berate me, but when she did the slave seal on her chest activated.

"Kyaaaaaa!"

"Myn.... Whore!"

Bitch turned to hear what Motoyasu was shouting. He had finally surfaced below.

"This is part of Mr. Iwatani's plan. You must respect it!"

The queen turned and shouted at Bitch.

Bitch would try to ruin my life whenever she got a chance.

"I have a suggestion. Mr. Kawasumi and Mr. Amaki will support the battle from the deck of the ship, focusing on ranged attacks."

"Very well."

"Fine by me."

"Motoyasu, if you can fight in the water, then please do so."

"I'd rather not!"

"You are the only one who can effectively attack in this situation. Doesn't this seem like good opportunity to earn the funds necessary to buy back my daughter's freedom?"

"Um . . . ."

He thought about disagreeing for a moment, before giving up and diving beneath the surface.

The legendary weapons could give the user skills that enabled better swimming, and if they were combined with a pekkul kigurumi, then you could really stay underwater for a really long time.

You didn't even have to have goggles on to see easily underwater.

"What about me?"

"Mr. Iwatani, I would like you to protect our ships in case that monster comes to attack us."

"That sounds like you want me in the water. If the monster dives to the ocean floor and starts charging upwards, you want me to block it!?"

"Naturally, I don't want you to do it if you don't think you will be able to."

"Oh, um . . . understood."

I didn't really know if I would be able to block a monster that big, but her plan was definitely the best one we had.

"Oh, and Ms. Raphtalia? Please use the ship's ballista to aim at the monster."

"What?"

Raphtalia was shocked she was being considered for the job. I could hardly believe it myself.

I guess it made sense. I couldn't picture her standing on its back and stabbing down at it with her sword. I guess that's all Motoyasu could really do though.

"It seems that your friend, Raphtalia, is quite powerful. If that's true, then I think she will be able to get the most out of our powerful ballista."

"Huh? I don't really understand what you are getting at."

I knew that a ballista was more powerful than the sort of bow that you could draw back with your hands. But why did it matter who used it? Itsuki might even have a skill or two specifically to use with ballistas. He was the Bow Hero, after all.

I couldn't think of a reason that Raphtalia would use it better than anyone else though.

Maybe there was some system that I didn't know about? Like how I hadn't known about the hero power up systems?

"Bows and ranged weapons still are subject to the stats of their users."

So guns and bows were similar to other weapons in this world?

In my world, the power behind a gunshot or an arrow didn't really depend on who used them. You were sure to die if you were hit. But I guess in this world the stats of the user had an effect. Maybe it worked by increasing the speed of the arrow or something like that.

It really was like a game.

Things like that happened all the time in games. Bows and guns and swords could all be just as powerful as any other weapon.

That wouldn't make sense in my world, but then again, we didn't have numbered stats in my world.

I had to think of this place as something completely different. If I treated it like the world I was used to, I was going to end up dead.

Thinking about it from the queen's perspective, it probably did make sense to let Raphtalia do the shooting.

"Got it. Okay Raphtalia, you attack the inter-dimensional whale using the ship's ballista."

"Oh . . . . Okay."

"I'll show you how it works, so please don't be worried about that. Now then Mr. Iwatani, take Filo with you and please protect out ship. We will be casting ceremonial magic to support you."

I remembered they had used collective ceremonial magic during the battle with the high priest. It had been extremely powerful. I think the queen had explained that it was normally reserved for wartime battles. I hoped it would be effective against the boss.

One more thing, up until now the heroes had been leading the charge in every wave that had come. Were we really supposed to act as supporting attackers in this fight?

"Leave it to me. Alright! Let's go, Filo!"

"Yeah!"

We climbed onto the deck railing and dove in to the ocean.

The water was still red due to the rucolu barrels.

The inter-dimensional whale had dove down deep below us.

That seemed to be its attack pattern—dive deep and then ram the ships from below.

Motoyasu was actually really impressive. He had his spear stuck in the side of the beast and was riding down with it.

But he didn't have any time to use a skill, and the boss was far more powerful than he was—so his attacks weren't having much effect.

What?! The whale turned towards the surface. Was it preparing to charge?

I took a deep breath and swam down under the boat, positioning myself beneath the hull.

I looked down into the depths and spotted the whale swimming far below.

I didn't know where it was planning to attack, which made it hard to think about defense.

Before it could attack, I pushed off from the hull and started swimming downward in the direction of the beast.

Filo was there with me, right by my side.

The first thing we'd have to do was get ourselves in a position to block the horn.

It wasn't going to be hard. The whale noticed us and leveled its horn. It was charging straight at us now!

Yes! Keep on coming, straight at me—you dumb whale.

At that moment, Motoyasu, Filo, and I were the only living things around the whale. All the other monsters had left the area.

Come on!

I readied myself and then it was on me. The horn was slicing through the water, threatening to impale me.

I felt the horn slam into me with a thundering crash, but my defenses were strong enough to withstand the attack.

But I didn't have anywhere to brace my feet, so I wasn't able to stop the whale from advancing.

The whale kept pushing towards the surface, and I felt my feet hit the underside of the ship's hull.

I couldn't do much else.

But either could the monster.

It started rocking back and forth, trying to fling me off of its horn.

As if I would let it!

I shot a glance at Filo.

She was in her filolial queen form, and she knew what I meant. She flipped through the water and kicked the whale hard.

And the monster reacted—it was thrown off balance!

While the monster reeled through the water, Motoyasu kept his attack up.

Because I'd stopped the monster for a moment, Motoyasu had found a free second to start using skills.

Above the water, the soldiers on the ship had been following the fight. Cannon balls and huge arrows rained down on the whale, and the water was filled with a booming and crashing sound.

The water was chaos. It was filled with white bubbles, and I couldn't see a thing.

But I kept my grip on the horn and pushed the monster back from the hull.

It was getting harder to breath.

Keeping my grip on the horn, I turned to the side and swam for the surface.

Huh? The whale looked surprised. I was pulling it through the water!

"Pufah!"

I stuck my head out of the water and took a deep breath.

"Huff . . . . Huff . . . ."

I filled my lungs and dove again. The whale was wriggling and writhing through the water. It couldn't get its horn free.

There was nothing else I could do.

The jewel-like bumps across its body were sending out magic spells left and right, but they weren't hurting me at all.

"Shooting Star Spear! Lightning Spear!"

The whale was on the surface of the ocean now. Motoyasu

climbed onto its back and used skill after skill.

"Take that! Hya! Hya!"

Filo was doing the same thing. Now that she had a place to stand, she was finally doing some real damage. Her sharp claws were shredding the monster's back.

Raphtalia got a lock on the monster with her ballista.

Itsuki was already shooting at it. Raphtalia's ballista was huge, so I was hoping that it had some serious attack power.

Everyone was pummeling the monster, and the water around it was turning a deep red.

There was a rush of wind when Raphtalia loosed the ballista's arrow. It connected with the monster and the air was filled with the sound of a successful attack.

Huh? Was Raphtalia's the most effective attack yet? Had we won?

"Shield Kiddo! Don't move!"

"What?"

L'Arc readied his scythe and jumped into the water.

"Flying Circle!"

A disc of light came from his weapon and sliced into the whale.

...?!

"Wha . . . ."

A massive spray of blood shot into the air and rained down on us. The whale's tail had been split in two.

" . . . ?!"

The inter-dimensional whale screamed in agony.

"Can't let him have all the fun!"

Filo shouted, and she reared back to deliver a decisive kick to the monster.

There was another spray of blood, and the whale's left flipper went flying. Her attack was really something.

But had L'Arc just done in one hit what had taken Filo this whole time to accomplish?

The whale started to twitch.

"Time to finish it! I'm going in!"

"Yes!"

L'Arc looked to Therese.

"Shining stone! Thunder rain!"

"Combo skill. Thunder rain flying circle!"

Therese's magic lightning struck L'Arc's scythe, and it seemed to charge it with energy. Raising the charged weapon, he shot a circle of light at the whale. Filo flapped her wings and attacked at the same time.

"Spiral strike!"

Their attacks hit at nearly the same time.

The whale was split into two pieces.

" . . . !"

It gave a final silent scream, and then died.

"Well that about does it, eh?"

L'Arc was standing on the corpse of the whale, pleased with himself.

"You guys sure are powerful."

Honestly, they were better fighters than Motoyasu was. How strong were they?

Something was strange. Had they been that powerful when we were all fighting together a few days ago?

I'd thought they were strong at the time, but I'd only thought they were strong for adventurers.

Motoyasu was as confused as I was.

"I tried real hard!" chirped Filo.

"Yeah, you did."

"Mr. Naofumi!"

Raphtalia was waving at me from the deck.

"Excellent. Now we just need to attack the rifts and end this thing."

I motioned to the queen so that she would command the ships to depart for the rifts.

But I heard a clang of metal on metal, and I felt eyes on me. I turned around.

It was L'Arc. He held his scythe out towards me and was grinning at me suspiciously.

Chapter Twelve: L'Arc Berg

Therese magically floated over and stood next to him.

"What's this about?"

I glared at them.

"Oh man. I really didn't think that you were the Shield Hero, kiddo."

"I told you so many times."

"You're right, you did. But I figured you shouldn't judge a book by its cover, you know? Kiddo. Or should I call you Naofumi?"

"Whatever you want. What are you up to?"

"Huh? Oh, I want you to know that I don't have anything against you personally."

"That's right. I don't either. I'm very sorry that things need to be this way, but . . . ."

I was getting a really bad feeling about this.

But I'd harbored doubts about that giant scythe of his for a while. Now I think I was finally getting my answer.

"We have to do it for the good of our world. You've got to die."

He moved so fast it was unbelievable. Before I could even see what was happening his scythe was slicing through the air.

Without thinking, I reacted. I guessed where the scythe would land and readied my shield to block it.

"Heh! You're pretty quick, kiddo."

"What are you doing?!"

'What are you doing to my master?!"

Filo jumped up and ran to attack them, but I held out a hand to stop her.

I don't know why I stopped her. I felt like if she made a little mistake, she wouldn't get out of it alive.

"I already told you."

All he'd said was that I had to die for the good of the world. What was that supposed to mean?"

"We must hold this adventurer accountable for raising arms against Mr. Iwatani, the Shield Hero! Everyone! Prepare for ceremonial magic casting!"

They had already started the spell, and they sent it in L'Arc's direction.

If their magic were as powerful as it looked, we'd all get caught up in it.

I looked to the queen and she caught my gaze.

I understood. She knew that we could survive the blast.

"Shooting star shield! Motoyasu, get over here!"

I quickly invited him to the party.

Surprisingly, he understood what was happening and immediately accepted. Then he ran into the range of my skill.

"This doesn't look good."

Therese raised her arms and her jewels sparkled. She was casting a spell.

What? The wind raised up, very powerfully, and began to swirl around us.

"All-encompassing power of the jewel, hear my plea and show yourself. My name is Therese Alexanderite. I am your friend. Lend me the power to destroy them!"

"Ceremonial magic judgment!"

Therese finished her spell a moment before the queen.

Then she removed her tiara and there was another jewel set into the center of her forehead.

"Shining stone! Shooting star rain of fire!"

Magic flames rained from the sky. But no, it wasn't like rain. Each one was a huge ball of fire.

"AAAAAAAAHHHHHH!"

"KYAAAAAAAAAAAAAA!"

Something like a meteor came shooting from the sky and shot straight through a ship, sinking it.

"Raphtalia!"

"I'm fine!"

Raphtalia, the queen, Itsuki, and his party all jumped from the sinking ship.

Dammit. The force of the sinking ship was forming a vortex. It was pulling people into it.

The queen tried to save them by teaming up with other people in a small boat and casting magic with them to calm the vortex.

The whole situation had moved in L'Arc's favor and Therese had only cast a single spell!

I'd seen a lot of different kinds of demi-humans and creatures since I arrived in this world, but I'd never seen anything like Therese.

She must have been something else entirely.

"Damn!"

"Ren! If you don't jump off that ship you're going to die!"

Ren looked worried, but he understood that his teammate was right—he jumped into the water.

He really wasn't much help, was he?

"Therese!"

"I know, I just had to keep them away!"

"All-encompassing power of the jewel, hear my plea and show yourself. My name is Therese Alexanderite. I am your friend. Protect them from the falling flames!"

"Shining stones, silent ocean!"

Huh? When Therese finished her spell the vortex vanished completely. The queen was staring at L'Arc, completely baffled.

"I don't want any unnecessary deaths."

"But you want to kill me? What kind of logic is that?!"

"It's not that we WANT to kill you. But we have to do what we have to do—I don't want anyone else to get involved."

"Then why are you trying to kill me?!"

"I guess we owe you that much. But I already told you we have to do it to save our world!"

"What does that mean?! Isn't THIS your world? How does it help anyone to kill a hero in the middle of a wave?!"

"Oh man, you don't even know that?"

"L'Arc isn't so good at explaining things."

"Shut up, Therese. Fine, I'll tell you, Naofumi. Our world is just what it sounds like—another world."

". . . ."

What was he talking about?

Could it really be what it sounded like?

It seemed like it was too much. It couldn't be true—and yet . . . .

During the last wave, we'd met an enemy named Glass.

If what L'Arc was saying was true, then were he and Glass from the same place? Where they the same enemy?

"It's just like the girl said. There are tons of fake heroes out there pretending to be you. Everyone who calls themselves a hero is lying. It took a lot of time to find you, Naofumi."

"What?!"

"What are you saying?!"

"Yeah! We are heroes!"

The other heroes jumped to their feet.

"Oh? Are you three pretending to be heroes too? Ha! Give me a break!"

L'Arc looked at the other three heroes and broke out into sincere laughter.

"You must be joking! You three are so WEAK! If you're going to pretend to be heroes, you'll have to be way stronger than that—like Naofumi here."

"What?!"

"You want to try me?!"

"Motoyasu, wait!"

But Motoyasu ignored me and ran at L'Arc, his spear readied.

"I already told you, we don't want to kill anyone we don't have to. We only need to kill the hero."

L'Arc waved his scythe.

"First form, wind slice!"

He had only flicked his wrist, but a massive tornado appeared and blew Motoyasu away.

"AHHHHHHH!"

Motoyasu flew through the air like a ragdoll and splashed into the ocean, where he floated face-up.

He'd defeated Motoyasu with a single hit?

"Guess they still have some fight in them?"

"Apparently. It's a waste of time, but I guess we need to get rid of them too."

"I suppose so."

L'Arc and Therese readied themselves for battle, then rushed to attack.

"Shining stones, explosive thunder rain!"

Just like last time, a bolt of lightning struck L'Arc's scythe, charging it.

"Combo skill, lightning firework!"

He spun the scythe between his hands, forming a quickly rotating disk. Innumerable beams of light shot from it— they shot from it and shot right through the people that were around the sinking ship.

I used shooting star shield and ran forward to protect the back line.

Raphtalia and Filo stood behind me, within the range of the protective barrier.

"What . . . what the . . . ."

"How . . . how could they?"

Luckily the queen and her immediate soldiers had been able to make it into the range of my skill, so they were safe. But the other heroes, and nearly all the other adventurers and sailors, had been shot straight through by the beams of light.

"Damn . . . ."

The actual attack wasn't too powerful, but the range was incredible.

I didn't know who L'Arc was, but his attacks were something serious to contend with. We'd have to be on our toes.

"I tried to make sure that wouldn't kill you all. If you interfere in my battle with Naofumi, I won't hold back next time."

I turned to see the damage. Most of the people looked like they were paralyzed. Luckily they had been in boats, so they didn't seem to be drowning.

"Such power . . . . Who are they . . . ?"

The queen began to chant a spell.

"Wait a second, queen. If that spell isn't powerful enough to kill us, you'd better not use it. It looks like they are only interested in me."

"That's the Naofumi I know! A quick thinker!"

"How cute—you think you know me after only a few days?"

"Spending bit of time with a person is enough to get the gist of his personality."

L'Arc was looking confident. He pointed at me.

"You must have a reason for stealing items from the defeated, Naofumi. You aren't the type to commit an evil act for no reason."

"Finally, someone who really understands what you're like, Mr. Naofumi."

"Don't say that. You're bumming me out."

They weren't wrong. They weren't wrong, but . . . .

"Damn! They betrayed my trust!"

I hate betrayal. But thinking back on it, I guess they'd never promised me anything.

They'd rejected my offer to stick together. I guess we were enemies that had accidently become friends.

Ha! What a joke.

"The flames have nearly died out. Raphtalia, Filo, we know these two, but we have to take them out!"

"It'll be tough, but let's do it, Mr. Naofumi!"

"Umm . . . . If they want to fight then I'll show them what I can do!"

"It's a fight just like any other fight."

"Just another fight? So you want to play it fair? I prefer to think of it as strategy."

"That's just like you, Naofumi. Come at me then! I came to this world to take your life!"

"Shining stones, explosive lightning rain!"

Just like when they had defeated the inter-dimensional whale, Therese's magic struck L'Arc's scythe.

He pivoted, then swung at us.

"Combo skill! Electric great circle!"

I assumed that the skill would break through my shooting star barrier, so I held up my shield to block the attack.

I was right. The barrier shattered with a deafening crack

and L'Arc's sizzling skill broke right through it, flying straight for me.

"HAAAAAA!"

The crackling circle of light slammed into to my shield and sent sparks flying in all directions.

The shield was strong enough to stop it, but if the skill had hit at a bad angle, there would have been real trouble to deal with.

"Hey, hey! You were able to stop my electric circle—pretty good!"

I had the Soul Eater Shield equipped, and its counter effect, soul eat, activated, sapping L'Arc of strength.

"What? What's that? Doesn't hurt much."

But he was shocked and thrown off guard. It was like he couldn't figure out what kind of attack he was dealing with.

Soul eat was a counter attack that activated whenever I successfully blocked an enemy's attack.

The shield itself moved, and it stole the enemy's magic power.

If the enemy was a hero, I wondered if it would decrease their SP.

It didn't deal any physical damage directly, but it did it in an indirect way.

If the enemy was good with magic, then they would find their spells less and less effective.

"Heh, you'll have to do better than that."

"I figured as much. You didn't even flinch. Therese!"

"Shining stones, karma fire!"

Therese cast a spell and sent it flying at me. The spell made something like a giant wave of lava, and it was rushing straight at me.

I wasn't sure if I was going to be able to withstand it.

"You better not forget about us!"

"Or meeeee!"

Raphtalia and Filo jumped forward from the back line and both started furiously attacking L'Arc.

"Ha!"

L'Arc back-stepped away from their attacks. They were within inches of connecting.

They kept up the barrage. Sometimes he dodged, sometimes he blocked, and sometimes he parried their weapons away.

Were they telegraphing their moves that much?

Therese continued to cast magic spells. I used the shield to charge forward, pushing L'Arc back so that I could block the spells.

But the second the magic hit me, it split apart and turned away.

For a split second, I thought I could hear a small voice saying "I'm sorry."

"What was that?"

"I know. You don't want to fight him."

Therese looked very sad. She was talking to her bracelet.

It was the bracelet I'd made for her.

"Therese! Use that spell on him!"

"Yes, I know!"

What were they talking about?! She turned to cast something on me.

It was starting to look like the only way out of this was straight through. We had to win the fight.

Besides, they weren't from this world, and they had come here specifically to kill me.

If that was true, then there was no way I was going to escape from the battle, and if there was no way to escape then there were plenty of people there that I had to protect. L'Arc and Therese said that they didn't want to hurt anyone else, but there was no way for them to escape.

"Raphtalia! Filo! I'm going to open him up to attack—you two rush in when you see a chance!"

"Yes!"

"Okay!"

I turned my gaze back to L'Arc. I was going to have to find some way to trip him up.

"Air strike shield! Second shield!"

I summoned two shields, one at his back and one at his

stomach—I was hoping to restrict his movement.

The normal way to use the skill was to summon a shield to block an enemy's attack—then you could use change shield to switch to a shield with a counter attack ability to deal some damage.

But when you were fighting against a person, or other enemies that could move quickly, there was another way to use the skill. And that was to summon the shields in such a way as to limit the enemy's movement.

My strategy was to think about how he might try to dodge an attack. I'd seen him back-step, so I summoned a shield behind him to prevent any retreat.

If he tried to jump back, he'd hit that shield, but what if there was another shield in front of him to block him moving forward?

That was my plan.

"Huh?"

L'Arc tried to dodge Raphtalia and Filo's attacks, but when he tried to move a clanging sound indicated he would not be able to.

"Now!"

"Hyaaaaaa!"

"Take that!"

Raphtalia sliced with her sword from the right. Filo swiped with her claws from the left.

"Floating scythe!"

L'Arc's empty hand was suddenly filled with another scythe, a mysterious one that seemed to float. He used the blade to block Raphtalia's attack and then pushed Filo back using the handle.

"That was close. Naofumi, I see what you mean about strategizing now. I'd figured the Shield Hero wouldn't have too many attacks up his sleeve, but I guess I better be more careful around you."

"We're not done yet! HAAAAA!"

Raphtalia reared back from the blocked attack and stabbed forward again.

A scythe was like a spear: the user blocked attacks with the handle. Which meant that it would be very difficult to block a stabbing attack.

"I'm not done with her!"

Filo flexed her arms and, bracing her foot, pushed back on the scythe handle that had blocked her last attack.

"Not so easy!"

L'Arc jumped straight up into the air, and both Raphtalia and Filo's attacks slipped into the space between the shields where he had been standing.

"Therese? Still not ready?!"

"It's ready!"

Therese raised her hands and began chanting a spell.

"All-encompassing power of the jewel, hear my plea and show yourself. My name is Therese Alexanderite. I am your friend. Destroy their unshakable protection!"

"Shining stones! Protection shatter!"

A flickering light flew at me. I wouldn't let it hit me!

I jumped to the side to avoid the spell. It flew past me, then it turned and kept coming like a guided missile.

"Mr. Naofumi!"

"I'm fine! Focus on your attack! You don't have the time to worry about me!"

"He's right. But Naofumi, you really need to pay attention too!"

" . . . ."

He blocked Raphtalia and Filo's attacks.

But I felt like they were getting closer to breaking through. If they were close, then there was one last thing I could try.

I kept dodging Therese's persistent spell as I chanted a spell of my own.

"That won't be easy! L'Arc!"

The light from her spell grew stronger, then expanded to completely engulf me. I felt it seeping into me.

I couldn't get away from it.

I felt like it was draining away my energy.

I quickly opened a menu to check my stats. Sure enough, my defense stat was blinking as the number dropped.

They'd noticed how high my defense rating was, and they were trying to deplete it with support magic

"Source of all power, I am the Shield Hero! Hear my words and heed them! Support them!"

"Zweite Aura!"

I had to respond with support magic of my own. I cast aura on Filo and Raphtalia, raising all of their stats!

It was affecting me too, raising my defense as it fell, effectively rendering their magic ineffective. Not only that, but it was raising all my other stats at the same time.

"Sorry to tell you, but that spell of yours won't really work on me."

"Guess you're right, kiddo. Therese!"

"Raphtalia, you focus your attacks on Therese. Filo, stick with me! We're taking out L'Arc!"

"Okay!"

"Understood!"

This time I would hold him down directly and get Filo to use her best attack on him.

He'd only be able to target me, and I wouldn't have to try and dodge his attacks.

"This is good. That's starting to hurt a little!"

L'Arc let out a sincere laugh, like he was actually enjoying himself. He swung his scythe at me.

Therese was dodging Raphtalia's attacks and casting a

spell. When she couldn't dodge, her bracelet flashed and a magic barrier appeared to block Raphtalia's sword.

"Naofumi, aren't you enjoying this too?

"I don't have the time to enjoy myself!"

But he was right in the way. I was getting so worked up by the battle that I didn't really have the time to remember why we were fighting in the first place.

That's what a direct battle was like. It wasn't about standing back and thinking and planning a strategy—it was about being there in the thick of it, reacting.

L'Arc. The guy was mysterious.

I knew he was my enemy, but I couldn't bring myself to hate him.

Did it mean that I was still holding back?

Was this the way a coward thought?

I couldn't laugh at the others who still treated this world like it was a game. We weren't supposed to enjoy battle and yet . . . .

I wanted to know. I wanted to know who would win.

He kept coming at me with the scythe. Sometimes I dodged and sometimes I blocked it and was showered with sparks. It was all very mesmerizing.

I didn't have any way to attack him. So I did what I could—I grabbed his wrist and held him back.

"Filo!"

"Yup!"

Filo crossed her arms and her claws filled with wind. She sent them flying at L'Arc.

"Wind claw!"

"Oh!"

There was a tearing sound, and two red lines appeared on L'Arc cheek and arms.

The cuts were not deep. But I still had a grip on him!

"Not bad! Let me repay you! Spirit scythe! Protection break!"

His scythe flashed brightly, and the tip touched my shoulder.

That was all.

And yet a searing spike of pain ran through my body, and my hand let go of his wrist almost on its own.

"Damn . . . ."

What?!"

L'Arc jumped away, dodging Filo's second attack.

"Well, looks like we found what works against the Shield Hero."

"Mr. Naofumi!"

Raphtalia shouted my name, though she was still locked in battle with Therese.

I was holding my shoulder to keep myself from bleeding out. I needed to get a healing spell cast, and fast.

"You're looking at me like you don't understand what just happened."

"Not quite."

I could think of a few explanations.

It could have been a defense ignoring attack.

Glass had done something similar when we'd fought during the last wave. It was one of the only ways to hurt someone with a high defense rating.

Those types of attacks dealt damage irrespective of your defense rating.

If I was dealing with something like that, then I'd have to give up the option of blocking the attack. The only way to avoid injury was to dodge.

The other possibility was not good at all.

"A defense rating attack."

"Bingo, kiddo. That defense rating of yours is a liability now, eh?"

When Glass had attacked us, I'd been using the Shield of Rage, which had a high defense rating anyway, so it was hard to figure out what was going on.

I'd only been touched by the tip of his scythe, but he'd dealt some serious damage. If he'd hit me with the full attack, I wasn't going to make it out of this with just a scratch.

Should I switch to a shield with a lower defense rating?

If I did that, I wouldn't be able to block his regular attacks though. This wasn't a good choice to be forced into.

Still, there was a weakness to defense ignoring attacks.

I didn't really know what kind of weapon he was using, but it seemed to be a lot like the hero's legendary weapons— and the legendary weapons had attack skills.

If that attack was one of those, then it would have a cool down time or it would use up his SP.

But I'd just hit him with soul eat, so he shouldn't have much SP left.

I assumed he wouldn't be able to use his new attack very many times.

"You might just decide not to block my next attack though."

"Yeah, there's no rule that says I can't just dodge."

Being the Shield Hero didn't mean that I had to use my shield all the time.

If he was only attacking me, it made since to prioritize avoiding his attacks.

"But I might not need to. I think that defense ignoring attack of yours has a major weakness."

I was half bluffing to see how he reacted.

I didn't know if he was going to answer me honestly, but I tried to think of a way around the attack regardless.

"It won't be effective against my indirect defense skills, like air strike shield and second shield."

It would probably break through the skill though.

But that was fine, as long as it didn't hit me directly. So I still had a way to block that attack.

If he was able to use the skill quickly, time after time, then I'd have to defend against it with a shield that had a lower defense rating.

The Chimera Viper Shield had a counter attack that would poison the enemy—that might work out well.

"Correct. It only works if I can hit you directly."

"You don't have to tell me the rest."

He didn't have to give away his plan. That was suicidal.

I didn't need him to do anything like that. I just needed to take the initiative and see what happened.

Besides, I still needed to keep an eye on Raphtalia and Filo. Filo continued attacking L'Arc, but he was quick on his feet, dodging all of her attacks with relative ease. If he used a ranged attack then I would have to jump in to defend the others.

"Let's get back to it!"

L'Arc swung his scythe. The blade was glowing.

That meant that he was using a defense-ignoring attack!

I turned on my feet and dodged it.

"Yikes!"

"Now!"

Filo ducked low and swung around behind him; her claws flashed.

"Hya!"

"Argh! Damn. That was a good one. I didn't think you were going to dodge that."

"Of course I would, right? Why should I try to block all the attacks? There's only one real job for a shielder; you know that I'm talking about?"

I only had to do one thing—protect. If the shield was the problem, then I just needed to dodge the attack.

I wasn't some sort of mindless wall for the party. You didn't need a person to do a job like that.

"This is getting better and better! Naofumi, I feel like I'm getting stronger the longer I fight you."

"Ha! Leveling up in the middle of a fight are you? Cut the jokes. You're no hero."

Perhaps thinking I'd found away around his best attack, L'Arc switched gears and started using another skill.

"First form, wind blade! Second form, sky blade!"

Two swirling tornadoes appeared, then they titled downwards like tunnels of violent wind.

The wind was so powerful I thought it might blow me away, but I was able to stand my ground.

Did he think he was going to defeat me with a normal attack like that?

I switched to the Chimera Viper Shield and blocked the attack.

"Huh? You changed your shield?"

"Yeah, now deal with the counter attack!"

The awakened version of the Chimera Viper Shield had a counter effect called snake fang (large).

The sculpted snake design of the shield came to life and bit L'Arc.

"Huh! It's . . . poison!"

L'Arc jumped back from the attack and held his head in his hands, reeling from the poison's effect.

While he was stumbling, Filo got in a few good attacks, though none of them were strong enough to knock him down.

"Master! I'm going to try a powerful attack, so you better stand back!"

"Got it!"

"Damn. That was tricky."

A bottle of medicine shot out of his scythe. He caught it and drank it. It was probably an antidote.

But there was something else. Another bottle! Soul-healing water! He'd figured out my plan.

But it was enough to confirm one thing: L'Arc had SP to deal with.

Traveling with Raphtalia, I'd realized that normal people didn't have any idea what SP was.

For most people, soul-healing water didn't do anything

more than help them concentrate—but for heroes, it was something else all together.

That meant that L'Arc was a hero or something else roughly equivalent.

"Master!"

Filo had finished charging her attack. All I had to do was give her an opportunity.

"Raphtalia!"

"Yes!"

She immediately knew what I meant. She started casting a spell. I'd needed her to keep Therese from interfering in our battle, but the time for concerns like that was over.

Therese noticed that Raphtalia had backed off her attacks, and she used the opportunity to immediately start casting a support spell.

But Raphtalia could swing her sword even as she chanted.

"Ah! You're very good!"

"I don't have another option, I have to attack and cast my spells at the same time against someone like you!"

"I am the source of all power. Hear my words and heed them. Hide!"

"First hiding!"

"Hiding Shield!"

Our combo skill could make an invisible shield. I set it to where I needed it.

"Change shield! Second shield!"

"Watch it!"

L'Arc, unable to see where the shield was, swung his scythe in a wide arc.

He was coming at us!

"What?!"

L'Arc's kneecap slammed into the invisible shield.

And I had changed it to the Two-Headed Black Dog Shield—with the special effect dog bite!

The shield warped into the shape of a dog and bit down on L'Arc—hard. He couldn't move.

"Spiral strike!"

Filo used the move she'd defeated the inter-dimensional whale with. She was flying straight for the immobilized L'Arc.

"Damn! That doesn't look good!"

L'Arc switched his scythe to his free hand and started to spin it. He was able to stop Filo's attack.

He must have been using some kind of defensive skill, because Filo's attack didn't seem to do any damage.

". . . ."

But Filo kept spinning and spinning, delivering attack after attack. Slowly, she seemed to be breaking through.

"That's not enough!"

The dog bite effect ran out. The shield vanished, and L'Arc jumped out of Filo's attack range.

But I wouldn't let him get away that easily.

"Shield prison!"

The third strongest shield skill I had, after air strike shield, was shield prison.

You could use it to hold an enemy in place or to protect yourself. It was perfect for restraining someone that tried to dodge all the time.

"Ugh! Dammit, Naofumi!"

With the shield prison in place, he couldn't avoid Filo's attack any longer. It connected.

"ARGH!"

What? He blocked her attack with his bare hand!?

Not even L'Arc was strong enough to pull that off. The attack broke through. He was bleeding, but not defeated.

"Damn. Not bad."

His arm was covered in gashes. He pressed his free hand against the wounds and held out his scythe.

"Guess that wasn't enough!" said Filo.

"Filo-chan. That was one impressive attack. I never thought you all would get this far."

"L'Arc!"

Therese shouted for him. Raphtalia had kept the pressure on her so consistently that she wasn't able to cast any sort of support magic on him at all. Raphtalia was really impressive. Therese kept flinging spells at her, but whenever she wasn't able to dodge them she bat them away with the blade of her sword.

And Therese must have been very powerful too—she was holding her own against all of Raphtalia's attacks, and she only had her magic to rely on.

If I had to fight them both at the same time, I don't think I could win.

"You know I really thought I could win. But it looks like I just don't have what it takes to beat you, Naofumi."

He was still acting like my superior.

I was amazed he could set aside the battle for a minute to talk.

I looked out at the ocean where an unconscious Motoyasu was floating. Ren and Itsuki were unable to fight. The fools. What would they have done in my situation?

This isn't how my game went! You're supposed to lose this fight! I was sure they would say something stupid like that.

If L'Arc or Therese were able to use a curative spell or medicine, then we'd have to start this all over again.

Then what?

I was about to think of how to end the battle when a great spray of water erupted before us, and a shadow appeared.

"How long are you going to take?"

"You?!"

An unexpected visitor landed right between us. I couldn't believe my eyes.

It made sense. I'd started to wonder about it myself. I'd felt there must have been a connection.

The person before me was so powerful. I hadn't stood a chance the last time we fought.

She had a refined face, long black hair, and pale skin. She wore a somber kimono, held a folding fan, and her fighting looked like dancing, like art. She had disappeared into a rift during the last wave.

She looked just as she had the last time I saw her. She exuded an oppressive sense of power over the whole area. She was staring straight at me.

It was Glass.

Chapter Thirteen: Soul-Healing Water

"Oh, if it isn't Glass? What are you up to?"

"Clearly I've defeated the enemy and come looking for you."

L'Arc was talking to Glass as if they knew each other.

Could it be? I'd considered the possibility before, but were they really connected?

From the look of it, they seemed to be friends. Damn! Filo and I had been about to win! With Glass in the mix, I didn't see that as a possibility anymore.

"Now then. Naofumi, was it? We've met before."

She regarded me quietly and spoke politely.

"I wasn't hoping to see you again."

"I'm impressed you made this much headway against L'Arc. And from the look of that shield, you hadn't even gotten serious yet."

"What?! He wasn't trying?"

L'Arc was shocked.

"Correct. When he fights for real, he uses a shield that's very different from the one he has equipped now."

"Oh, then I guess I really never stood a chance."

It's not that I wasn't fighting for real. It's that the Wrath Shield asks too much from me.

"Heh. This guy was using a defense rating attack—I couldn't use my best shield because of that."

"I see."

Glass opened a folding fan and pointed it at me.

"Then I suppose I will have to join this fight myself."

"I'd really rather not fight you, but I guess I don't have a choice."

I took a step forward and readied my shield.

"Counting the wave boss, this makes round three."

Honestly I was annoyed. I didn't want to keep fighting without a break.

But the other heroes were useless, and the queen couldn't do anything to help. How was I supposed to fight these people without any support?

"Ha!"

She snapped open her fan and swiped at me. Her attack flowed like water.

Based on what I'd seen the last time we'd fought, I didn't have to worry too much unless I was using the Wrath Shield.

I raised my shield and blocked her attack.

Soul eat activated and drained Glass's . . . SP?

"What? That shield!"

Understanding the shield I was using, Glass took a long jump backwards.

What was happening? Glass was behaving like it was the first time she'd ever been hurt.

And her attack had felt much weaker than the last time we'd fought. What was happening?

I had the Soul Eater Shield equipped.

It had a counter effect called soul eat, which stole the enemy's SP.

If the enemy didn't have SP, it stole their magic power.

"L'Arc, you understand, right?"

"Yeah."

L'Arc stepped forward and Glass opened her fan wide.

"Circle dance break! Tortoise shell shatter!"

I felt like she was moving slower than she had last time too.

I used air strike shield to block her attack.

"Naofumi, I'm coming!"

L'Arc spun around my skill and moved in close to use his defense rating attack.

"Don't even try!"

Before he could hit me, Filo reached out and grabbed the handle of his scythe, preventing the attack from connecting.

That was smart. If she held the handle then she could throw off his control of the blade.

"Ms. Glass! There's no choice!"

Therese pulled out a gemstone and threw it at Raphtalia.

"All-encompassing power of the jewel, hear my plea and show yourself. My name is Therese Alexanderite. I am your friend. Lend me your last light! Surrender yourself for the sake of our future!"

"Shining stone, shrinking explosion!"

"?!"

Raphtalia ran to get distance from Therese.

It was the right move. A second later there was an ear-splitting blast and a great rush of searing wind.

Had the gemstone exploded?

Her magic was so strange. From what I'd seen up until know, Therese's magic worked by using gemstones.

If she would blow one up, did that mean that we were winning?

"Mr. Naofumi!"

Therese used the confusion of the explosion to reunite with L'Arc and Glass.

Raphtalia did the same, running back to Filo and I.

With us all back together, there was only one thing left to do.

"Shooting star shield!"

A force field appeared around us.

"L'Arc, hurry and show me your wounds."

"Sorry, Therese . . . ."

Therese used magic to heal his gashed arm.

"You're much stronger then the last time we met. You really are a hero."

"I know."

"It's hard to call it a fair fight. But I won't hold back now."

Glass opened her fan wide and prepared to use a skill. It had defeated the other three heroes in one shot the last time we met. I remembered it.

At the same time, Therese was preparing a spell.

This wasn't looking good. Were they about to use a combo skill!?

"All-encompassing power of the jewel, hear my plea and show yourself. My name is Therese Alexanderite. I am your friend. Defeat them with a storm of ice!"

"Shining stones, blizzard!"

"Combination form. Reverse hail snow moon flower!"

Like cherry blossoms on the breeze, the wind carried daggers of ice on in a quickening squall.

"Shield prison!"

I used shield prison inside of the shooting star shield force field to protect us.

A few seconds after Glass initiated her attack the force field shattered. The shield prison rocked in the winds and ice.

I could feel the attack power rattling the shields around us. The winds died down just as the shield prison's effect time wore out.

"He survived our combo skill?"

"We've gotten stronger since the last time we met. Don't forget it."

"It seems I've underestimated you."

I thought I saw an expression of anxiety flit over her face.

Exactly. This fight felt a lot different than the last one had.

If we'd been able to survive that attack from Glass, it was proof that we'd become a lot more powerful since the last time we met.

But there was something even more intriguing than that. I had to know why Glass had seemed so intimidated by the Soul Eater Shield.

It looked like she had jumped back, almost scared, from its counter attack.

Alright, it was time for our attack now.

"Raphtalia, Filo, it's going to be tough, but try to keep L'Arc and Therese at bay and focus your attacks on Glass. If you can't avoid them entirely, you can let a few of their attacks through. Don't worry, I'll protect you."

"Alright."

"What are you gonna do?"

"Don't worry about me."

"Mkay!"

We all agreed on the plan and turned to begin the attack.

"Shooting star shield!"

See, the force field also prevented anyone not in your

party from crossing into range. So we couldn't get a grip on them and restrain them, but by keeping my party members safe within the force field we were free to focus on attacking.

But if the enemy's attacks exceeded what the field could withstand, then it would break instantly. So I'd have to keep an eye on it.

Raphtalia and Filo used the force field as a shield and drew Glass and L'Arc's attacks.

Glass attacked and attacked, again and again, her impatience growing increasingly evident.

Finally, there was a splintering sound as the force field reached its limit and broke.

"Now! Circle dance form, tortoise . . . ."

"Hya!"

Filo drew back and clawed ferociously at Glass's fan.

"You! Get off!"

Glass swung the fan to try and knock Filo back.

Now!

"Air strike shield! Change shield!"

I turned the air strike shield into what I had been using since the start—the Soul Eater Shield.

Glass's attack was flying at Filo, but my skill was faster. Her attack collided with the shield.

"What?! No . . . ."

The soul eat counter attack activated, and Glass immediately made to dodge it.

I knew it!"

That confirmed it. Glass was weak against the soul eat attack.

"Raphtalia!"

"What is it?"

"Do you have the magic sword?"

"Yes."

"That's our trump card this time. Give it all your power and thrust it into her!"

We didn't have any other way to use it, so we might as well put it to use while we could.

"Understood! Hyaaaaa!"

"Not so fast!"

L'Arc dashed over to cut her off.

"Don't forget about meeee!"

Filo crosscut and stopped L'Arc from advancing. Now nothing was in Raphtalia's way.

I followed her, bringing up the rear.

"Ms. Glass!"

Therese crossed her wrists and chanted a spell.

"All-encompassing power of the jewel, here my plea and show yourself. My name is Therese Alexanderite. I am your friend. Halt their advance with a wall of flame!"

"Shining stones, flame wall!"

A wall of raging flames surged up to protect them.

I leveled my shield and kept running right for it.

The force field was reaching its limit. The air was filled with crackling snaps—the wall must have been very powerful.

But it wasn't enough.

"I . . . I can't stop them!"

"Better not underestimate us!"

L'Arc and the others were so strong it was remarkable.

Honestly, I thought they might even be more powerful than the high priest had been, and he had a replica of the legendary weapons.

But they weren't powerful enough to stop me.

Their best attacks were the defense ignoring and the defense rating attacks. Once I found away around those, I knew how to defeat them.

Still, if they got a chance to pummel us with close range attacks, we might not get control of the battle again.

We had to finish it before L'Arc got a chance to interfere!

"Raphtalia!"

"Yes!"

She fixed her grip on her magic sword and thrust it at Glass.

"I don't think so!"

Glass judged the path of the blade and blocked with her fan.

This had happened in our last fight, and it had broken Raphtalia's blade.

"Not quite!"

But the magic sword didn't have a physical blade to break.

Raphtalia held back her magic power just before the blade hit the fan, and the blade wavered and vanished. Judging the timing, Raphtalia pivoted and then the blade reappeared—thrusting straight into Glass's stomach.

But it hadn't pierced through her. Was the attack power too low?

"What?!"

Glass was speechless.

For a single moment, the blade of the magic sword sparked.

"ARRRGHHHHHHH!"

Raphtalia screamed as she focused all her remaining magic power into the blade. It sparked and crackled and slipped into Glass.

"NOOOOOOOOOOOO!"

Glass wrapped her hands around the crackling blade and tried to pull it out. But Raphtalia focused further, pressing the sword in deeper before releasing her grip and jumping away.

The blade sparked again and then exploded with a blinding flash.

"Whoa!"

The light was so bright that I could hardly keep my eyes open.

I ran to Raphtalia and used my shield to block the light.

"Glass!"

L'Arc shout to Glass and tried to wrest himself free from Filo.

The area was filling with smoke. That's how powerful the magic explosion had been.

We'd hit Glass in her weakest point. I hoped that would end the battle.

The smoke cleared.

Huff . . . .

"It's . . . ."

Huff . . . .

"No problem at all . . . ."

Glass was still standing. She held her stomach and was breathing heavily. She looked like she might collapse at any moment.

Damn! It hadn't been a finishing move after all.

But it had done plenty of damage. If there was a time for a follow-up attack, it was now.

"Ms. Glass. We must retreat for now."

"No . . . . Not yet. I mustn't retreat!"

"Glass! Dammit! Move!"

"Hey!"

L'Arc threw off Filo and ran to Glass's side.

"Filo, are you okay?"

"Yup!"

Alright, we could still fight.

We'd backed Glass into a corner. Now even if they used restorative magic, she'd still be exhausted.

And I still had the Wrath Shield if I needed it.

As a last resort I could get the timing right and use iron maiden.

After powering up, the Air Strike Shield skill had a higher defense than it had.

So it was probably safe to assume that the attack power of iron maiden had gone up as well. If I defended with the Soul Eater Shield, then I could get back my lost SP too. And I could always drink a soul-healing water and use the skill in succession.

"Glass. Stay still."

What? Something that looked like soul-healing water was dribbling out of L'Arc scythe and falling onto Glass.

That was all, but a strange look immediately crossed Glass's face. She looked relieved.

"Rapid energy recovery?!"

Glass was as surprised as I was. What was going on?!

"Naofumi, you're really something. You haven't left us any spare room to maneuver, have you? I wanted to hang on to this, but you've forced me to play my trump card."

L'Arc kept pouring the soul-healing water over Glass.

Her cheeks immediately flushed a healthy red.

I couldn't explain it, but she looked even more powerful than she had before.

"L'Arc, what is this?"

"For me it's a drink that refills my skill power. But for you it's an amazingly powerful power up tool."

"Oh yes. I see."

Glass was on her feet in a flash. She narrowed her eyes at me.

I was getting a bad feeling about this.

"I'm going."

Glass said it, and then she was right in front of me—before I could even blink!

Had she teleported? No, she had just moved so quickly that I hadn't been able to follow her.

Luckily my shield was already positioned between us.

"Hyaaa!"

The strongest attack yet slammed against my shield. I felt it reverberate in my hands.

"Damn!"

The attack had been so powerful my arm felt numb.

What was going on? I'd been able to withstand her most powerful attacks just a few minutes ago!

All he did was pour some soul-healing water on her—why was she suddenly so powerful?

Glass could not have been human. She had to be something else. The Soul Eater Shield's counter attack had been really effective against her too.

That would mean that she became more powerful when her SP was increased or something like that.

"Mr. Naofumi!"

"Master?!"

Thinking that Glass had nearly broken through my defenses, Raphtalia and Filo rushed foreword.

"Wait! Stay back! Don't expose yourselves to attack!"

Glass was extraordinarily powerful. I'd blocked her attack with my best shield, and she'd nearly broken it. If she scored a direct hit against Raphtalia or Filo, they would probably die. I don't think they were fast enough to avoid Glass's attacks either.

But Filo didn't listen. She was already past me, using her fastest attack.

"Haikuikku!"

Filo rushed at Glass, and her claws flashed time and time again.

"Ugh . . . ."

Glass tried to brush off Filo's attacks, but Filo had grown too powerful. Unable to ignore them, Glass was forced to jump back.

"Circle dance, tortoise shell break!"

Glass's fan began to glow. She aimed a defense ignoring attack at my shoulder.

"Argh!"

Pain shot through my shoulder. I held it to try and regain my composure.

"I'm coming, Naofumi! This is it!"

L'Arc swung his scythe. It was a defense rating attack.

"Shooting Star Shield!"

The force field appeared just in time to stop his scythe.

And then the field broke—but his attack didn't make it through.

"Damn. You just won't give up, will you? I already used my trump card, and you're still standing!"

"We haven't lost yet!"

But we were running out of options.

"L'Arc, stand down. I'll finish this by using all my power."

"Right!"

L'Arc and Therese got as far from Glass as they could. What was she planning?!

"Circle dance of nothingness."

Her fan grew very large, and then another fan materialized next to it.

She snapped the fan shut, and they released blades of energy as she did.

Then she held the closed fans over her head.

The circle path they formed as they rose remained in the air, glowing like the moon.

It was so beautiful, but I couldn't afford to be distracted. I readied my shield and braced myself.

She brought the fans back down with force.

"Moon break!"

"Ah!"

I quickly switched to the Wrath Shield and held it over my head.

There was plenty of distance between Glass and I, but innumerable blades of energy rained down on me from above.

I couldn't dodge them. They were too fast!

I did all I could to block them with the shield, but I couldn't keep it up much longer. Raphtalia and Filo were in danger!

"Raphtalia! Filo! Get out of here!"

"Y . . . yes!"

"Okay!"

They escaped to the left and right, away from me.

The shield was taking a serious beating from the energy blades. It felt like it might break at any moment.

"Ugggghhhh . . . ."

The attack ceased. The shield had survived it.

But I soon realized my shoulder had been cut anyway.

Even though the shield had survived the attack.

The attack was over. The blades stopped falling.

I turned to survey the damage. The ocean itself was split in two.

Just how powerful was she? I was surprised I had even survived.

Huff . . . huff . . . .

Huff . . . huff . . . .

Glass and I were both exhausted.

The Wrath Shield started to glow.

"It's my turn now!"

Damn. It hurt. It hurt so bad!

Dark curse burning activated, burning everything.

Dark flames shot up from the ground and swirled around me.

"L'Arc! Therese! Stay back!"

"Right!"

I couldn't let them get away! I immediately expanded the flames, burning the whole area.

Glass slapped open her fan to defend herself.

"Arrrghhh!"

The flames finally died down, but Glass was still standing there, exhausted from the effort.

My attack had been extremely powerful. How had she survived it?!

Did I need to use iron maiden?

The problem was whether I could use change shield (attack) without it breaking.

Actually, she might break the actual iron maiden. Glass's attack had been powerful enough to nearly break the Wrath Shield. I couldn't be sure that she wouldn't destroy the iron maiden.

Glass began to use her powerful ocean-splitting attack again.

"Glass! It's too dangerous! Stop it!"

"If we don't defeat him now, he will only grow more powerful! Even if I don't survive, we have to defeat him. If we don't . . . do you understand what I'm saying?"

"I feel the same way."

I held my hand out and prepared to use shield prison.

"Mr. Naofumi!"

"Master!"

"Stay BACK!"

If they were swept up in this, they would die for sure. Glass was just too powerful.

After this attack exchange, which of us would be left standing?

"My queen . . . fueeee . . . ."

"What?!"

Suddenly, I don't know how, but suddenly the queen was

standing behind Glass. Had she used the confusion of the self-curse burning to sneak over? Another person in a squirrel kigurumi was clinging to a barrel, floating on the sea.

The queen's hand shot out, and she used magic to send the barrel flying at me.

"Mr. Iwatani! Take it!"

A barrel? Why? The barrel came flying and landed between Glass and I.

For a second I thought she was just trying to make a distraction. But then I recognized the barrel.

"That's . . . Shooting star shield!"

"What's that?!"

The force field appeared, and I jumped back to where Raphtalia and Filo were standing.

Glass was still preparing for her attack when the explosive rucolu barrel exploded forcefully.

We'd been fighting on top of the inter-dimensional whale, and that's where the barrel exploded.

The whole area was immediately filled with the smell of rucolu and a thick red mist.

"This . . . this is . . . ."

Glass couldn't see in the thick red fog. She held her face in her hands and stumbled left and right.

"What is that? Could it be? The barrels they used to turn the sea red?"

The mist didn't make it through the shooting star shield force field.

"Raphtalia, Filo, you understand?"

"Yes!"

It would be dangerous, but it was our only chance.

"This . . . ."

"Hya!"

"Yah!"

We all moved through the mist and maneuvered behind Glass. Raphtalia and Filo went right up to the force field boundary and attacked her from behind.

"Argh!"

After each attack, we moved back to hide in the mist.

Whenever Filo stuck her face out of the force field, she sniffed the air and made a disturbed face.

"It stinks! If they're stuck out there, they're not gonna like it!"

"Damn . . . ."

"Ugh . . . . You guys don't stop!"

I could hear L'Arc shouting. They weren't able to attack because they couldn't find us in the mist.

There was a splash. L'Arc and the others had dove into the water. They swam. Then they climbed up on the hull of the sinking ship. If they used more soul-healing water on Glass to heal and power up, the fight would not turn in our favor again.

"Didn't expect an attack like that. This isn't looking good."

"L'Arc! We're finishing this now!"

I still had iron maiden.

And I still had blood sacrifice, but I couldn't use that here. If I hit L'Arc with iron maiden, I thought that would end the battle.

"It's not over yet."

Therese stood next to L'Arc.

Maybe I could use iron maiden on both of them at the same time . . . ?

"Not yet!"

A tornado appeared and the mist vanished. Glass was standing there, breathing heavily. She was holding her head in her hands and stumbling left and right.

Damn these people were tough! Come on. What was it going to take to end this?

We'd tried strategy after strategy, and nothing was enough to finish them.

I had no other choice. I had to use my last trick.

"Glass, I'm sure you understand. I have to finish this!"

I thought about whether to use it on L'Arc or on Glass. They were both very powerful. But L'Arc's attacks were trickier, so I decided to focus on him first.

"Shield prison!"

"Oh!"

L'Arc was caught in the shield prison.

"Stop!"

Glass immediately started pummeling the prison with long range attacks while L'Arc rocked it from the inside.

It wasn't strong enough to survive both attacks, and it broke.

Damn. It took too long to set up the iron maiden attack.

First I had to trap them in the shield prison, use change shield (attack), and then I was free to use iron maiden. But if it took so long that they could break out of the shield prison first, I couldn't do it.

"That was close!"

I had no other choice. I'd have to keep using self-curse burning. But to use that I'd have to survive one of their attacks. In the very worst case, I would have to use blood sacrifice and kill them both at the same time.

Suddenly I heard a beep.

00:59

The numbers appeared in my field of view.

I remembered something like this happening the last time we fought Glass. She had retreated immediately after the counter appeared.

Would she escape again? I couldn't let her.

We were about to win. It was time to put an end to all this!

"It seems there really is no other choice, is there L'Arc?"

In a flash, Glass was right before me.

"No . . . Ms. Glass!"

She opened her fan.

When Therese saw her, she covered her mouth with both hands. She looked terrified.

What was happening? After all those attacks, did this mean that they still had a trump card?

"Glass!"

L'Arc was furious. He ran behind her and hooked his arms around her torso, restraining her.

"What are you doing? Let me go!"

"You can't do it. You haven't thought about what will happen!"

"Think L'Arc. Think of how powerful he is. We must be prepared to give our all if we are to defeat him."

"But Glass . . . ."

L'Arc leaned over and whispered in Glass's ear. She suddenly looked very surprised.

L'Arc and Therese both nodded.

"Very well. Then we must retreat today."

She nodded slowly. What could he have said?

I didn't care what their strategy was. I couldn't let them escape this time.

"You think I'm letting you go?"

"Try to stop us. Naofumi, next time we will emerge victorious."

Glass immediately used a ranged attack, filling the area with gale-force winds.

What? The soldiers in the boats were all being sucked up with the wind!

"Looks like you guys won this one. Naofumi. I don't like that name. Is kiddo all right with you?"

"Why?!"

L'Arc didn't seem worried at all. He waved to us as they jumped into a rift.

"I bid you farewell. Goodbye."

Therese cast a spell, saving the soldiers from the winds. Then she threw a gemstone down and it exploded, making room for her escape.

"Wait!"

We chased after them, but they were too fast. We couldn't reach them before they were already in the rift.

I hesitated for a split-second. I wondered if we should follow them. But it was too late. The rift closed.

"Dammit! We were so close!"

They'd escaped.

We'd grown so powerful that I really thought we were going to defeat Glass this time. But we were never able to land a winning blow.

The next time we met, we'd be starting all over.

With their defense ignoring and defense rating attacks, they had too many tricks up their sleeves.

I was breathing hard—exhausted. All I could do was survey the destruction the wave had left in its wake.

Epilogue: The Problem We Face

"So, it looks like the other heroes proved themselves useless in yet another battle."

After the wave, we all went back to Cal Mira.

The other heroes regained consciousness right around the time we arrived at the island, and they were taken to a hospital to recuperate.

Honestly, how could they be so weak that L'Arc and Glass hadn't even worried about bothering with them?

What a bunch of useless jerks they were proving to be!

Did they think the whole game was just a series of events the player was forced to lose?

"To think there is such power in the world. We must find a way to defeat them."

The queen was thinking over the day's events and muttering to herself.

"Thank you for your help there at the end. If you hadn't stepped in, who knows what might have happened."

"Naturally. Though I was wondering something, Mr. Iwatani. After Raphtalia and Filo were out of range from the rucolu mist, why didn't you breathe some in?"

"Huh?"

"I have heard that you do not get drunk from the rucolu."

"That's true."

"Well the fruits and the alcohol which they produce has another short term effect beyond drunkenness. It increases the user's magic power and concentration. It may have helped you."

"What?"

Did that mean that if I was fighting in rucolu mist, I could continuously replenish my magic and SP?

Glass had been able to break the shield prison, but if I had unlimited SP, I could have used iron maiden time after time?

Damn! If I'd known that, we might have won!

"You could have told me that earlier."

"Unfortunately I only just thought of it now."

In her defense, it had been a pretty tense situation back there.

And my only way of attacking took too long, anyway. They were able to break the shield prison before I got a chance to use it.

My only real remaining option was to try and keep using counter attacks to slowly wear them down.

Glass had been so powerful after the soul-healing water that neither Raphtalia nor Filo had been able to get a decisive blow in. It's not that they were weak or anything like that.

They'd both been fighting really well before Glass had been powered up.

What did we have to do to beat them?

And what did they want? I gathered from their conversation that their goal was to kill the heroes. But L'Arc had gone to lengths to avoid any unnecessary casualties. He'd only been concerned with me at the time.

Were they really bad guys?

They were definitely my enemy—but why did they want to kill the heroes?

But who were we fighting, anyway?

Sure, we were fighting the waves. It was supposed to be simple.

The waves would produce monsters. We had to protect the civilians and defeat the monsters. I knew that much.

But then a person—Glass—appeared.

At first I thought that it was another monster, a smarter, more terrifying one. But that theory didn't make sense anymore.

And her allies, L'Arc and Therese, had been around since long before the waves had come.

They must have come from the other side.

I hadn't even thought about it until now, but just what was on the other side of the rifts?

What were the waves of destruction, really?

In this world, they were only spoken of as legendary waves of destruction.

But what about Glass and L'Arc? There must have been real people on the other side.

I had plenty of theories, but no way to figure out what was true.

Theory #1

Glass and the others were trying to invade this world. The monsters were their solders. But there was a problem with that idea. Glass and L'Arc had fought and defeated some of those monsters. And it didn't explain why they wanted to kill the heroes.

Theory #2

Glass and the others stood to benefit from killing the heroes. But how? And why? And what was on the other side of the rifts?

Theory #3

Fitoria had said that if the heroes died the world would have no way to stand against the waves. Is that what they wanted? What would happen if the waves overran the world? We wouldn't know unless we lost. If the world was destroyed then there was no point to any of this. There was no way to tell.

I couldn't figure out what they were after.

"It seems that Cal Mira is still in the midst of the activation event. What would you like to do?"

The queen asked.

There was some sort of level cap around level 80, and I'd felt the leveling efficiency drop off substantially when we crossed level 70. That meant there was no reason to stay on the islands much longer. The only real thing left to do was to fight the boss characters on the island interiors for their drop items.

Raphtalia and Filo had gotten some good weapons. All that was left to do was gather up more rare materials and see what the weapon shop owner could do with them.

"I think we'll head back to Melromarc pretty soon."

"Very well. I will prepare a ship for your return. But the ocean is very rough now due to the wave, so it will take a little time."

"That's fine."

"I cannot praise you and your achievements highly enough, Mr. Iwatani. We will do all that we can to assist you. Let us move forward against the waves, against whatever difficulties we encounter."

That was nice, but her cooperation wasn't really the issue. I was the only hero that was pulling his share of the load here.

"The problem is the other heroes."

"Yes."

They hadn't helped at all. Actually they hadn't helped during the last wave either.

They would probably say that they hadn't leveled enough or make some other excuse. But we were past the time for excuses.

They were too weak.

I didn't say that to try and feel better about myself, either.

Maybe the problem was they hadn't put all of their respective power up systems into use.

"I think we're going to need to have another meeting about them."

"I agree. And it had better be soon."

The queen seemed to understand the situation.

Honestly, the other heroes weren't truly much stronger than a typical adventurer.

Sure, they had access to special skills, so they had power for short term immediate attacks.

But that wasn't the same as having real power.

If the other heroes could become as powerful as I truly am, would we have such a hard time fighting Glass?

The queen had said that the high priest's replica weapon was not even a quarter as powerful as a real hero's legendary weapon.

After all we'd been through on the islands, I felt I was

finally strong enough to withstand how powerful the high priest's attacks had been.

That meant that the heroes were capable of being at least as strong as I was now.

If the heroes with strong attacks matched my current power level, then could we have realistically lost to Glass?

"Yeah."

That sense of crisis I had when the waves came hadn't left me yet.

No matter how powerful I became, all I could really do was protect others. That was a limitation I was going to have to face.

If you can only protect, then there was no way to win.

If we didn't find some way around that problem, then we were not going to survive the next encounter.

I felt like I finally understood why Fitoria had wanted us to cooperate and grow more powerful.

Not to mention that if we lost a hero, the waves would get that much more difficult to deal with.

Those three were obnoxious and didn't know how to shut up and listen, but we needed them to be stronger as a whole. I was a little worried about what they would do when they got stronger. But whatever happened, it was better than dying.

"I'm a little tired right now. Let me get some rest, then we'll meet with the other heroes tomorrow."

"As you wish, Mr. Iwatani."

The queen bowed deeply and walked back to the soldiers.

I stepped back and turned—Raphtalia and Filo were right there waiting for me.

"We survived another one, didn't we, Mr. Naofumi?"

"Yeah."

"I don't feel like I was very useful."

"That's not true."

Both Raphtalia and Filo had fought well. So had L'Arc and Therese.

Honestly, until L'Arc used that soul-healing water, we were about to win.

Judging from that, Raphtalia and Filo must have been far more powerful than the other heroes.

It must have been due to my maturation adjustments skills and the effects of the class up ceremony.

"That fan lady was really strong!"

"Yeah."

"I wanna get stronger, so I can help you more, master!"

"I'd like that too."

I didn't know what the leveling or power cap would be on them after the class up ceremony, but they had gotten really powerful already. If the other heroes weren't able to step up to the task, I'd have to depend on these two to take up the slack.

They were my only party members.

"We might need to have more power on our side."

"Yes, we may not be able to go much further without more help."

Raphtalia immediately understood what I had meant.

She didn't ask any unnecessary follow-up questions like "aren't we enough?"

The country's soldiers could help us in a pinch, but we weren't going to be able to depend on them for a decisive victory.

We needed . . . we needed more help, someone that could help us defeat Glass and L'Arc even if the other heroes were not around.

We needed another party member.

But I had my personal traumas to deal with too.

If we increased the size of the party, then I opened myself up to the possibility of further betrayal.

I found out Melty wouldn't betray us, so I could trust her.

But could I say the same thing about our next party member?

I needed to find someone else I could trust.

That was why I wanted to invite L'Arc and Therese to join, but they turned out to be the enemy.

I'd trusted them too quickly. I must have been looking for someone to trust. L'Arc and Therese had been friendly enough that I had just fallen into it.

They'd gotten worried about us and come looking for us in the middle of the night. I'd really wanted to trust them.

It's hard. Things just don't go the way you want them to.

We still needed to fight against the waves and against Glass.

"What's wrong, master?"

"Huh? It's nothing. I was thinking we should get some rest."

"Good idea. I'm very tired."

"Master! Let's go to the baths!"

"Oh okay. We need to rest up tonight. We'll be busy again when morning comes."

"Yes!"

"Yay!"

So we went back to our room and rested, preparing for the next day.

The next fight, and the next wave, would be upon us soon.

Before then, we had to find some way to overcome the problems we faced.

We all had to be stronger than we were.

Extra Chapter: The Cal Mira Hot Springs

It was the fourth night since we'd arrived in the islands.

I went to soak in the hotel's outdoor bath, thinking that it might help my curse heal faster.

I'd been going there every night.

The tubs were large and Japanese-styled. There were large parasols covering the center of the baths, and a bamboo partition ran down the center to separate the sexes. The best part about it was the unobstructed view of the ocean you had from the baths.

The floor of the baths was made from stone, which also gave it all a very Japanese feel. It made me feel strangely homesick.

"Ah . . . ."

I sunk down into the water and sighed, looking up at the sky.

The water was the perfect temperature. It was a great place to relax.

I'd been visiting the baths every day, so I was starting to feel pretty good.

The sluggish feeling that had been bothering me was going away. A glance at my stats showed that I wasn't fully healed yet though.

Maybe I had just gotten used to feeling exhausted.

I mulled over such thoughts, barely holding onto them for a moment, as I sunk into the water and relaxed.

"Well, well. If it isn't Naofumi."

Motoyasu came walking into the baths.

Where was his spear? I looked closer, and sure enough he still had it. He'd changed it into a very small spear, and it was swinging at his waist.

I couldn't begrudge him that. I'd done the same thing. My shield was very small and slung over my back.

I wasn't allowed to ever set the shield down, but I could change where I held it—so at least I could relax a little.

Motoyasu poured some of the bath water over himself to warm up before entering the full bath.

"How's your hangover?"

"How can you even say that to me?"

"I never told you to eat them. I was just eating some fruit, minding my own business."

"Well you're obviously from a different Japan than I am. I'll assume there's some differences in the way our bodies work."

"Assume whatever you want."

I'd never been drunk before. Besides, I'm sure Bitch and the other girls were waiting on him hand and foot. He was probably loving it.

He's lucky he got out of it with only a hangover to complain about.

"Hey! The water is pretty great!"

Motoyasu was shouting to someone. Who was it?

"I already know that much. How many days have we visited the baths now?"

Itsuki and his crew came shuffling in.

They were followed shortly by Ren and his party.

"Master!"

Filo was in her filolial queen form, and she came jumping over the partition into the men's baths.

"Huh? What do you want?"

"I want to sit with you!"

"You're a bird. Go to a different bath. Or just leave the baths and go swimming."

"I don't wanna!"

She could be a real brat when she wanted to.

"You better clean any feathers out when you leave."

"Yay!"

"Stuck in a bath with Filo-chan . . . ."

Motoyasu came sliding over, an intrigued look on his face.

Filo used me as a human shield and hid behind me. She was too large to really hide though.

"Filo-chan. Why don't you turn into your angel form?"

"I don't wanna!"

Damn he was persistent. I guess he really had a thing for angels.

But why did Filo insist on sitting in the men's baths? Sometimes I just didn't understand her.

Motoyasu started to get excited.

"Hey guys! So out of all the girls in our parties, who do you think is the cutest?"

Oh jeez . . . . They talked about the stupidest things. I sighed loudly.

We weren't on vacation here. Or is that how Motoyasu was treating his time in this world?

Ren and Itsuki looked annoyed too.

"Hey guys, did you? You know . . . do it? I . . . well . . . heh, heh . . . ."

He was getting really obnoxious. What was he after?

He sounded like a stupid kid, giggling over everything. Was he really a ladies' man back in his world?

I couldn't stand his company. I'd just got in the baths, but I was already thinking about leaving.

"So did you do it with Raphtalia?

"Don't bring me into this."

We weren't on such friendly terms, Motoyasu and I.

Wasn't he the one who believed all the things Bitch was saying about me?

Did the heroes need to be so light-hearted? This guy was an idiot.

"Oh lighten up. Tell us!"

Had he forgotten about Bitch? What was with him?

"I'll start then. Maybe I should start by telling you my ranking of the pretty ladies?"

"No thanks."

"Unnecessary."

"Not my thing."

Ren, Itsuki, and I all refused.

"Well if I had to name my top four, it would be Bitch, Raphtalia, Filo-chan, and Rishia."

" . . . ."

What kind of girl did he like? Those four were all over the place.

I guess he just needed a pretty face.

"I understand what you mean. Bitch is a princess, after all. Apparently she has some personality issues, but she was always nice to me."

Itsuki jumped in on the conversation. Armor leaned over and whispered something in his ear.

I could kind of overhear what he was saying. He was telling Itsuki what kind of girls he liked.

The whole lot of them were idiots.

"Well they say the queen isn't very nice, but that's never bothered me."

Now Ren was joining in too. Didn't he just say these conversations weren't his thing?

They were all letting Motoyasu control the conversation.

It was easy enough to complain about it, but I really didn't want to be included.

"Am I cuuuute?"

Filo asked me.

"Whatever."

"Boooo."

"I think you're the cutest! So why don't you turn into your angel form?"

"I don't wanna!"

Did Motoyasu really like her that much?

Why didn't he just raise his own filolial then? He'd get the same results.

"Rishia is cute too, isn't she? Itsuki, I'm jealous."

"No . . . She's, uh . . . ."

Itsuki looked suddenly embarrassed.

"Who's Rishia?"

Ren had already forgotten about her. She was the one Itsuki's whole party treated like a slave.

She was quite soft-spoken, so she must not have made an impression on Ren.

"Sounds like you all pretty much agree with me."

"I guess so. As long as we're just talking about their faces."

" . . . ."

Ren and I stayed silent and refused to contribute.

What were they talking about? I guess this is just what guys were like.

"I'm gonna go back over with big sister!"

"Yeah, you'd better. This bath is full of dangerous wack-os."

"Okay!"

Filo waved and jumped back over the partition.

Motoyasu shuffled over to the partition.

"If we are heroes and men, it's an understood rule, isn't it? We'd better have a . . . peek."

"What are you talking about?!"

"Come on, you know you want to."

Itsuki, the warrior of justice, didn't have anything to say about this?

"You mustn't."

Said Itsuki, but he didn't stop Motoyasu. He shuffled over to join him.

Big surprise there. So the heroes were all horn-balls? Give me a break.

Armor and the other men were all getting excited. They all lined up against the partition.

"Damn . . . . It's a little too tall. Itsuki, give me a boost! If we jump, we'll give ourselves away."

"What are you saying? You're the taller one. You should give me a boost!"

"But then I wouldn't get a glimpse of paradise!"

Is that the only issue they had to debate? Who was going to boost who?

"Idiots . . . ."

Ren muttered to himself, but he made no motion to leave.

"I've had about enough."

I said, and I climbed out of the water.

I'd only been in for a few minutes, but I didn't want to get swept up in whatever trouble they were fomenting.

No sense in playing with fire.

Especially not after all I'd been through, with Bitch framing me and all. I didn't need to give anyone the opportunity to accuse me of character faults.

If I didn't leave, I was sure to get blamed for the whole thing.

"What's up with you, Naofumi? Don't you want to hang out?"

"Not particularly."

What were we supposed to do, just look at women's bodies?

I got sick just thinking about Bitch.

I was sure that I'd have a crime pinned on me if I didn't get out of there fast.

I would just wait for Raphtalia and Filo to meet me back at the room.

"If you want to peep, do it when I'm not around!"

I said, and I tried to leave for the changing room.

But . . . .

"Huh? It's Shield Kiddo!"

L'Arc came out of the changing room and into the baths.

"Did you come for the baths too, kiddo?"

He had terrible timing. Why did he have to come now?

"I heard these are the best springs on the island. Therese is here too. Are your friends here?"

I cursed myself silently and then, even though he hadn't asked, started to explain the whole situation.

"We're staying here."

"Oh yeah? You must have some serious cash."

"I'm about to leave. Those guys are all about to start peeping on the girls. If you don't want to end up in trouble, you'd better leave too."

I explained it all to L'Arc and prepared to make my exit. But something about the way he was listening made me nervous.

"Hold on a second. Did you say peeping?"

L'Arc grabbed my hand.

Why? Was he angry?

He seemed like he had a sense of justice and was stubborn enough to stick too it. Was he going to try and stop them?

"And you're not going to participate in something that fun?"

We apparently had another horn-ball to deal with.

He looked over at Motoyasu, who was trying to position himself to see over the wall.

"I guess they're my comrades!"

"What?!"

"Come on!"

I could hardly believe my eyes. He was siding with them?

"Come on, kiddo!"

"No thanks."

"Don't bother with him! He's as stubborn as they come!"

"But . . . but this is man's highest calling? What are we for, if not to worship a woman's naked body?"

They were so rude! Did they even think about how the women might feel being peeped on?

L'Arc and Motoyasu were so excited that their perspective was the only one being heard.

I liked L'Arc, but I'll have to knock him down a few ranks.

"Hey Naofumi, how far have you gotten with Raphtalia? Certainly you've thought about it?"

"That girl he's with? I bet he's gone pretty far!"

It's like I had two Motoyasu's to deal with. I slapped my hand to my forehead and sighed.

"How many times do I have to tell you that it's not like that?"

"Yeah, well you know that she's thinking about it."

"Nice . . . . I've been trying to get Therese into that kind of mood . . . ."

I'd thought they were an item this whole time.

They seemed so close, that I had just assumed they were dating or something.

But if he was trying to peep, then I guess not.

And here they were trying to peep on each other's party members. It's like they were trying to ruin my reputation even further than they already had.

"Nonsense. This is all nonsense!"

"So there's no action at all? Maybe L'Arc could tell us something?"

"Nothing good."

"No, I mean like . . . hasn't Raphtalia tried to instigate anything?"

"Instigate? No. She's only a child."

"Are you dense? You mean she's never taken her clothes off or anything? It's hard to tell with all those clothes and armor on, but she's stylish under all that, right? I can feel how attractive and classy she is under those clothes. I can't ignore it!"

If I didn't tell them something, I'd never get them to leave me alone.

What a pain.

"Sigh . . . well actually, a while back . . . ."

It was when we were traveling around as merchants.

We were in a village that was pretty famous for its springs.

The hotel had baths attached, so I soaked in them.

"Mr. Naofumi . . . ."

I was back at the room working on accessories, when Raphtalia came in from the pools.

She was wrapped in a towel, and I remember that she looked very embarrassed.

I don't know what she was thinking, but she stood there and untied the towel. She dropped it, showing off her body.

"What do you think?"

Her body was kept up well. I'd known that her breasts were large from a time we'd hugged, but they were larger than I'd even thought. They must have gotten in the way during battle.

Her whole body was soft though. It was hard to believe she was capable of such power in a fight.

Her hair was wet, and the scars that had been on her back had faded away.

She'd shown me her scars before, and I'd applied medicine to them.

But now she was standing there before me, naked, looking embarrassed.

So I said, "They look much better than before. Compared to when we met, the scars are like night and day—I can't even really see them."

"Oh? Is that, um . . . all?"

"Was there something else?"

Her jaw dropped like she couldn't believe my reaction.

"If you don't get dressed, you'll catch a cold."

"Hey! Big-sister is naaaaaaked!"

Filo ran into the room and started shouting.

Then she pulled off her dress, becoming naked herself, and charged at me.

"I wanna play too!"

"No! We're not playing!"

They wrestled a little, but that was all.

"So that happened."

"You idiot!"

L'Arc and Motoyasu were so disappointed they acted like they wanted to beat me up.

I caught their fists and pushed them back.

"What's wrong with you two?"

"How can you ignore such brazen appeal? What a waste!"

"Yeah, yeah! If a woman shows you her body, you can't just turn it down! That's rude!"

"What are you talking about? I already told you, Raphtalia is only a child. Plus she's so serious she'll drive you crazy. She definitely doesn't think about stuff like that."

I guess it was only natural for men to interpret everything from a perverted angle, but they had to learn to separate reality from fantasy.

Besides, you needed to be careful.

What would happen if we were in the middle of fighting the waves and we found out she was pregnant? Then she wouldn't be able to fight.

Raphtalia lived with purpose. She didn't have time for things like that. She hated distraction.

I thought it was my job to create an environment where Raphtalia could best focus on her fighting skills.

"Quite stoic, aren't you?"

"Hey, kiddo, you don't play for the other team, do you?"

Motoyasu took that as a sign and stepped back from us. L'Arc was twisting his finger into some bizarre gesture.

How was I supposed to understand his sign language?

"Everyone watch out! This one's after you! Pervert on the loose!"

L'Arc covered his butt with his hands as if to protect it.

What?! Now I knew what he was saying!

"You calling me a gay? Shut up!"

Why did they have to treat me like I was gay just because I wasn't doing it with Raphtalia?

I couldn't stand to be around these people anymore.

"I don't know how you're going to explain this all to the girls or to the hotel, but that's up to you. I'm not going to save you."

"Are you serious? I don't believe you."

L'Arc and Motoyasu were stunned. They watched me prepare to leave the baths in silence.

I couldn't afford to get wrapped up in another scandal, so
I needed to avoid it when I saw one coming.

"Alright then, strategy meeting! Do we try and look over
the top, or do we try to make a peephole?"

They all huddled and actually started discussing it.

They had gotten other men adventurers in the baths to get
in on it too.

There were quite a few people.

If that was charisma I didn't need it.

I wondered if peeping was treated differently in this world
than it was in mine. Back in my Japan, baths in the Edo period
apparently had peepholes installed.

This hotel had the baths separated by sex, but a lot of the
other hotels had had unisex baths.

Why didn't they just go to one of those?

Maybe there was no thrill in that. Maybe they only liked it
if they were stealing a glimpse in secret.

Idiots.

I didn't want to get involved, so I left the baths and went
back to my room.

"Whew."

I was cooling off in my room.

Eventually, I heard footsteps approaching. Raphtalia came in, wrapped in a towel.

"Mr. Naofumi!"

"What? Did Motoyasu and L'Arc get caught peeping?"

"Oh, yes! L'Arc and the other heroes are all hanging their heads in shame."

"Yeah? Good. They deserve it."

Of course they were going to get caught. The girls weren't stupid.

If Motoyasu was in the baths anyone could tell what would happen.

"But what about you, Mr. Naofumi?"

"What, do I have to peep too?"

Raphtalia looked disappointed in my answer. She stood there, crestfallen.

Her reaction was not what I would have expected.

"Here I thought maybe you'd come around . . . ."

"Come around?"

What was she talking about?

I'd more than come around. I'd heard enough from the other heroes.

"What's wrong big sister?"

Filo came tottering into the room and saw Rapthalia looking crestfallen.

"I don't know."

What was she so upset about?

I don't know for sure. I mean, of course she would hate to be peeped on by a guy like me.

Did she . . . did she want me to look?

No. Raphtalia wasn't like that.

She was just confused because of all the nonsense the other guys had said.

"Are you okay? Are you upset that L'Arc and the others were spying on you?"

"They didn't see me! Filo spotted them and I covered myself!"

"That's good."

She looked exhausted, even though she had just left the baths. I guess it was because of all the crazy excitement on the men's side.

"Whew . . . Mr. Naofumi?"

"What?"

"Considering what's going on do you want to go to a private bath? It might be kind of small, but that might be nice too."

"Um . . . ."

I knit my eyebrows together and made my stance evident.

I mean . . . I'd just gotten out of the baths. Still, it had been a short soak.

"You don't have to turn it down so forcefully. I just thought it would be good for your curse."

"Yeah . . . you might be right."

I was getting a weird feeling about it. She was right about the curse though.

"Come on, Mr. Naofumi."

"Sigh . . . alright."

So I lifted myself up from the bed and decided to go to the baths again. It was good for the curse, after all.

"It's over here."

Raphtalia led me down the hall and out to the other side of the hotel, where there was a private room that required a key to get in. It was on the other side of the building from the main baths. It faced the island's interior, rather than the ocean.

I could see why the hotel didn't show it off. The scenery wasn't so great.

It was supposed to be for families, so it was just Raphtalia, Filo, and I.

Raphtalia kept her chest covered with a towel, and Filo was also wrapped in a towel. They beckoned to me from the bath. I couldn't forget what L'Arc and Motoyasu had said, but they were wrong. Raphtalia wasn't looking for a sexual relationship with me.

Yeah, she didn't look embarrassed at all.

They were poisoning my mind.

I pushed their stupid ideas out of my mind and entered the bath.

"The water is very nice."

"Yeah, it is."

"How is your curse doing?"

"I think it's doing a lot better."

It would probably be a while until it was completely healed. If I kept soaking in hot springs like this, it would clear up eventually.

"Oooh! Master! A star in she sky just sparkled!"

"Huh?"

I looked up just in time to see a shooting star streak by.

"Oh . . . it's gone . . . ."

But then there came another. And another.

Raphtalia watched the stars streaming through the sky and clasped her hands together as if in prayer.

I guess people in this world liked to wish on shooting stars too.

You know I could see the stars way better in this world than in Japan. I'd been so busy since I got here I never had taken the time to look upwards.

"What did you wish for, Mr. Naofumi?"

"Oh nothing. What about you, Raphtalia? Did you wish for something?"

"Yes."

"I hope it comes true."

"Yes. Me too."

It wasn't hard to guess what she'd wished for.

It was probably for world peace or to reunite with her friends from the village.

The whole scene was very romantic. I leaned back and watched the stars.

Eventually we left the bath and started walking back to the room.

"Peeping? L'Arc, how old do you think you are? You might get away with that back home, but you need to follow the rules here!"

L'Arc and the other guys were all getting a lecture in the hallway.

Therese was lecturing L'Arc, while Bitch and her retinue were yelling at the other heroes.

They deserved it. How funny that I got to see their punishment.

It wasn't worth worrying about them. They were going to enjoy life however they wanted.

They would just accept the lecture as a compromise on their part. I'd read about things like this in manga, so I knew how it worked.

Still . . . I wasn't like them.

"Oh! Kiddo was in a private bath with the girls. Not fair!"

"L'Arc, pay attention!"

He was pointing at me, but Therese wouldn't take the bait and let him change the subject. She sent on berating him.

So they went on pretending like they caught me in the act, but we ignored them and went straight back to our room.

I was sure there would be plenty of hardship down the road. L'Arc was an idiot, but he was fun. Next time, maybe, I'd join in on their fun—if only a little.

Of course, I'd make sure I had Raphtalia's permission first to make sure I didn't end up getting yelled at in the hallway.

Character Design:
Therese

テリス

イレズミ

鎌

ラルクベルク

The Rising of the Shield Hero Vol. 5
© Aneko Yusagi 2014
First published by KADOKAWA in 2014 in Japan.
English translation rights arranged by One Peace Books
under the license from KADOKAWA CORPORATION, Japan

ISBN: 978-1-935548-67-6

Written by Aneko Yusagi
Character design by Minami Seira
English edition published by One Peace Books 2016

Printed in Canada

4 5 6 7 8 9 10 11 12 13 14 15

One Peace Books
43-32 22nd Street STE 204 Long Island City New York 11101
www.onepeacebooks.com